FAREWELL
—— *to* ——
VANCOUVER ISLAND

Lorna Hunting

Published by Goldcrest Books
www.goldcrestbooks.com
publish@goldcrestbooks.com

ISBN: 978-1-9192133-2-3

*This book is for
Dr Christopher K. Roberts*

Distances as the crow flies:

    Colville to Victoria – 57 miles

    Victoria to New Westminster – 57 miles

    New Westminster to Fort Langley – 15 miles

    Fort Langley to Harrison – 42 miles

The fastest mode of travel at this time was by water. The above map is based on one published in 1858 by Kinahan Cornwallis.

Note:

    Place names are those current in 1858.

    New Westminster will develop into modern-day Vancouver.

    Colville on Vancouver Island will become Nanaimo.

    Victoria will become the capital city of the Province of British Columbia.

THE COLVILLE SERIES

In the spring of 1854, a number of English colliers signed five-year contracts with the Hudson's Bay Company to open up the coal mines on Vancouver Island in Canada. They and their families set sail to pass around the Horn in a southern hemisphere winter to arrive in Colville in November of the same year.

The lives of these bold pioneers are imagined in *New Beginnings on Vancouver Island* and *Called to Vancouver Island*. These are fiction based on fact. In May 1858 one of these colliers, Sam Gray, broke his contract and deserted to become a digger in the goldfields of the Fraser River Valley on the mainland.

This is Sam's story.

PART ONE

CHAPTER ONE

Victoria, Vancouver Island, Canada
Thursday May 13th 1858

The Triple X was enjoying a roaring trade. As Sam approached, two men shot through its swing doors to land in the muddy street below the boardwalk. After picking themselves up and wiping their soiled hands on their breeches, they stumbled into the next-door bar.

Sam had heard tell how everything had changed in Victoria since the discovery of gold in the Fraser River Valley. The changes had not been exaggerated. If anything, the influx of miners from San Francisco had been underreported. Throughout the settlement there was a great sense of urgency. The boardwalks teemed with men from all walks of life thrown together in one heaving mass of male humanity, all in a hurry, all with the yellow gleam of gold in their eyes.

Sam paused for a moment on the Triple X's threshold listening to the diggers carousing within. Then, thinking he was less likely to be noticed in a crowd than lingering suspiciously in the street like the fugitive he now was, he ventured inside. The place was heaving. A few of the drinkers glanced quizzically in his direction then, to his intense relief, returned to their glasses. The majority paid him no attention at all. Despite this general lack of interest, he felt immediately out of place, not least because he was dressed in the flat cap, pale grey shirt and canvas breeches of a collier. He was lacking the uniform diggers' red-and-blue shirt, the brass belt-buckle, the hatband and boots. And they all spoke so differently. They were Yankees through and through, and he was a Cumberland collier from Whitehaven.

At least, he used to be a collier. Now he was an absconder. A fugitive. A contract breaker, or whatever the official word for it was. It was possible a desertion report had already been filed, and Hudson's Bay Company officers could be looking for him at this very moment. If he was stopped and questioned, his British accent would be a dead giveaway.

He could do with a double whiskey, if only to quell his nerves, but he needed to find Stag. The crowd, pushing and shoving, forced him to move sideways, bumping into the tables where people were playing cards until, leading with a sharp elbow to the fore, he managed to forge a path to the counter. The noise was incessant, and when a bartender finally turned his attention to him, Sam had trouble making himself understood.

'I'm looking for Stag Liddell,' he said, with a mouth so dry he found difficulty in formulating the words.

The bartender leaned forward and cupped his ear. 'What?'

'Stag Liddell. S-T-A-G. I'm here to see Stag.'

Another man working alongside, with long white cuffs from wrist to elbow, came over and explained. 'He wants the Britisher, the one who rented the storage out back.' He grinned at Sam. 'Lucky for you I can lip-read. Years of working in places like this.' He pointed to a closed door tucked away in a corner to his left. 'You'll find him through there.'

Sam thanked him with a curt nod and, relieved he didn't have to carry on any further conversation, elbowed his way over to the door. Opening it with some difficulty, because the latch was bent, he found himself in a small yard lit by a rusty oil lamp suspended from an overhead pole. The lamp cast an eerie, pale yellow light. On one side three sad-looking mules were tethered to a rail. They lifted their heads and examined him with bleary eyes. Directly opposite them was an outbuilding that appeared to have recently received a fresh coat of paint. A wooden sign above the door read 'Liddell's General Supplies'.

A shadow passed across the window. From its size and shape, Sam guessed it to be Stag. He knocked then entered quickly, closing the door behind him and narrowly avoiding knocking over a pile of iron buckets. Shovels of varying sizes, picks, spades, tin drinking-bottles and other gold-mining bits of kit were hanging from iron hooks and thick nails hammered into the timbered walls and ceiling.

For a split second when Stag glanced up and saw Sam, his eyes showed amazement, as if he'd seen an apparition. He ran his fingers through his hair then laughed and clapped Sam on the back. 'Well, damn me, Sam Gray. What are *you* doing here?'

'Passing through.'

'Where to? Company business?'

'No. I'm away to the goldfields.'

Stag scratched his head. 'Really? The Fraser River Valley?'

Sam nodded.

There was a pause. Stag's weathered face lost its laughter lines and his brow threatened a frown. 'Well, blow me. I take it you've bought yourself out of your contract?'

Sam shook his head. 'I've broken my contract. I'm standing before you nothing less than a common criminal hoping, as my marra, you will help me.' He looked down at his boots, expecting Stag to be shocked by this confession.

'How'd you know where to find me?'

Still looking down, Sam replied, 'I asked your good wife. I said I'd something for you and wanted to send it.' His comment to Stag's wife Kate, safely still in Colville, had been the first lie he'd told to facilitate his escape.

'Company officers'll be searching for you.' Stag bade Sam sit on a stool to warm himself by a small stove. He pulled up another for himself. 'I can't believe you're telling me you've deserted the mines. You, of all people.'

Sam sucked in his cheeks. 'I'd no choice. I'm going to make some brass then move on to San Francisco to begin a new life.'

Stag appeared to digest this unexpected news for a short while before clearing his throat and asking, 'What about Grace? Kate and I are expecting you two to get married.'

Sam had been trying not to think about Grace, the woman who had rejected him. 'I asked her to wait, then meet me in San Francisco.'

'This is becoming more and more extraordinary. What did she say?'

'That she'd a life in Colville, had made good friends and wouldn't break her missionary contract.' Sam swallowed, still raw from their difficult conversation. 'Or rather, that she *couldn't* break her contract. She said it would set a bad example, with her being a missionary.'

Stag let out a low whistle. 'I can understand that, knowing her sound Christian principles and loyalty to her work, but we thought you and she would get together. Especially after...'

Stag's voice trailed away, but the name he'd left unsaid hung in the air. *Especially after Evie.* The pain twisted in Sam's gut. His wife Evie had been lost to him, taken by the sea. Now it came to him for the first time that his friends must have been relieved to see him grow closer to Grace, convinced he'd finally found happiness.

He looked away and shrugged. 'It's not to be. Grace is in my past now.' Since leaving Colville he'd done his best to sublimate the overwhelming feeling of despair he'd experienced when it had slowly dawned on him she was rejecting him. Now he was learning those painful feelings were not as deeply buried as he'd thought. He suspected they would always be there, waiting to ambush him every time he thought of Colville.

'In the cold light of day, you can't be surprised she turned you down, can you?' Stag said. 'You were asking a lot. Especially as Grace is a missionary.'

As usual, Stag was talking sense. 'Aye. Well, we took our farewells,' Sam said. 'We're on different paths now.'

Stag's sharp gaze was on him. 'Did you tell her you were seeking me out?'

Sam twisted his cap in his hands. 'No. I didn't want her to have to lie for me. I thought it best she knew only what was necessary – that I was leaving to make brass, then heading for San Francisco.'

'The city lights.' Stag took in a breath, and Sam prepared himself for the lecture he knew he was about to receive. 'What if you don't find any gold? Or you have an accident? Lots of folk do. Getting to the goldfields is a danger in itself. Then there's landslides, rough water, bears, Indians and even the other diggers.'

'I know, but I have to do it. It's all I can think about. You won't shop me, will you?'

Stag sighed. 'Of course not. I don't work for the Company anymore. My contract's finished.' He got up from his stool and put his hand on Sam's shoulder, giving it a squeeze. 'I don't have to say I've seen you and I won't, but it's not too late to change your mind. You could go back and say you had an aberration. That would be that, I'm sure of it. The Company won't want to lose a collier as experienced as you. There'd be some disciplinary action, a fine maybe, then it would all be over.' He stepped back. 'What must Grace think of you as a deserter?'

'It don't matter now what Grace thinks. Colville has too many memories associated with death that plague me. Lives lost and hopes thwarted. I want a new life away from all that.' Sam looked away, ashamed he'd let his emotions burst out. His eyes fell on the ordered shelves, the boxes of hardware, the neatly stacked tins, the coiled ropes, and the buckets hanging from the walls, and he felt a pang of envy at Stag's settled life. What wouldn't he give not to feel this restless urge? 'I'm looking for peace,' he said.

'Peace? What kind of peace?'

'Peace of mind and release from the ghosts of my past. Colville is where I lost my wife and where I was rejected.'

The two friends then fell into an awkward silence. The memory of his wife Evie's lifeless body, dragged from under the log boom and laid out on the dock, her sodden hair plastered to her cheeks, leapt into Sam's mind. This and the wretched conversation with Grace seemed destined to live in the deep recesses of his mind, and he thought they probably always would.

Sam looked round again at the well-ordered stock room. Stag had meant it when he'd said he was starting up a business in Victoria. 'I'm doing what you're doing,' he said. 'A new start. The Company officers know I'm friendly with you, so I must move on.'

Stag pursed his lips. 'They'll go to my tent and be directed here. I'm well known now I've this lock-up store, so it'll not take them long to find me. Aye, you can't stay here.'

'Can you find me somewhere to lie low? And how quickly can I get out of here to the diggings?'

Stag's brow creased in thought. 'I'd say two days to set you up before you can even leave. You'll need full kit and a digging licence. Then there's the transportation across to New Westminster and up the Fraser River Valley. It's a long trek from here.'

'Can you help me?' Sam put his hand in his bag and pulled out some dollar bills. 'I've brass to pay my way. I called in most of my wages afore I left.'

'You'll need that for passage across to the mainland and to register a claim. If you can get on a boat, that is.'

'If?' Sam had assumed there'd be plenty of boats heading his way.

'Everyone and their mad dog wants a passage to the mouth of the Fraser River right now.' Stag pulled out his pocket watch. 'We've to move fast. I may be able to pull in a few favours to get you a passage.'

'And the licence? I know I've to have one.'

'That's no problem. Ask no questions, but you'll remember I used to issue those for the Company. First thing is to get you a bolt-hole and I may have the perfect place. Upstairs.'

'Upstairs? Isn't that too close?'

'Come and meet Daphne du Bois. She'll look after you. For a price, mind you.'

'Who is she?'

'This is Daphne's place. I rent this space. She keeps house upstairs with her niece, Lisa. It's where they carry out their business.'

'Their business?'

Stag smiled. 'They entertain gentlemen friends.'

Sam leaned forward. 'You mean they keep a whorehouse?'

'A pleasure palace is what *they* choose to call it.'

CHAPTER TWO

Sam followed Stag up a set of well-worn ladder-like steps fixed to the outside of the main building. Stag knocked loudly on the door at the top, while Sam held back, wondering what and who to expect. As far as whorehouses went, he was a complete innocent.

Stag smiled at him. 'You can uncross your brow. They'll not be working while the bars are still doing good business.'

A woman's voice invited them in. Once inside, Sam looked around, open-mouthed, asking himself how this happened. *How did I, Sam Gray from Whitehaven in Cumberland, end up here?* It was a shock after coming up the dusty stained steps with their creaky handrail to suddenly find himself in such lavishness. Red velvet curtains with gold-braid ties adorned two windows looking out into the street below. There were matching wing chairs with footstools. The room was filled with rich perfume and the lingering haze of expensive cigar smoke.

A chaise longue leant lazily against one wall. Over its side was draped a shawl fashioned from cream Chinese silk. Daphne du Bois, her auburn hair piled on top of her head, walked forward to meet them, her skirt brushing against the shawl's fringe.

'Ah, my tenant.' She looked over Stag's shoulder and her eyes lit up. 'You've brought a friend. Please sit, both of you.'

'Meet Sam Gray, my best friend and "marra", as we say in Cumberland.'

Daphne put out a hand encased in shiny, silky gloves that reached beyond her elbows. 'Pleased to meet you, I'm sure.' She had a Yankee accent, like the diggers in the bar, but spoke with a gentler, more feminine tone.

Sam felt the smoothness of her glove in his palm. He thought she held his hand for a little longer than was usual and wondered if he was imagining it.

While Stag was explaining Sam's situation and predicament to Daphne, a younger woman appeared.

Daphne performed the introductions. 'This is my niece, Lisa. Lisa, you know Stag. This is his friend Sam.'

Just as Daphne had done, Lisa extended a gloved hand to Sam and smiled. This time he did not imagine it. She placed her other hand over his, so he could not withdraw his own without seeming impolite, and looked right into his eyes as she gave his fingers a gentle squeeze. Sam felt himself blush, and no wonder. He had never seen such a beautiful creature in all his life. Everything about her was perfect. Her green eyes, her smooth skin, the light line of freckles across her nose and her full, rounded lips. Her skirt was of a light blue material and her bodice so tight, it must be what people meant when they referred to a corset. Her breasts, rising in majestic domes, were bordered by intricate embroidered black lace that traced the bodice's edge. Dark blue lace ran in wavy lines from her shoulders to her waist. Sam was sure even her toes, within their tightly-laced satin boots, would be flawless too.

Sam had always imagined 'ladies of the night', as he'd heard them referred to, as coarse and bawdy. He'd seen such women plying their trade to visiting sailors down by the docks in Whitehaven and to local colliers in back alleys, and there had always been a look of desperation about them. He'd never been tempted; he was too frightened of the possible repercussions and could never understand why any man would want to go with such women. Daphne and Lisa could not have been further from his idea of whores.

Stag's voice broke into his thoughts. 'I know my store couldn't be any nearer,' he was saying, 'but to my mind will a Company officer think of looking here? What do you say?'

Daphne was looking at Sam as if assessing him. *Is she wondering if I'm too much of a danger? Is she worrying about lost trade? Is she wondering how much I'm prepared to pay?*

It was clear Daphne was in charge, for she didn't consult Lisa at all. 'We've the back room we use for overnighters, but it'll mean we lose two nights' takings. Can you make that up to me? And food?'

'I've funds,' said Sam.

'He's a good lad,' said Stag. 'He'll not cause you trouble.'

Sam was beginning to appreciate the irony of just how dependent he'd become on others in his quest for independence. 'I'd appreciate your help,' he said. 'I'm just trying to start a new life, like you've begun a new life here in Victoria.'

Daphne nodded. 'Two days, but no more, and you're to stay in your room when we've clients.'

Sam hadn't thought of whores as having 'clients'. In fact, he'd never even thought of them as having a business.

'What about the barmen downstairs? They know I came in and asked for Stag.'

Daphne waved her hand as if swatting away a fly. 'They work for me and I pay them well. When I've had a quiet word with them, it'll be as if you were never here.'

It was clear Daphne du Bois had financial acumen. But then, when Sam thought about it, she'd come all the way from San Francisco to a strange place, set up a bar with an upstairs whorehouse and was renting an outhouse to Stag. You needed to be sharp to do that. Very sharp.

Daphne and Lisa disappeared downstairs, leaving Stag and Sam alone. Sam leaned forward. He had to ask. 'Stag, how do you know Daphne and Lisa?'

'I rent the storeroom, at a good price I may add, and I see them all the time.'

'You didn't know them before that?'

'Everyone knows Daphne and Lisa. Being seen out and about when they're not working is how they drum up business.'

'I mean...' Sam paused.

Stag laughed. 'You mean, do I *really* know them? In the biblical sense?'

Sam felt his cheeks redden. 'Aye, just wondering. Marra to marra, you understand. No further.'

'They are both delightful in physique and mind, but no. Firstly, I love my wife. Secondly, I've vowed never to mix business with pleasure. And thirdly, you must put your mind to who else has climbed the stairs on their way up here. No, they're safe from me and they know it. We've a purely business relationship that revolves solely around the storeroom rent.'

'You're just friends?'

'Aye. I know we're always saying it, but things are different here. We're not in Whitehaven any longer. We could never have been friends with the likes of Daphne and Lisa back home. You put your finger on it when you said we're all here to try and make new lives for ourselves. And if you're worried about their morality, they go to church every Sunday.' He laughed. 'I have to give those two credit, turning up every week in their Sunday best. It's probably the most lucrative advertising they do.'

When Daphne returned, she showed Sam into a room decorated in the same splendid manner as the reception room – all red velvet, gold cord and plushness. The bed, as he'd expected, took centre stage. There was one wooden chair which was probably for customers' clothes, a washstand with basin and jug, and towels – a tower of towels. A round table in the corner held two glasses and a decanter, which he judged by the colour of its contents to be liquor. Looking more closely he could see the curtains had seen better days. They were worn where they scraped the floor, giving an air of faded glory.

It was at this point the reality of his situation came home. *Have I done the right thing? Perhaps I should have stayed in Colville and made a life with Grace after all. I don't suppose we'll ever meet again now.* The last thought was too overwhelming to dwell on, and besides, it was too late for regrets.

Sam turned his mind to the next two days. Stag had insisted he remain indoors and not set foot in the streets, because he was so obviously a collier. Despite washing himself several times on the trip down, there was still coal ingrained in the creases of his face. His hands, too, were colliers' hands. He wore his occupation on his body. There was nothing in the slightest of the Yankee about him. In daylight he was an oddity on the streets of Victoria and would easily be picked out. He could see the sense of staying inside, but he felt helpless at the thought of spending two days idly twiddling his thumbs.

CHAPTER THREE

The next morning Sam awoke to a loud, aggressive banging. A minute later Lisa, wearing a lot less than she'd been wearing the evening before, ran into his room and shut the door. Sam was instantly alert and afraid.

'Quick,' she whispered, putting a finger to her lips.

Sam had no time to protest as she climbed into his bed. 'Stay underneath me,' she said, still in a whisper. 'A Company man's here looking for you.'

Sam's heart sank. Not only was he going to be discovered, but it would get back to the Colville community he'd been found sheltering under a whore. He would never live that down, no matter how loudly he protested the situation and his innocence. Men would snigger and tease him and the womenfolk would look at him with distaste.

There was the sound of a man's gruff voice followed by Daphne's reply.

'Mr Cotton, we never entertain colliers in this establishment for the simple reason they can't pay. Why take a collier when you can hook a digger, or a Frisco salesman with gold who'll leave a big tip? If you don't believe me, take a look.'

Real fear coursed through Sam's body and he understood now the expression of 'blood running cold'. *Why is she saying such a thing? He'll come in here and see me.*

Lisa, taking her weight on her knees, raised her body and pulled the sheets around her to form a tent so when the Company man opened the door Sam's face would be hidden from view. He would only be discovered if the intruder walked right into the room. She turned her head when the door opened and let out a string of the worst expletives Sam had ever heard – not even from the roughest drunken sailors on the quay in Whitehaven.

To Sam's shock and surprise, she ended with '…and after this intrusion, don't think you can resume your Wednesday afternoons without a gift in a fancy ribboned box and a flask of decent grog.' Mr Cotton retreated, spluttering an apology, and took his leave of Daphne before departing.

Lisa lowered her body onto Sam's and looked at him with questioning eyes. 'Shall we continue?' she asked. 'No charge.'

When Sam hesitated, Lisa propped herself on her elbows and raised an eyebrow. Still shaken from the fear of his near discovery, Sam could only gawp at her.

'Ah, you hesitate. It's my guess you've a lady friend back home to return to.'

It was true enough he'd had a lady friend in Colville,

but since Grace had unequivocally rejected his proposal of marriage, he could hardly agree she was one he was going to return to. There was also the added impediment that as a runaway Company deserter he was unable to return there.

Lisa took his silence as confirmation and Sam decided not to correct her.

'You're off to make your fortune for her? Will she wait for you?'

'She's a missionary.'

She let out an unruly laugh. 'Lordy be. Well, I didn't reckon on that. I can't do this to a missionary's fella. Ain't right, whichever which way you look at it.' She rolled off him and got out of bed. 'It's early, but if you git dressed, I'll cook up some grits.'

Sam was left wondering if he'd missed an opportunity a more adventurous man would have embraced gladly, both mentally and physically. He'd only had to say yes, or even perhaps given a slight nod, but he hadn't, and although a tiny part of him wondered what it would have been like to savour the delights of the perfect Lisa, the rest of him knew he'd done the right thing.

The following morning Stag appeared, carrying a large canvas bag. He set it down on the floor and pulled out three crumpled Yankee digger's red-and-blue shirts, some thick striped trousers, a brass eagle belt-buckle and some well-worn hiking boots that threatened to engulf Sam's kneecaps.

Sam disappeared into the bedroom to change, reappearing a few minutes later feeling very different. The shirt sleeves were too long and Lisa stepped forward to roll them up. She pointed to one of their full-length mirrors, saying, 'Take a look at yourself in that. You may not sound like a Yankee, but at least you look like one now.'

'Yes, siree,' said Sam, 'Indeedy ah do.'

Daphne laughed. 'Not bad, but safer to keep your mouth shut. That Britisher accent of yours is distinctive.'

Sam examined his new uniform. He had to admit, he really did look the part. 'There's pockets in the shirt as well as the trousers, front and back.' He put his hand inside the right-hand shirt pocket. 'Deep ones too.'

'Make sure you keep them buttoned up tight at all times. There's plenty light-fingered enough to relieve you of your baccy pouch and any other valuables. It's dog eat dog out there, I've heard.'

Stag brought out a Colt revolver and laid it on a table. 'And there's this.'

Sam hadn't given a thought to carrying a gun. A knife, aye, but a gun? He knew he had to pick it up, but he hesitated.

'You *can* shoot, can't you?' asked Daphne.

'I've used a rifle in younger days for vermin – pigeons, rabbits, foxes, that kind of thing – but not a handgun like this.'

'Well, you can't go without one, even if you never use it,' said Stag.

'Everyone's carrying one these days,' said Lisa,

admiring herself in the mirror. 'I make them take them off at the door and put them in there.' She pointed to a highly polished mahogany box on a side table.

Stag handed the gun to Sam. 'It's not loaded, but always treat it as if it is.'

'I know that,' said Sam, gingerly turning the gun over in his hands.

'You can practise in the woods when you get there. I've arranged a passage for you and sent your mining kit on ahead under the name of Sam Jenkins. Your boat sails at 8 pm.'

Sam put the gun down and offered his hand. 'I really appreciate all you're doing for me.'

Stag took the outstretched hand in his. 'That's what a marra's for, to be there when he's needed. Only real problem I can see is, it'll still be light when you leave. Our main difficulty is smuggling you from here to the boat.'

Lisa turned round. '*We* can get him there.'

'How?' asked Sam, stealing a glance at Stag.

Lisa raised her skirt sufficiently to reveal a shapely calf. Giving a little twirl she said, 'We'll hide you under our skirts.'

Daphne chuckled. 'Of course, we can use the buggy trick.'

'Don't see why it won't work.' Lisa flashed Sam a smile.

'With that level of risk,' Daphne told him, 'it's gonna cost you more. We'll be taking a big risk ourselves, you understand.'

'Now I'm even more confused,' said Sam. 'What's the buggy trick?'

Daphne leaned forward. 'Every now and then Lisa and I take a buggy and ride up to Esquimalt, Victoria's deep harbour where the big ships come in. We put on our finery, and if it so happens that the *Burnham Green*'s come in from Frisco, we take a liquid delivery, secrete it under our skirts, and bring it back.'

Sam raised an eyebrow. 'You smuggle liquor into town?'

'Top-quality rum at an excellent price. We're friendly with a few of the loaders down there. They come over as if to pass the time of day and when no one's looking they slip us liquor. Works a treat every time.'

'You do this yourselves?' Sam was both impressed and surprised.

'Involve someone else and be forced to give them a cut? Nope, that'd be bad business.'

'The men working up there know us,' said Lisa. 'Some of them are clients. We'll not stand out as anything unusual. You'll be well hidden.'

'You'll just not have to sneeze or cough,' said Daphne. 'Then the game'll be up and we'll all be in for a whole might of trouble. They'll throw the book at us for assisting a Company deserter.'

Sam was shocked to hear someone refer to him as a deserter. Although he knew it was true, it still stung his ears. Regarding the plan, he didn't know what to think, but a lift was a lift, and they'd left him in no doubt he'd be rewarding them handsomely.

❉ ❉ ❉

As part of Sam's kit, Stag had found him a small digger's rocker with closely meshed sieves for catching gold. Despite being heavier than the more traditional pan, Stag had told him, a rocker was at least five times more efficient. Sam spent all afternoon in his room putting it together and taking it apart. He was glad of the diversion. It was frustrating being cooped up listening to all the excitement going on outside in the street: the whoops of delight from drunken diggers, the cursing of the buggy drivers as they edged gingerly from pothole to pothole and the clomp of heavy boots on the boardwalk. At one point he laughed out loud at the thought that there must be many a twenty-five-year-old male would think being cooped up in a whorehouse for two days was the equivalent of having died and gone to heaven.

Learning to put a rocker together was tedious, but he needed to be proficient. Stag had drummed into him how vital it was to get the different sieves lined up properly so the gold separated from the gravel. The rocker was to be taken apart every two hours and the sieves washed clean.

'If all else fails,' Stag told him, 'there'll be some 49er old-timer from the Frisco gold rush who'll help you out, in exchange for an hour or two of your time hearing out his stories.'

CHAPTER FOUR

When the time came for Sam to take his leave, he didn't need to put on a brave face. He was surprised at how easy it had been to find the courage and strength to change direction once he was set on what he wanted.

Sitting on the plush chaise longue waiting for the ladies to finish prettying themselves, he asked Stag, 'How long do you think they'll look for me?'

Stag, standing with his back to the window, shrugged. 'The last time someone deserted word came back they'd landed up in Frisco, so the alert was called off, but his name's still in the register. That's four years back.'

'He's free?'

'Aye, unless he sets foot on land where the Company can reach him. Then he'll be arrested and locked up. I don't suppose *you'll* ever want to come back as a deserter. Although you can always buy yourself out of your contract if you make enough brass. Then you really could be a free man.'

'I'm know I'm doing the right thing,' Sam said, wondering if Stag believed him.

'You've to understand, it's not just about making a new life. Sad memories are everywhere in Colville. I lost my wife to the water there and when I found love again I was spurned. I'm hoping the memories won't follow me to San Francisco.'

'I don't think running away'll free you of remembering.'

'I just can't go back.' Sam prickled at the thought. 'Not now.'

Stag pulled a piece of paper from his pocket. 'Here's your government digging licence.'

Sam thanked him profusely and opened his bag. 'It's ten dollars, isn't it?'

Stag put out a hand. 'No need. Ask no questions how I got it, just accept it. They'll check you've a licence when you board the ship – no licence, no passage – so I've made it out in the name of Samuel Jenkins.' He held out another piece of paper. 'Do you remember Billy Botcher?'

'I do.' Sam remembered Billy well: a lively sailor on the ship carrying the colliers from Whitehaven to Vancouver Island, who'd been good to everyone regardless of their position and had taken time to entertain the children.

'He's got a general goods business in San Francisco. He helped me set up here and gave me excellent credit terms. I don't know what he's doing now. He told me he travels a lot looking for business, but here's the address he gave me last time I saw him. When you get to San Francisco you should drop by and see him. He'll be a useful contact.'

Sam took the paper. 'Thank you. Will you remember me to Billy and tell him to expect me?'

'I don't think that's a good idea. You don't want to leave any tracks that can be followed up or cause him any aggravation if he returns to Victoria. He'll know you when he sees you. What message shall I send to Grace?'

Sam didn't answer immediately. He wanted to say 'Tell her, when you see her, that I miss her,' but instead he said, 'Tell her I'm safe and well.'

Stag put on his hat and slapped Sam's back. 'Mind how you go. I mean it, it's tough out there.'

Sam reciprocated the backslap and the two men shook hands.

'Thank you,' Sam said again. 'You've been a good marra to me all these years.'

'And you to me.' Stag was at the threshold when he turned back. 'I almost forgot; you need a hat.' He took off his own and brushed it round the brim with his elbow. 'Here, take mine. Can't say as it'll bring you luck, but I'd like you to have it.'

Sam accepted it and thanked him. Having felt completely in control of his emotions up to that moment, he was caught unawares by an overwhelming wave of sadness. He would probably never see his Cumberland marra again.

❋ ❋ ❋

When it was time to leave the Triple X, Sam crept down the stairs, his heart in his mouth, doing his best to avoid pulling too hard on the squeaky handrail. After reaching the bottom he climbed into the buggy and hid under the women's skirts. He was able to squash himself between the many petticoat layers so he wasn't pushed up against the women's actual legs. He felt a cover being thrown over their knees and it was only then he realised he was going to be short of air. Not short enough that he would suffocate, but he would be unbearably hot and that might set off a coughing fit when he needed to be silent. He'd anticipated a degree of jolting from potholes, but not the stuffy, all-encompassing heat.

Out on the open road, Sam lifted up a corner of Lisa's skirt to let in some air. When he went to let it fall, he felt Lisa's hand; she was holding the layers to let in air, having presumably realised his predicament. No doubt it was warm for them too having his body heat so close.

When the buggy stopped, Sam heard Lisa's voice.

'Well, if it isn't Mr Cotton, our favourite Company man again, out and about around town.'

Icy fingers of dread wrapped themselves round Sam's heart. *Is this all going to be for nothing?* There was the loud crunch of riding boots on gravel. Then he heard Mr Cotton's voice.

'Good evening, ladies, what brings you here today?'

'Ooh, Mr Cotton,' said Lisa. 'You sound like a Customs man. We're here to pick up the diamonds we ordered in San Francisco some months back.'

'Diamonds? To buy?' Sam could hear the surprise in Cotton's voice.

'Of course, to buy. There ain't nothing sale or return about us, is there, Lisa?' Daphne giggled.

Despite his fear of being found out, Sam had to smother a chuckle. Miss du Bois had a good line in banter.

Mr Cotton began to laugh. 'Well, I shouldn't be surprised, since you've a damn good business in town, but I don't believe you.'

He's flirting with them, thought Sam.

'You can see right through us, can't you?' Daphne said. 'You're right, we're here to take the air, like we sometimes do. Anyways, what are *you* doing out here?'

'We're keeping a check on licences and men in and out.'

'Still looking for that deserter?' asked Lisa.

Sam could imagine her tilting her head to one side, her face one big smile, eyelids fluttering.

'Yes. Heard anything?'

'I haven't. What about you, Aunt Daphne?'

'I don't suppose it's anything, but I heard a blacksmith came into the bar earlier this afternoon, said he'd seen someone dressed like a collier up by Dr Helmcken's house. Was asking about licences and spoke like a Britisher.'

'You didn't think to report it?'

'Like you say, Mr Cotton, sir, I run a business. I've no time for running around sending messages up to the fort.'

'That's right,' said Lisa. 'We're working girls. We work hard.'

Cotton gave a chortle. 'I've noticed that, but this evening you've time for a little run out?'

Sam didn't miss the irony in his voice.

'Best get over there,' said Daphne, ignoring the taunt. 'It'll take no time on your horse. Look at the poor dejected thing. If that ain't a bored animal, my name's not Daphne du Bois.'

Cotton sniggered. 'We all know it isn't.'

Sam imagined a look of disdain spreading over Daphne's face. She seemed to enjoy a feisty love-hate relationship with the man.

'We've got better things to do than listen to you calling me out, haven't we, Lisa? You'd best git after that Britisher.'

'Good evening, ladies, enjoy your ride.'

To his relief Sam, heard the sound of boots walking away, then the squeaking of a saddle. When the sound of the horse's hooves had retreated to nothing, the cover was drawn back and Sam pulled himself up onto his knees.

'Your ship's to the left. Over there.' Daphne was pointing to a steamer. 'Git down quickly then go round the front of the buggy and walk slowly. Don't run. Keep your head down and your mouth shut.'

'Thank you –' began Sam.

'Don't waste time on thanks. Git going.'

Sam's legs had been folded for so long, they wobbled like a half-set jelly when required to bear his body weight, but after a quick grimace he kept on going, head high, with a wide stride. He felt genuine regret he hadn't been able to thank Daphne and Lisa as sincerely as he'd have liked to.

A queue had formed to board and he added himself to it, conscious this was the first of the many checks he had to get through. A boatman chewing baccy, with brown spit rolling down his chin, was lolling against the gangway examining licences. He was obviously bored because he barely looked at Sam's papers. On board there was standing room. The first mate was too busy directing operations to pay much attention to the latest arrival amongst so many, and Sam didn't have to say more than confirm his new name. A second boatman, standing guard over an untidy pile of kit bundles, directed him to the one with the label 'Sam Jenkins'. Relieved it had arrived, he examined the contents – a rocker, a long-handled shovel, a pick-axe, a heavy hammer, some rope, an iron spoon, a cup and bowl, and a cumbersome bundle consisting of a blanket tied round with thick string, containing a change of clothes. All Sam's possessions in the whole world were laid out in front of him. His hand went automatically to his waist, where his remaining dollars were secreted in a bag along with a good supply of baccy.

He found what he hoped would prove to be a quiet spot for the journey, where he could turn his back on his fellow travellers and keep himself to himself. He needed to be able to sound at least a bit like a Yankee and he listened carefully to the voices around him, practising the intonations in his head. He knew he had plenty to learn on all fronts, but he was a quick learner and had youth, strength, and a good ear.

The ship departed with a lengthy blow on the horn accompanied by rousing farewell cheers from the diggers on board. Those waiting on the quay for other ships raised their hats and waved. The atmosphere was jubilant. Sam wished he could share in the celebration, but travelling under an assumed name, and as a deserter, there was too much sweat on his brow, both literally and metaphorically, to be able to share in the excitement. Everyone on board was restless with anticipation, pacing back and forth in what little space was available. Many men asked others to watch their kit while they swayed on their feet and retched over the side. As they headed towards the Gulf of Georgia, and being tossed around, Sam too threw up. Whether his seasickness was caused by anxiety or the motion of the ship, he didn't care. All that mattered was that he was on his way to a new life.

CHAPTER FIVE

Dawn was breaking as the *SS Burnham Green* arrived at the mouth of the Fraser River to be met by a line of Company boats blockading the entrance to facilitate the checking of digging permits. To the north, huge majestic mountains carpeted with trees kept watch over the valley. Sam's jaw dropped. It was the sort of landscape that couldn't fail to take a visitor's breath away.

After the ship's papers were checked they were allowed free passage past Sea Island to steam up the northern arm of the river and on to New Westminster. They were now in calmer water. It took a while to dock, but with ships of all sizes coming and going, and with the usual activities of mariners on the quayside providing entertainment, there was a great deal to see. Sam watched the bars and stores taking down their shutters and opening up for the day.

On disembarkation, compared to the cursory licence check when Sam left Esquimalt, things were very different. An HBC officer, a beefy fellow seemingly full of his own importance, was checking licences and logging each digger's name in a thick ledger. When it came to Sam's turn his hands were shaking and he was worried he might show his nerves in his voice.

The officer glanced at him and held out his hand for the licence. 'Where're you from?' he asked.

'Frisco,' Sam replied, hoping his careful eavesdropping on his Yankee fellow travellers was going to pay off.

'Where you headed?'

'Fort Hope.' He sent up a silent prayer. *Dear God, if you hear me, help me out. Get me past this man.*

In a monotone, grown bored with having to repeat the same information over and over, the officer said, 'You can take a riverboat to Fort Langley, but after that you'll need portage. Steamers don't pass that far up river. Bringing any trade goods?'

Sam shook his head. Stag had warned him the Governor had recently issued instructions that all trade goods were to be seized to protect the Company's monopoly. It hadn't worried him, as he'd more than enough to carry as it was, but he could see a selection of spades, buckets, knives and axes piled high on the quay. He assumed they were confiscated goods from others in ignorance of the new regulations or hoping to flaunt them.

The officer pointed to his right towards a straggly line of untidily dressed men, all smoking pipes or chewing baccy. 'Over there for boats,' he said. It seemed strange to see him write 'Samuel Jenkins', not 'Samuel Gray', in his ledger. 'I'd get in line now,' the officer went on. 'There's a good three-hour wait to book a place.' He turned his attention to the man behind him.

Sam, with most of his kit strapped to his body and his blanket-roll on his shoulders, his rocker hooked over his arm, made his way slowly towards the boat queue.

Thank you, God. Thank you.

At the front of the line there was a makeshift sign nailed high up on a pole that said 'Langley $6'. As Sam approached the other diggers, he reviewed their kits in relation to his own. Every man had a bedding bundle tied round with thick twine. The taller and stronger the man, the bigger and heavier their rocker. Most men seemed to be lining up in pairs. Sam had already decided, if it worked out for him, he was going to go it alone. If there were to be any spoils, he wanted them all for himself. No good trusting a stranger with gold at stake, especially a Yankee. Besides, the last thing he wanted was to have a partner who'd want to know all about him and his past.

He'd been standing for half an hour when a stocky, broad-shouldered man came down the line, stopping to exchange words with each digger. When whatever he was offering was declined, he shrugged his shoulders and moved on to the next. After a short while the man reached the digger in front of Sam and he listened in.

'I've a seat in my river boat. Just one more and I can leave.'

'How much?' the digger asked.

'Twelve dollars.'

The digger pulled a face. 'You expect someone to pay double?'

'Sure I do. You'll still be waiting in line by the time my riverboat reaches the first up-river fur-trading encampment.'

'*I'll* take it,' said Sam.

The man looked him up and down before holding out his hand. 'Tug. Tug Tait's the name.'

'Sam. Sam…Jenkins,' he said, hoping he sounded like a Yankee.

Sam judged Tug to be about twenty, maybe twenty-five years older than himself, making him old enough be his father. He had the deeply wrinkled face of a man who'd spent most of his life outdoors and enjoyed strong baccy. It was an honest, open face, and when he smiled, the wrinkles spread out from the corners of his eyes in wide arcs to halfway down his cheeks. His brow was heavy over a flattish nose and he sported a moustache over a cleanly shaven chin.

Tug pointed to a wooden shack with 'Colonial Bar' painted in tall black letters over its doorway.

'Show me the colour of your money in there and if you've the twelve dollars the seat's yours. We leave in an hour. The river's a tad high, but she's still navigable.'

As Sam picked up his rocker and moved away from the line, the man who'd been in front of him shouted out, 'When you've handed over the money, make sure you stick to that boatman like glue. Looks to me the type to do a runner.'

Tug turned to the shouter. 'That's slander, that is,' he said. 'Everyone in these parts knows I'm an honest man. Tug. Tug Tait's the name.'

* * *

Installed with Tug and three strangers at a discreet table in a corner of the Colonial Bar, directly under a large glitzy mirror that had seen better days in a nice home someplace else, Sam handed over the twelve dollars. Tug extracted a beaten-up drawstring leather purse from his belt, deposited the cash in it, then introduced Sam to his three fellow travellers. The first was a thirty-something Yankee with smooth, almost manicured clerk's hands who spoke softly with an educated voice. Tug then introduced a pair of lanky identical twins, who were probably in their mid-twenties, around Sam's age. One twin wore a felt hat and the other a straw one. With their uniform beards, without the hats it would have been impossible to distinguish between the two. Sam had no idea what their professions might be.

With the financial transaction and introductions completed, Tug turned to Sam.

'What weapons have you?'

Sam pulled out his Colt with what he hoped was a flourish.

Tug leant back and held up a hand, palm facing outwards. 'Put it down. Never wave a gun around. A loaded gun can go off without you even touching it. I knew a young lad went to sleep with his Colt under his blanket. Forgot about it, went to make his bunk in the morning, pulled back his blanket and the gun went off. Killed him outright. Is yours loaded?'

Sam shook his head, putting the gun down. 'I'm only intending to use it for killing animals for food.'

Tug picked the gun up and inspected it. 'You've another, haven't you.' It was a statement, not a question.

'No, just this one.'

The clerk shook his head. 'No second revolver?'

'No. Isn't one enough?'

The felt-hatted twin frowned. 'We've got two and we each keep one loaded.'

'Why do I need two?' asked Sam, feeling very much the new recruit.

Tug handed the gun back. 'Lose your revolver and with no spare you maybe can't eat or protect yourself from animals and Indians. You've a choice: you can buy another here, or pick one up at Fort Langley. There are several gun stores there.'

The twin spoke again. 'It'll be cheaper here. There's portage to pay on everything up-river. I know, I've been working for a supplier writing out invoices. Some of the prices are four times what they should be and rising all the time.'

Although he judged Tug an honest man, Sam was mindful of what the man in the line had said about sticking with him after he'd handed over his money. 'I'll get another revolver at Fort Langley,' he said.

Tug nodded. 'I wouldn't go wandering around here on your own if I were you. You're already a marked man.'

Sam's stomach turned over. Had he been unmasked so soon? After a short pause during which he could feel his throat closing up he managed to say, 'How do you mean?'

'You've just paid double the rate for a trip with me up to Fort Langley without questioning it. That means you've brass on you. That'll have been noticed. Best stay here until we're ready to leave. Safety in numbers.'

Sam felt a wave of relief pass through him.

The boat turned out to be what Sam would have called a skiff back in Cumberland. For a moment he thought he'd been duped and that there was no way it could ride against the current. Then, when he looked around, he saw Tug's boat was the same as most of the others. Maybe a skiff was what they called a riverboat on the Fraser River. It was just big enough to take all five men and their kit. When they set off, Tug had to juggle to find a place amongst the other riverboats and canoes all heading up to Fort Langley, but it seemed to Sam he knew what he was doing.

CHAPTER SIX

If Sam thought the Victoria and mainland streets were alive with diggers, they were empty compared to those of Fort Langley. The settlement was seething with men all wanting a ride to Fort Hope. There were rows of circular canvas army tents along the riverbank bridle path. Outside the tents men were sorting their kit, sharpening knives, chatting and arguing. The diggers Sam had nudged elbows with in Victoria had been starting their journey, full of excited enthusiasm and goodwill. Here in Langley, stymied by the lack of up-river transportation, tempers flared quickly, with every man having access to a gun and a sharp knife. It didn't take a stranger such as Sam long to realise Langley was a dangerous place to be, especially when carrying kit and while trying to keep out of other men's way. On top of everything, they were in the shadow of the fort. The bastion and the long rectangular buildings were full of Company men, many of them likely alert to Sam's desertion.

As he mingled with the crowds alongside Tug and the twins – the clerk having abandoned them at the quay – Sam found himself continually on alert. He avoided looking people in the eye and dodged the drunks, trying not to knock into anyone who might turn on him aggressively. Added to the difficulties of moving around was the smell of the place. The odour of human detritus and unwashed bodies mingled with that of burnt meat, whale-oil lamps and wood fires assaulting his nose and mouth.

Tug led the group to a store selling the same mining-kit essentials Sam had seen in Stag's store in Victoria. This, though, was an emporium at least ten, or perhaps even a dozen times the size, with an enormous counter behind which several assistants were hard at work. As soon as they entered, a man with huge shoulders, rounded like a bear's, rushed out from behind the counter to greet Tug as a long-lost prodigal son.

'Tug, my good friend. Welcome.' He extended a hand and then, seeing Sam and the twins, a broad grin spread over his face. 'Ah, you've brought me business. Some greenhorns.'

Tug introduced them, pausing at Sam to say, 'This one's looking for a Colt.'

'We've plenty. Come over to the counter.'

Sam was uncomfortable with the twins' continued scrutiny and wished they would leave him alone and go off on their own, but it seemed they were determined to stick to him and Tug, like flies caught on a sticky paper trap. Within a few minutes, four handguns appeared on the counter. Sam stared at them, not sure what he was expected to do. They all looked the same to him, except for one which had ivory panels and silver stars set into the grip. He wasn't going to go for that one. He didn't do fancy in metal goods.

'Go on,' said the storekeeper. 'They won't bite.'

The twins laughed in unison.

Tug picked one up and held it. 'It's all about feel and weight. It's true they won't bite, but always remember they can kill.'

Sam moved the fancy-handled gun to one side then picked up and held each of the others in turn. Tug was right. They all looked the same, but one definitely felt easier in his hand.

'How much is this?' he asked, turning the gun over.

When the storekeeper named his price, one of the twins drew in his breath and whistled. 'That's four times the cost in Victoria.'

The storekeeper began some well-rehearsed sales patter. There was laughter in his eyes as he spoke. 'These guns are experienced travellers. They've come all the way from San Francisco, calling in at Victoria and New Westminster, admiring the scenery along the way, and now they're here in Fort Langley. They've survived storms at sea, tidal waters, Indians, and not least...' He paused and lowered his voice. '...evaded Customs and Excise men. Nothing comes cheap up-river.'

Sam struggled not to laugh. The twin, who didn't seem to have cottoned on to the tongue-in-cheek explanation, was rescued by his brother, who put a hand on his arm. 'I think we'll have a scout round and leave these good men to get on with their business.'

They walked off, the storekeeper's chuckling ringing in their ears.

'Can we negotiate?' asked Sam.

The storekeeper pointed to Tug.' 'Since this here fella's a friend of mine, I can knock you a dollar off.'

'Done,' said Sam.

'You'll be needing to feed it?'

For a moment Sam wondered what he meant, then gave a nod. They negotiated on the number of bullets he might need and were at the point when the storekeeper was going to announce the grand total when there was a loud shout from near the door.

Sam turned to see a store assistant, one hand round the neck of a burly guy with broad shoulders, and the other fastening his right arm against his body. The man snarled and cursed as a second assistant rushed up to grab his left arm. A hunting knife with a deadly serrated blade fell from under his waistcoat and clattered to the floor.

'Him again,' said the storekeeper. 'I've thrown him out for thieving before. Thinks we're suckers, but I tell you, all my assistants have eyes in the back of their heads, especially where our stock's concerned. You'd think that jackass'd know that by now.'

'Who is he?' asked Sam. He wouldn't like to meet the thief in a darkly lit back-alley – or a well-lit room, for that matter. There was an evil look to him.

'That, my dear friend, is Bulley. Aptly named. Bulley by name and bully by nature.'

'Is that his real name?'

'Who knows? There's many here travelling under a new name.'

Aye, I can confirm that, Sam thought.

'Main thing is,' Tug went on, 'he's a reputation in these parts for trouble. He's a real villain and he'll steal your last meal soon as look at you. Take a good look at him and never sit down to a card table when he's in the room.'

The 'villain', still pinioned by the two assistants, was discharging obscenities. Sam had a good look at him. Bulley was the sort of man who took up a lot of space. Back home in Cumberland he would be described as 'brawny'. His head was set on a thick neck framed by strong shoulders. Beneath his bushy eyebrows his black crows' eyes darted around, checking and searching – whether looking for opportunity or checking for danger, Sam couldn't be sure. The man's arms seemed overlong for his body and ended in hands which, for the size of the rest of him, had surprisingly stubby fingers. He was the sort of man who could intimidate without saying a word, just by standing too close or giving the evil eye. A man who could outstare the devil.

'Listen good, Bulley,' the storekeeper said. 'Next time you darken our door there'll be no time for questions. I'm gonna blast your head off. It's not as if I can't lay my hands on a loaded gun quickly in here.' He turned to his assistants. 'Take him outside and deal with him in the way we usually deal with thieves.'

Bulley spat out, but the storekeeper had anticipated this and stepped back out of range. The men disappeared and a few moments later Sam heard a loud yell. The two assistants then returned alone and took up their stations at the counter.

After settling up, Sam left the emporium with Tug and stepped out onto the boardwalk. There was no sign of Bulley, although all human kind was on display: Britishers and Yankees, native Indians, Chinese and Africans, as well as mixed heritage folk. The men who stood out were those who were blatantly not used to manual work. They struggled carrying their pans and rockers, and their blanket-rolls kept slipping from their carriers.

Sam pointed out a man scrabbling around on his knees on the ground, trying to gather up the bits of his kit that had slipped from his grasp. '*He* don't look like a man who knows how to sharpen an axe,' he commented.

'Easy pickings,' said Tug. 'Weak men like him and the perpetual drunks are the ones the card sharps and dice rollers single out. I don't think they'll target you. You look like you can swing a hammer without needing to be in a rage.'

Sam wondered what Tug would say if he knew of his years as a collier, wielding a pickaxe and coal carting. He'd have liked to tell him. Instead, he nodded in agreement. When he'd decided to go digging, the state of his physique and his coaling skills had never occurred to him. Now he could see his strength provided him with an unexpected welcome advantage over many of his fellow diggers.

Tug took Sam by the arm. 'You'll join me for a whiskey at my expense, won't you?'

'I'll be glad to.'

As they were at the bar, an old-timer with a fine head of grey hair and teeth coated brown by baccy juice, addressed Sam. 'You headed up-river?'

'Fort Hope,' Sam replied. He suspected the man was angling for a free drink.

The old-timer surprised him by slapping a gold US dollar on the bar to pay for his own drink.

'I was headed up there,' he told Sam, 'but my instinct tells me to head north.'

'Your instinct?' asked Sam.

'You're talking with a San Franciscan 49er. Name's Wilson.'

Tug leaned forward, interested. 'I guess that means you know a thing or two about gold-digging.'

This was the very thing Sam would have said, but he was still mindful of his accent. Better if Tug did the talking for the two of them.

Wilson drew himself up. 'I sure as hell do know and I can tell you heading east is not the way to go.' He pulled out a pipe and tapped the bowl on the side of a brass ashtray, watching as dead ash fell out in a neat pile. 'Us 49ers can smell gold in the wind. Like those men with forked sticks that shake when they find water. I'm taking the steamer north to Harrison Lake in a couple of days.' He paused to fill his pipe. Sam found him entertaining, but he could see Tug was taking in every word. It was as if he thought the old man had got wind of something.

'I'll bet you didn't know the steamers could get that far,' Wilson went on. 'There's one done it right up to Port Douglas at the top of the lake. I'll wager steamers'll soon reach Hope and Yale going that way. That'll help clear the log-jam of men here in Langley.'

Tug slammed his dollar on the bar. 'You'll have another with us, won't you, old friend?'

'Don't mind if I do.' Wilson nodded. 'Mark my words, the Harrison Lake area is going to expand in no time. There's virgin land up there to claim and that means gold just lying around to be picked up when they've cleared it.'

They chatted for another twenty minutes and listened to Wilson's stories until he said he'd some folk to meet and had to be on his way.

'What do you make of all that?' Sam asked, when Wilson was out of hearing distance.

'I make a lot of it,' said Tug. 'There's sense in what he says in not following the herd. You might want to think on it and change your plans.'

'Shall we tell the others?'

'Not that clerk. He won't last two days digging a claim. He'll likely end up behind a counter in a bar, or keeping door on a whorehouse. Anyway, he ran off when we docked and I ain't seen him since.'

'And the twins? What about them?'

'Nay, they're brothers, that's what's wrong with them – specially where gold's concerned.'

'Why?'

'Cain and Abel, that's why. They'll likely end up strangling or shooting each other. But I can suggest they travel with you if you want me to. They'll be company.'

Sam shook his head. He wasn't looking for company – people probed and asked questions to pass the time. 'I need to thank you for all your help and advice,' he said.

'No bother.' There was a short silence before Tug added, 'Besides, you remind me of someone I've lost to this life.'

Sam wondered who it was. A brother? A son perhaps? Tug didn't pause for breath long enough for him to ask.

'You've youth, strength and enthusiasm. I'm hoping you've enough brass round that waist of yours to buy up a Harrison Lake claim right now.'

Sam looked down at his shirt. The outline of his money pouch was there for all to see. It had worked its way round under his shirt from the hollow of his back to his front.

'If you decide to go north, the Harrison steamer leaves the day after tomorrow. You can buy a ticket at the dock. It beats sitting round here for a couple of weeks hankering for a ride east, knocking into people, gambling and womanising in full view of everyone. Dammit, there's little else to pass the time. Think it over. Besides, Harrison is off the beaten track, and I reckon you're looking for somewhere you can hide yourself away for a while.'

Sam froze. 'Why do you think I'm wanting to hide away?'

'I've been in the Company office at the fort, read the latest notices, and with your phoney Yankee accent I reckon I know who you really are.'

Sam's whole body tensed. His muscles tightened, priming in preparation for flight, ready to run. *But where to?* He felt his throat close up. The instinct to get up and run was so strong, he was having trouble fighting it.

'When we met you were in a hurry,' Tug said. 'You don't say much in a group, probably to hide your Britisher accent, though I reckon you're an honest fella. If you've got this far, Lady Luck's gotta be on your side, but I'd drop the Yankee accent. There's plenty of Britishers up here, like the government engineers. You'll not stand out like you would have done down-river.'

'Who are the British engineers?' *They might turn me in.*

'They're government staff from Britain, so they're not looking for you. I've heard they'll be working to the north of Harrison surveying. It's not as if you murdered someone.'

'What makes you say that?' It hadn't occurred to Sam people might think he was a common criminal.

'If you had, it would say so on the poster in big black letters: "SAM GRAY – MURDERER". I'm surprised you didn't change your first name, but it's too late now. It's not my business to be a blabbermouth, but I may not be the only one to make the connection. I'd move on as quick as you can from here. Seems the Company intends making an example of you, if they're putting posters as far up the river as this.'

Sam began thanking Tug for all the help he'd given him, but he brushed his words aside with the sweep of a hand. 'Like I said, you remind me of someone I've lost. You take care now, and if you need it there's always a bunk at my place in New Westminster. Just ask for me at the Colonial Bar. And good luck – you're gonna need it.'

After Tug left, Sam, feeling quite alone again, with thoughts whirling around over what to do, found a stretcher-bunk in a large bunkhouse tent as far away from the fort as he could. The bunkhouse was run by a garrulous French Canadian charging three dollars a night, including evening grub. Twenty other men were boarded there. While allocating the stretcher-bunk the French Canadian pointed to a pile of skins in one of the corners.

'You can take one of those, but I want it back first thing. If you lose it or it gets taken off you in the night, it's ten bucks to replace, so tie it round yourself. Each skin's branded with its stretcher number.'

After a supper of charred squirrel, which Sam ate sitting on his stretcher to keep himself to himself, he was ready to bunk down. Glad he'd brought his own blanket, he was beginning to unroll it when one of the other men stopped him.

'I can tell *you're* a greenhorn. Your rolled-up blanket is your pillow in this neck of the woods. Open it out and as soon as you're dead to the world it'll be off your bed and into someone else's pack, before you can whistle up a hound dog.'

Sam thanked the man and accepted the skin allocated to his stretcher. It was stiff and stank, but he was too tired to worry. He tied it round his body and put both revolvers under his blanket-roll, where he could feel them.

He was woken in the early hours by a drunken latecomer tripping over the end of his stretcher, and lay awake thinking of the places and the people he'd left behind. He'd been dreadfully shaken by Tug identifying him. He'd lulled himself into what was now, with hindsight, a false sense of security. The idea of hiding away from the main mining areas was new to Sam. He'd intended to be lost in the crowd, but the more he thought about Tug's suggestion that he change tack and head for Harrison, the more it seemed the right thing to do, if only to get him out of Langley as quickly as possible. To sit around risking someone else questioning his identity was foolish. By the time the French Canadian began clunking pans and dropping lids in his efforts to produce twenty breakfasts, Sam had come to a decision.

During the following day he ran into the twins, who confirmed they were heading up to Fort Hope. He was probably imagining it, but he had the impression they were looking at him sideways, studying him. He felt unprotected and uneasy in their presence – so much so he pretended he too was still heading up to Fort Hope. Even if the twins hadn't guessed he was the deserter, it might occur to them later. They held no allegiance to Sam and he expected the reward money, whatever was being offered, would be welcome to them. That decided it for him: he would go in the opposite direction to the twins.

CHAPTER SEVEN

As the Harrison steamer pulled away from Fort Langley's dock – with a great deal of black smoke, airborne smuts, and churning of Fraser River water – to his dismay, Sam recognised the villain Bulley leaning against the ship's rail. He was struggling to light a cigar, but the draught created by the steamer's headway was making it an impossible task. After a few minutes he gave up and, with an irritated toss of his head, slotted the cigar into a well-worn leather case. There was something different about Bulley from the other men and it took Sam a few moments to realise what it was: he was the only man on the boat who was not accompanied by a digging kit.

Out of the corner of his eye, Sam watched as Bulley moved among the passengers. Several times he sidled up to a group of men and, each time, Sam could see he was moving in too close.

He's a 'dipper', thought Sam. *He's looking for an opportunity to pickpocket.*

Sam put his hand to his waistcoat, feeling for his pocket watch. It wasn't valuable, but it was his and he wanted to keep it. Then he let his hand fall and chastised himself. He wasn't anywhere near the man. Besides, dippers often watched as people checked their body for valuables and then moved in, knowing exactly where to strike. Better to move away altogether.

Anyways, if I see him pick a pocket what am I going to do? Nothing, that's what. I don't want to draw attention to myself. It was a real relief when, after more hours than Sam had anticipated, they docked at Harrison. Here, the river opened out into the long, glacial Harrison Lake, stretching as far as the eye could see. From his upper-deck vantage point Sam surveyed the town as he and the other passengers waited for clearance to disembark. One street ran along the water's edge and he guessed that would be called Front Street. A narrow track, which he anticipated would be named High or Main Street, had a few hastily constructed clapboard buildings on either side of it.

The settlement, like Langley, seemed to consist mostly of tents, both large and small. The sawmill stood out as the largest and tallest construction. A few outlier cabins had been built a short walk from the waterfront, and from the large wooden wheels attached to them Sam guessed they were for draining mine shafts and would require a large number of operatives. Definitely not the sort of operation he was intending to become a part of. He'd not left Colville's mines to sweat underground somewhere else.

It was evident that little thought of planning or orderliness had been employed in the layout of the town –

it had exploded in all directions. The word 'shambles' came to mind. The whole landscape was denuded of trees, as if a tornado had swept into town leaving sad, lonely stumps of varying heights wherever the eye wandered. There were no fallen timbers on the ground; every trunk and branch had been utilised for buildings and boardwalks. It was clear it was the lumber the men needed, for building and fuel, and not the land the trees grew on. The town's inhabitants had settled there to desecrate, not cultivate. On first impression it was a depressing, godforsaken place, and Sam seriously wondered if he'd made a dreadful mistake.

When the whistle blew to announce they could disembark, he and every other man from the steamer except Bulley made straight for the claims office, only to find it was closed, although people were inside sitting at desks, surrounded by papers. A notice announced its doors would open again at 6 am sharp the next day. There was much muttering amongst the new arrivals. 'Another goddamn hold-up' was a phrase much bandied about, but there was nothing anyone could do.

Sam set off to find a bunkhouse. After dismissing one because it was too expensive and another because the stretchers were narrower than he wanted and placed far too close to each other, he found one run by a jovial, middle-aged, overweight German called Herr Steiner with enormous sideburns and a thick German accent. At two dollars fifty it was a cheaper and smaller establishment than the one he'd used in Fort Langley, having only twelve stretchers laid out four to a row. He agreed terms, paid his money, and was allocated stretcher number eight.

With his digging kit stowed under the watchful eye of Herr Steiner for safekeeping, Sam left the bunkhouse and wandered around to get a feel for the place. The sun was just starting to drop, but he was curious, and enough time and light remained for a quick exploration. He began walking along Main Street's raised boardwalk, which ran between the clapboard buildings, but it was too narrow for its purpose. Not wanting to risk confrontation by bumping into someone and annoying them, he took some steps down and started walking on the muddy track. His boots made a sloppy, slurping noise with every step, and he had to keep his wits about him as he dodged piles of mule- and oxen-droppings.

He passed a doctor's rooms, a general store and three noisy saloon bars. As he reached the end of the boardwalk, he saw a sign in the top half of a window announcing 'Muldoon's – First-class barber, dentist, boot, shoe and clothing repairer'. Casting a curious glance through the bottom half of the lit window, to his surprise he saw a young lady, perhaps a few years younger than himself, sitting behind a desk sewing. He'd seen few women since he'd left Victoria, and those he had, he'd assumed from the style of their dress, were good-time gals. He stepped back up onto the boardwalk to get a better view and the movement must have caught the young lady's eye. She glanced up. As soon as she saw him peering in, she frowned and shook her head. He immediately stepped back and returned to slurping along in the mud. After a few yards, there being so much that was new to attract his attention, the young lady slipped from his mind.

On returning to Herr Steiner's bunkhouse for supper, he found his companions were an assorted crew, all with one aim – to make their fortunes. Two Californians had come up through Oregon to evade the authorities in Victoria and escape the licence fee. Four professional men from Seattle had thrown everything to the winds in the hope of earning what one had called 'an easy buck'. Three French Canadians, with long rifles, ate separately, speaking amongst themselves in what Sam assumed was French, but which no one else seemed to understand. Herr Steiner chatted and sang to himself over his cooking pots in German, but spoke to everyone else in broken English.

Sam turned in at ten o'clock. After lying awake on his stretcher for an hour listening to the intermittent snoring of the man on his right, he made the decision he must keep himself to himself, even if this made him appear unfriendly. He'd realised from Tug that trying to hide his Britishness was doomed to failure, and pretending to be something he wasn't was going to make him stand out more than acting the person he was: just another Englishman of the hundreds out there hoping to make their fortune. All he needed to do now he was through the official barriers was to keep to the story that he'd arrived recently from England by boat, that he'd spent a short while in Victoria and that he was now a digger. If anyone asked about the voyage over, he could say plenty about it in detail. It wasn't the sort of journey you forgot, even after four years.

CHAPTER EIGHT

Miss Kitty Muldoon didn't suffer fools gladly. When she saw the young man gawping at her through their window, her first thought was 'what an idiot'. Her second thought was that if she didn't want to be gawped at, she should remember to draw the blinds as dusk approached. Being one of only a handful of women in Harrison she was used to being stared at, but that didn't stop it irritating her. Soon after their arrival, Pa had instructed her to ignore the men outside the store at all times, while being gracious to those entering its portals.

'Every man coming through our door is a bringer of bucks,' he'd said, and Kitty had taken notice. Pa had said as soon as they made enough bucks, however long that took, they could return home to San Francisco, and that couldn't be soon enough for Kitty. When she'd pressed him about how many bucks they needed, he'd chuckled. 'The combined weight of us both in gold,' he'd said. Then he'd laughed loudly at the impossibility of such an idea.

'Services, that's what diggers want,' he'd told her back home, a tumbler of ginger beer in his hand. When Kitty had remonstrated, he'd replied, 'They're out prospecting all hours. No time for looking after themselves.'

'Can't they cut each other's hair and pull each other's teeth?'

Her father finished his ginger beer and reached across the table for the stoneware flagon for a refill. 'Maybe to start with, but earn a bit of brass through hard graft and a man wants to treat himself to a hot shave and a haircut. Wants others to know he's got spare brass to throw around looking after himself. You know, it's not the diggers that make the money, it's the storekeepers, the doctors, the people that transport them and take them home. Folk such as ourselves offering services, we're the ones going to make the big bucks.'

'But dentistry?'

'Anyone can pull teeth. All you need is a pair of pliers and the strength and nerve to do it. That's the foundation of the profession. And maybe not fainting at the sight of a bit of blood and the sound of a grown man crying.'

Kitty knew her pa had nerve aplenty, and pliers could be found in every hardware store.

'Diggers won't be bothered about qualifications,' he went on. 'They'll not want the sort of dentist that's studied for years and demands high fees, they'll want the rotten tooth pulled and the pain gone with it. With your ma gone now, there's nothing to keep us here, and we could make enough to buy our own barbershop.'

They'd given up their shop lease and before Kitty knew it, they'd arrived at Harrison, with pliers and scissors galore, where Pa had rented an office with living quarters above. He found a carpenter who could make the sort of chair he wanted that tilted back, and in what seemed no more than the twinkling of an eye, they were all set up.

To give her father his due, he'd bought a dental textbook, and in the three months since they'd arrived he'd pulled well over twenty teeth by her count, with no complaints except for a few disagreeable comments concerning the bill.

Kitty often thought how different it would have been if her mother hadn't passed away; she'd never have let her husband leave San Francisco and gallivant off on what she'd have called a fool's errand, let alone take their daughter with him.

But her father had been adamant. 'Kathryn, I can't leave you here on your own. I care for you far too much, and besides, you can be a support to your poor old pa. We'll be back quicker with two of us working.'

Kitty knew there was no point arguing with him when he called her by her full name. He rarely did so and usually only when he'd been drinking, but when he did, it meant he'd have no truck with dissent. Besides, there hadn't been much she could say against it; he was probably right.

Her responsibilities lay with clothing and footwear. Not only could she mend and darn, she could also run up a pair of trousers or a shirt in no time. They could make more money as a team, but it seemed to her no matter how many bucks they made, it was never quite enough to live in the style her father envisaged for their San Franciscan future.

Kitty heard the steamer's whistle blow as it prepared

for the return trip to Fort Langley, and soon afterwards three diggers dropped by the store, all fresh in from the previous day. One digger had brought in a pair of trousers that needed the knees strengthening with leather protector patches, another enquired how much it would cost for a hot-towel shave, then left saying he'd call again another time, and the third asked about having a tooth pulled.

'They've made me come,' he said. 'It's not so bad that chewing on a spot of baccy and a big slug of Irish whiskey can't ease it, but that's getting expensive.'

The side of the man's cheek was dreadfully swollen. 'Tobacco and whiskey might ease it for a while,' Kitty told him, 'but they won't cure it. Anyway, who's made you come?'

'Them in the bunkhouse, saying I've kept them awake all night with my moaning and groaning. I told 'em if I can sleep through it then so can they, but they've thrown me out until I gits it seen to.'

'I can see you're in real pain,' said Kitty. 'I'm sure Mr Muldoon will be free in a few minutes.'

The digger glanced towards the door. 'I'm not so sure it isn't passing off a bit. Reckon it's sorting itself out.'

Kitty laughed. 'You're not telling me you're afraid, are you? A big strapping digger like you?' Then she played her trump card, which seemed to work most times. 'I can come in and hold your hand if it'll help.'

The digger looked sheepish. 'Now then, there's no need for that.'

Kitty smiled. 'I'll let him know you're here.'

* * *

While the digger was having his tooth pulled, Sam was at the front of the queue in the claims office. There were two receiving desks covered in papers and maps, with a clerk sitting behind each one. Sam handed over his licence. The man took his name, wrote it in a thin ledger with marbled sides, then asked if he wanted a new claim or to buy one someone had abandoned.

'Abandoned? Why would I want one of those? No one would abandon a paying claim, would they?'

The man behind the desk yawned. 'People get rich and go home, they get sick, have accidents, many lose heart and sometimes they even die. Then their claim goes begging and we list it as abandoned.'

Sam wished he'd thought to ask Tug or the old-timer the finer details about staking a claim.

The clerk looked beyond him at the long queue of men. 'You'll have to decide. There's others waiting. Do you want one that's already staked or are you going to stake out your own? You can't register a claim on virgin land until you've struck gold.' He seemed to take pity on him. 'If you want virgin land then you're responsible for the security of your stakes until you get a strike. You'll have to pay someone to watch your stake markers don't get moved at night or you'll have to sleep out there yourself. Rain or shine.'

'Further to walk from the bunkhouse every day too,' added the man in the queue behind him. 'You need to think on that, but you need to do it right now. You're not the only fish swimming up-river in here today, wanting to git goin'.'

Sam didn't turn and acknowledge the speaker directly, but he registered his reasonable irritation. 'Is there a registered working claim available?'

The clerk rifled through his pile of papers and pulled out a yellow form. 'There's this gravel bar fronting the lake.' He held up a map marked with lots of rectangular boxes. 'This here's the one – number 73.' He jabbed at a spot on the paper. 'Worked by a digger name of F. J. Carter. A Scotsman.' The clerk turned around and said to his neighbour, 'That Scotsman, Carter, he did all right, didn't he?'

'Out at Abbot's Bar?'

'Yes, that one. Red hair. Head, chest and beard.'

'Well, he must have struck something or it wouldn't be registered.'

The clerk turned back. 'It's on a small bar just up the lake a bit from town.'

Sam looked at the map again. A green hashed area was adjoining the claim. 'What's that?' he asked.

'Indian encampment.'

'Will that be a problem?'

'Needn't be. There's a few encampments scattered through the claims area. You can look at it two ways. There's a ready labour supply if you need help or get into trouble. We had one man stuck in mud up to his neck for two days and by the time we realised and got him out it was too late. That'd never happen to you 'cos the Indians'd see you. Worth thinking about as a sole digger.'

The man was making a good point.

'On the other hand, they can be curious and you might

find them coming to stand and watch, which can be off-putting. But you can always send them packing with a bit of baccy. They all like a smoke, men and women.'

Sam was in two minds. A workable claim would save him a lot of trouble and mean he could start digging straight away.

'Carter was often in the saloon bar spending the proceeds. Why shouldn't it pay out for you?'

'But why did he leave it?'

The clerk consulted his neighbour again.

'Got knifed in a Langley bar brawl. I remember them auctioning off his kit on the quay.'

'I'll take it,' said Sam.

CHAPTER NINE

After winning a stunning ten ounces in gold nuggets on the first day, then nothing at all for a week, Sam decided he'd been sold a pup. His rocker saw no pay dirt at all. The apron underneath to catch the gold dust remained stubbornly un-stretched and empty.

The heat from the sun made him sweat, and more than once he thought how much harder it was digging above ground than working down the mine, where the heat was of a different kind. It was hard work tilting the rocker and changing the sieves. He'd soon realised it really took two men to use a rocker efficiently, and one of the friendlier French Canadians in the bunkhouse had suggested he hire an Indian. He'd thought about it, but didn't want to lose control.

Some groups had set up 'Long Tom' rockers that stretched twelve feet in length and required several men to shovel in the pay dirt at one end, then another man to add water, and another to agitate the muddy torrent as it passed by, racing and churning its way through the boxes. Finally there would be another man waiting at the end of the line to oversee the apron catching the gold. While Sam envied them the opportunity to swap places amongst themselves, or take a short rest, he had no desire to join them. His winnings would be for him and him alone.

Things improved gradually. By the end of the second week, he'd rocked thirty ounces in nuggets and dust and was elated. Back in the bunkhouse that evening one of the professionals, a doctor, boasted he'd made $200 in dust that day. The way the other diggers looked at him with undisguised envy troubled Sam and made him determined that no matter what joy the day brought him, he would always say it had been a bad day.

June began with unseasonably heavy rain, halting all operations. As each day passed and conditions worsened, the diggers became tetchier and more frustrated. The odd rainy morning or afternoon could be tolerated and worked through, or else seen as being useful for sharpening tools, or for catching up on lost sleep. Continuous rain waterlogged everything. It became impossible to operate any size of rocker or pan effectively.

Walking around became more and more hazardous as the uneven tracks, saturated with animal droppings mixed with the heavy rain, turned into raging, muddy torrents. The Main Street boardwalk became so slippery, folk were in danger of twisting their ankles and breaking their wrists if they fell off. On waterlogged days the diggers stuck to their bunkhouses, playing cards, rolling dice, arguing, reminiscing about the 'Frisco 49' gold rush and boasting about their diggings. Others became withdrawn and depressed. Under normal conditions everyone worked with speed and there was a general restlessness, but for some, when the rain was at its worst their brains seemed to wind down as well. These men even began speaking more slowly, such was their general malaise.

The rain proved a welcome boost for the Muldoon business as diggers took the opportunity to have their beards trimmed and check their clothing. Kitty couldn't remember ever having held a needle in her hand for so many days on end. The pads of her middle fingers were sore where she'd caught the skin. Hating to use a thimble, even though she knew she ought to, after a couple of days she'd given in and resorted to one.

At the end of the week, a day finally began with a clear sky and everyone breathed a sigh of relief. Everyone except Kitty, who held her breath. As the week progressed and the work piled up, Pa had wound himself up like a tight spring. He'd worked all hours, refusing food, not sleeping and becoming embarrassingly vociferous. It couldn't go on, and now the weather had changed and things were going to be back to normal, the screw had to unwind.

Around midday Kitty's fears were confirmed when Pa appeared in his Sunday best. They couldn't go to church in Harrison because there wasn't one, but there he was in his best bib and tucker.

'Pa, I think you've got your days muddled up. It's Monday today, not Sunday.'

'Is it, indeed? Well, I'm all dressed up now so I might as well take a stroll and show myself off.'

'Pa, you know what happens when you get like this.'

He gave a wicked, playful laugh, his eyes bright. 'When I get dressed up?'

'No, when you head out to a bar.'

'Ah, if I become strident you mean?'

'That's exactly what I mean and you know it.'

'No, no. no. Not today.' He opened the shop door and made a big show of sniffing the air. 'No, it's not a strident day. Not today.'

The door banged behind him.

As he trudged back into town, Sam distracted himself by singling out stones in his path, fixing his eye on them and giving them a good kicking. If they landed directly in front of him, he kicked them again. If they didn't, he selected another. He recognised the activity for the ruse that it was: to stop him dwelling on the fruitless day he'd endured. The rain had stopped, but the soil and the lake water were carrying so much dirt and debris the rocker sieves were clogging up within fifteen minutes. Normally he changed them after two hours or so, but he'd soon realised he was on a mission to nowhere. Better to pack up early afternoon and write off the rest of the day.

He was ten minutes from the bunkhouse, having just passed the doctor's office, when he saw a smartly dressed middle-aged man with well-cared-for whiskers exit a saloon bar and pause in front of one of its windows. He was unsteady on his feet. If he advanced any further, he was likely to slip off the boardwalk and fall the three feet below to land in the mud. Sam wondered if he was ill, and watched as he put out a hand to stabilise himself against the saloon window frame. At the same time another man was advancing on the opposite side of the street. Sam recognised him immediately. It was the first time he'd seen Bulley since they'd arrived together on the ferry.

Has he been here all the time and our paths not crossed, or has he been somewhere and returned? He was definitely the sort of man you couldn't walk by without noticing.

The well-dressed man's face lit up. 'Bulley, when are you going to settle up with me?'

Sam, now close enough to see the man's eyes were watery and red, realised he was swaying because he was drunk. Some passing diggers paused to watch.

Bulley sneered and kept on walking.

'I'm talking to you, Bulley.' The voice had an edge to it – that of a drunk sensing he's being ignored while determined to be heard.

Bulley stopped and looked across. 'I don't owe you nothing,' he said. 'Be on your way.'

The drunk tottered down the three steps leading from the boardwalk onto the mud and began weaving his way across the street, his eyes fixed on Bulley. It was now obvious to all that he was not only drunk, but angry. 'You owe me for a hot shave and haircut.' He glanced at the gathered diggers and addressed them, slurring his words. 'See that man, there?' he said, pointing. 'He's a thief.'

The situation had the makings of turning nasty, but what to do?

A voice rang out from the crowd. 'If he owes you money now's not the time to ask for it, Frank. You're drunk.'

Another voice joined in. 'Don't be a jackass. Go home, Frank, sleep it off. You can sort this out another time.'

Bulley frowned, making his ugly face even more off-putting. With spread legs and fisted hands, he adopted a belligerent pose as the man advanced. 'I tell you, you're mixing me up with someone else.'

Sam thought that highly unlikely; Bulley was a once seen, never forgotten encounter.

'I ain't mixing you up with nobody. You came in two days ago, said you'd be right back with the money and never showed up.' Frank turned to the crowd. 'My daughter'll vouch he's the same man.'

Bulley leered. 'Now, she's someone I could be interested in. I need someone to keep my lap warm.' He wriggled, spreading his fingers against his thighs.

Frank's cheeks, originally flushed from the liquor, were now red with fury. Having reached the other side of the street, he raised a foot onto the steps leading up to the boardwalk. Bulley stepped down onto the second step to meet him. Frank took a drunken swing and Bulley neatly avoided it, laughing at the wide miss. At this point Sam expected Bulley to step back onto the boardwalk and move on. He was younger and sober. Frank was older and the worse for wear in drink. Sam was wrong. Bulley's black crow eyes widened and, stepping forward, he grasped the lapels of Frank's jacket, pulled him forward slightly to gain momentum, then pushed him away so roughly he overbalanced and landed on his back in the muddy thoroughfare to thrash about like an upturned sheep. Bulley inspected his hands before wiping them ostentatiously on his breeches.

'That'll teach you to accuse an innocent man of theft,' he said, turning his back on where Frank lay sprawled in the mud, and walking away.

Sam looked to the small crowd of diggers still watching. He was expecting them to react in some way, to help Frank, but with the show over they began dispersing and it became apparent no one wanted to become involved.

'Can't someone at least take him home?' Sam called after them.

A digger, spade in hand, called out, 'You can deliver him to his daughter if you want to, Britisher, but I'd drop him off at the bath house first. He's Frank Muldoon.' He pointed down the street. 'You'll find his barbershop on the left at the end of this row. Don't worry, he'll be back to himself in the morning. It's not the first time he's had to be escorted home and I'm guessing it won't be the last.'

The man tipped his cap and continued on his way. Sam helped Frank up from the street. It seemed there was no part of him free from mud and he stank of alcohol and animal waste. 'Come on, let's get you to the bath house.'

As they walked in step, Frank, in a slurry voice, kept repeating how Bulley had stolen from him. Sam said nothing; he was pondering the name Muldoon. It wasn't until after he'd dropped Frank off at the bath house in the care of a Chinese attendant and found himself at the barbershop that he remembered where he'd seen it. He rapped on the window glass. The young lady who had frowned at him through the window on his first stroll through the town was sitting at a table sewing. She looked up and mouthed, 'We're closed.'

He rapped again. This time she shook her head and waved him away.

He went to the shop door and knocked authoritatively. After a short delay he heard footsteps. She opened the door just enough for them to converse. 'We're closed. Pa's not here if you're wanting a haircut.'

Sam was momentarily lost for words. She was much prettier in the flesh than through the window. She was practically attired – not overdressed in flounces and lace, like the other women he'd seen in the town. No fancy ribbons and furbelows. Her hair was dark, parted in the middle and pulled back. *Just like Grace's*, he thought. Although this superficial similarity put him off his stride, he still managed to notice her nice looks.

'If you've a bad tooth, you'll have to come back later.'

Sam pulled himself together. 'I'm not here for a haircut.'

'Then what *are* you here for?'

'If you're Miss Muldoon, I've come about your pa.'

'Yes, I'm his daughter, Miss Kitty.' There was a short pause while she looked him up and down. It was obvious she was reluctant to admit a stranger. 'Trouble?' she asked.

'A bit of a spat in the street. I've taken him to the bath house.'

'Is he hurt?'

'Just his pride.'

Kitty stepped back and opened the door fully. She smoothed her hair, saying, 'I was expecting this. You'd better come in.'

She led the way down a narrow hallway with a door off each side and steep stairs at the end, then turned right into a small room that clearly doubled as the barbershop's waiting-room and her workroom. Its window looked out onto the boardwalk. A sewing machine stood on a small table in one corner, alongside a pile of hand-sewing. On the floor beside the desk was an oval Indian-weave basket overflowing with bits of material, and beside that some neatly folded diggers' clothing.

'Sit down,' she said, indicating four chairs with their backs against the front wall, two of which stood either side of the window he'd looked through that first evening. Sam chose the chair that looked the sturdiest and least uncomfortable. He felt awkward intruding on a private family matter.

'Thank you for looking after Pa. Sometimes he falls asleep and if it's not in one of the saloons, it's the devil to track him down. What happened?' She sat down behind the desk, picked up a short length of lace and began running it through her fingers.

Sam told her about Bulley, omitting the crude remark he'd made about her, while Kitty listened and fidgeted with the lace. When he'd finished, she put down the lace and shrugged. 'I knew Gregory Bulley was going to be trouble and not pay up, although I'm surprised he's still here in Harrison.'

'His first name's Gregory?'

'Yes. At least, that's the name he gave me when he came for the haircut. He's got a face like a starved bird.'

Sam laughed.

'Why are you laughing?' she asked, a puzzled look on her face.

'It's that he reminds me of a bird too. A big black crow.'

Kitty smiled. 'Definitely not a sweet robin redbreast.'

'What's he doing here?' Sam asked.

'He's a trader. Brings all manner of things in over the border. Nails, hammers, cigars. Sometimes liquor. Plays cards, I understand. A bit of a drifter.'

'Just looking at him could bring on a bilious attack.'

Kitty shivered and screwed up her face. She stood up. 'Pa'll need clean clothes.'

'I can drop them at the bath house if you want. Save you going.'

'Will you?'

'It's no trouble. Besides, it's no place for a lady.'

To his amusement, she blushed.

'You've mud on *you* too. I expect it's where it's rubbed off Pa.'

Sam looked down. He hadn't realised how mucky he was. 'I'm a digger. A spot of mud don't bother me these days.' *You fool. She knows you're a digger. What else could you be, dressed as you are?* Just as when he'd been with Tug, under different circumstances he'd have told her he'd been a collier for over ten years, but he couldn't take the risk.

Kitty left to collect Pa's clean clothes and Sam heard her footsteps on the uncarpeted floorboards above. He went and stood in front of an oval mirror. There were streaks of mud where he'd wiped his fingers across his cheeks and forehead. He rubbed the marks, but he was only making things worse. Kitty must have noticed his attempt to clean himself up, because when she returned she invited him into the barbershop, handed him a towel and poured some hot water into an enamel basin.

When he'd cleaned off the easily removable top layer of dirt and was more presentable, she handed him a canvas bag.

'Here's Pa's clothes. Please tell them at the bath house I'll settle up tomorrow for their services if they'll call round.'

As Sam took the bag he noticed she had what back home they'd called 'piano fingers' – long, dainty ones with short, clean, rounded nails.

'Do you want me to collect him and bring him home? He was very unsteady on his feet.' Sam found himself hoping she would say yes so he could see her again, but he was disappointed.

'No, it's kind of you to offer, but they'll let him sleep it off. They know what to do on a strident day.'

'A what?'

'A strident day.' She gave a deep sigh. 'We never use the words "drunk" nor the more genteel "worse for wear". Pa might, when he's sober, refer to "an upset" or say "things got a little out of hand", but never once has he admitted to being "drunk".'

Sam suspected she wanted to share her troubles and it was perhaps acceptable to enquire further. 'Has he always been fond of liquor?'

'Since Ma died, a year back. As far as he's concerned, he's a religious teetotaller, apart from when he isn't, which all Harrison knows is more or less every four or five weeks.'

Sam had heard of people who were sober for a long time then, for whatever reason, would take to drink again.

'I take it today's one of his "strident days", then?'

Kitty nodded. 'I tell him people laugh behind his back, him being all dressed up and that, but he takes delight in it. Even chuckles and says how lucky he is to be able to entertain so many people.'

As Sam was about to leave, Kitty asked his name.

'Sam. Sam Jenkins.'

It was the first untruth he told her.

CHAPTER TEN

The next ten days passed with variable takings from the diggings. Sam's buckskin purse, where he kept his 'poke' – his gold stash – was beginning to swell nicely. It was no 'easy buck', but unlike the bunkhouse's doctor, he hadn't expected it to be. He calculated he'd taken about $267, which was half a year's wages coal-mining for HBC. Sometimes at the back of his mind when he dreamt of Evie, which he did occasionally and woke feeling sad and unsettled, he wondered how much it would cost to buy his freedom from the Company and return to Colville to his old life. He assumed he might have to reimburse his passage from England, although as part of his contract he'd worked off some of the cost of that during the voyage. And there would definitely be some sort of penalty. He couldn't remember exactly what his contract said and whether the penalty was financial or a spell in the lock-up, but the main thing was, he wasn't the same person who'd left his family over four years previously in Whitehaven. He was older, harder, more worldly-wise; they'd never recognise him back home and he'd little in common with them now. In reality, he was bound for San Francisco, and it was this plan he tried to focus on in his stretcher, listening to the continual snoring and incoherent mumblings of his sleeping companions. He would start some sort of business. Maybe carpentry. He was good with his hands and he knew about wood.

With some of the other diggers receiving letters, and having been gone for five weeks, Sam thought he should write to Stag in Victoria and let him know he was still alive.

Dear Stag,
June 21st

All is well and I am in good health. I have a small claim that is providing a good poke. It is a very different life here. I work all hours every day. The food is monotonous, but there is plenty. Tell my friends I am well and I will write again.

Yours,

S. Jenkins.

He re-read the letter carefully to make sure there was no indication as to his whereabouts. By 'friends' Stag would know he meant Grace. Having no idea whose hands his letter might pass through, he was not prepared to take any chances, even with his identity disguised. He was still fearful at any moment he would be correctly identified and arrested. It needed only a small slip to be unmasked.

He addressed the letter to Stag at the Triple X and

handed it, along with one dollar, to one of the steamship's crew, asking him to give it to Tug at the Colonial Bar to ensure it went on one of the Victoria-bound ships.

That evening Sam told Herr Steiner he'd sent the letter. The German looked dubious. 'I hope you didn't give it to a scamper.'

'A scamper? What's that?'

'Maybe not the right word. Someone who runs off with your money then throws the letter over the side of the boat. Some are scampers. Maybe not. Perhaps it's scarpers.'

Sam shrugged. 'Do you mean a swindler?'

Herr Steiner broke into a big grin. 'That's it.'

'Too late now,' said Sam. It had occurred to him that the letter might not get through, but there was no harm in trying, and he could afford the dollar. An hour later, sitting on his stretcher listening to the relentless pounding of the rain on the sailcloth roof, Sam began examining his shirts. They were in a dismal state. He only had three and he didn't want to waste money buying a new one, not with portage rates slapped on the price. He was wondering if he could ask Miss Muldoon to do some repairs when Pierre, the French Canadian in the next stretcher, pulled up a stool and sat beside him. Usually they only exchanged nods, but this time he seemed to want to engage in chat.

'How long you planning on staying?' he asked.

'Six months maybe.'

Pierre laughed. 'I'll believe that when I see your empty stretcher.'

'You think I'll stay longer?'

'*Oui, bien sûr.* Of course. A digger is never satisfied,

especially a man without a wife. You'll think maybe another week, then that turns into a month. You look at your poke – it's heavy, you have money, so maybe you get a little lazy. You think you'll take a few days off and gamble, make some easy money. The man you thought was a bit simple, the one who kept losing, turns out to be a card shark. You lose more with dice. You're cross with yourself, but you made a good poke before, so you can make it again. The result? You have to stay a couple more months. Then you go down river back to Fort Langley when the winter sets in. You spend your money in the saloon bars, go with the girls, you have a good time. The spring comes and you are here again.' He paused. 'Unless –'

'Unless?'

A fat gob of tobacco juice flew out of Pierre's mouth and landed on the bare earth between them. 'Unless you've a lady waiting.'

Sam gave a smile that he hoped said nothing and everything at the same time.

Pierre tapped his nose. 'Ah, there's a sweetheart. Your heart is captured, is it not?'

Sam kept smiling, as if he was shy. It was not a subject he wished to pursue.

'Ha, I am right.' Pierre slapped his thigh. 'Then maybe you *will* be leaving us in a few months. In the meantime, watch out for the card sharps and the new pretty ladies down the road.'

'Pretty ladies?'

'There's a whorehouse set up two doors down from

the doctor's office. Opened for business back end of last week. I'm surprised you don't know. I bet you if it wasn't raining there'd be a queue outside trailing right down to the lakeside and back.'

'Thanks for the advice. I'm not a gambling man and those ladies'll be safe from me.'

Sam laughed to himself. Pierre obviously thought him a very staid fellow. He'd have loved to tell him how he'd escaped discovery at the Triple X. That would have revised Pierre's opinion of him, perhaps even earned a look of respect or awe, but mostly Sam tried not to look back. He was firmly fixed on the future. It was just that now and then things people did, or said, dragged him into the past. He guessed it would always be like that, although he had to admit that thinking of his wife Evie now was not as painful as it used to be in Colville. She had been taken from him still loving him. She had not rejected him, as Grace had done.

CHAPTER ELEVEN

Almost three weeks had passed since her father's 'strident' episode and his run-in with Bulley. Kitty, to her surprise, several times found herself wondering what had become of Sam Jenkins. Twice, when walking to the general store for supplies, she thought she'd seen him. On both occasions it occurred to her a more brazen woman would have called out or run after him and waylaid him, but that wasn't her way. Besides, what could she say to him except to thank him once again for his kindness in helping her father?

Men requiring the Muldoons' services rarely made appointments, so when the door opened, setting off a jangling bell, Kitty never knew who was arriving. When she looked up one day and saw Sam, her first thought was that she wished she'd paid more attention to her hair that morning. He was holding a rolled-up ball of clothing which he put down on her sewing table.

'I've some business for you.' Unrolling the ball, he produced two shirts. 'Can you do anything with these?'

Kitty could see immediately they were almost beyond repair. 'I can turn the collars and stitch up some of the seams for you, but you've had good wear from them.'

Sam looked embarrassed. 'Hmm. What you're saying is they're past it.'

She began folding one of the shirts. 'Not beyond redemption. More on their last legs.'

'So, I need new ones?'

'No need for that just yet. I can give them a bit more life and you probably won't be wearing a shirt for the next couple of months, with it being summer.'

'But…?' He tilted his head on one side, gazing at her.

'But come autumn you're going to need something more substantial.'

'Is that something you can provide?'

'Oh, yes. You're staying for the summer, then?' The thought pleased her.

'Depends on my digging.'

'Where's your claim?'

'Abbot's Bar, next to the encampment. I plan to stay until September or maybe October, while the steamers are still running.'

'Then what will you do?'

'I'm going to San Francisco.'

Kitty couldn't hold back her excitement at his words. 'That's wonderful. Pa and I are going back there when we've made enough and I can't wait. A winter here will kill me, I'm sure, even if we spend it at Fort Langley. What will you do there?'

'I'm going to open a business. Maybe as a joiner or carpenter.'

'Is that what you did before you came here?'

'Sort of.'

It was as if shutters came down over Sam's face. Shutters that had letters written on them saying 'Ask me no more.' Kitty knew she'd overstepped some line, but in her defence, she hadn't known it was there, and it was at this point she decided he must be married.

The door from the barbershop opened and Frank walked in.

'Pa, this is Sam Jenkins. He's brought some mending for me.' Kitty hoped Sam would realise she didn't expect her father to recognise him from their previous encounter.

'Pleased to make your acquaintance, sir,' he said, casting a glance at Kitty sending her a half-smile. She was relieved when he made no mention of Bulley or the drinking.

Mr Muldoon accepted his hand, although seemingly not with much enthusiasm.

'Got yourself a paying claim?' he asked.

'I reckon it's much like any other. I get rewarded by the extent of my labours.'

'Ah, the harder you work the better you do?' Mr Muldoon lifted his chin and looked down his nose at Sam, like a schoolteacher delivering a proverb to a pupil.

'Something like that,' said Sam.

'Got yourself a bunkhouse?'

'Herr Steiner's.'

'He'll see you right. Need any teeth pulled, you know where to come?'

'I do,' said Sam, although Kitty deduced from his

expression that the prospect of having Frank Muldoon leaning over him with a pair of pliers was not something he wanted to dwell on. 'I must be on my way.'

'I'll get on with the shirts tomorrow,' said Kitty. She didn't want him to leave, even though he was most likely married. She wanted him to stay so she could talk about San Francisco, and he seemed good company.

CHAPTER TWELVE

The following day, June 26th, was glorious. No clouds and just enough breeze to keep the temperature at a workable level. It was perfect for the diggers and dreadful for the storekeepers, whose establishments remained devoid of customers all day. Those not digging were washing heavy items like blankets and jackets and hanging them out to dry, or sitting in the sun watching others work.

Kitty, setting her chair out on the boardwalk, began working on Sam's shirts. Turning the collars was straightforward; the problems began with the sleeves. The elbows were worked right through and at the top, where they joined the main body of the shirt, the material had frayed at the seams. These she thought she could repair with a strong blanket stitch, but the elbows would need patches. She rummaged around in her sewing box, found the strong brown thread she sometimes used for leather repairs, and set to.

After an hour she was joined by her father. He looked up and down the empty High Street. 'These sultry days are the devil's drudge for business. There's no one about until the sun goes down and even then, they've worked such long days they're too tired to think of anything other than a game of cards or a couple of whiskey shots.'

'We could stay open later.'

'And run the risk of some drunks stumbling in causing mayhem? No, I don't think so. Thank the dear Lord for toothache. That's all we've got to hope for on days like this.' He looked down at her sewing. 'Seeing to that young digger's shirts? What was his name?'

'Sam. Sam Jenkins.'

'What are you going to charge him?'

'I don't know. It depends how long it takes me.'

'Don't forget the thread and patching material costs. It's not just time. Three bucks minimum, I'd say.'

'That's more than a night in a bunkhouse.'

'We need every cent we can get.'

'Pa, we've had this conversation lots of times. If I charge too much they won't come again. It's not like taking a tooth out, where they're so pleased to get rid of the pain. If need be, they can set to with a needle and thread themselves. I'm a convenience, not a necessity.'

'That's where the barbering comes in. Teeth can only be got rid of once, but hair and beards keep right on growing.' He looked up at the sky. 'A bit more of this sunshine and some of those winter beards are going to be mighty itchy.' He rubbed his hands together and went back inside.

Kitty followed him half an hour later with the finished shirts. With it being such a slack day there was no reason why she couldn't deliver the shirts herself. She could drop them off at the bunkhouse, but then she wouldn't see Sam. Or, under the pretext of a walk, she could visit him at Abbot's Bar. She knew where the Indian encampment was, so she would probably see him if she went that way. Then she could casually mention in passing that the shirts were ready for collection.

The dilemma was solved when her father asked her to take a notice about Muldoon's services to be put up at the sawmill. She could deliver it then amble back, taking in Abbot's Bar.

Sam thought his eyes were deceiving him. Kitty was walking towards him wearing a wide-brimmed straw bonnet, raising her skirts and picking her way gingerly amongst the tree stumps and uneven ground. The phrase 'a sight for sore eyes' passed through his mind. He stopped the rocker and wiped his brow with the back of his hand, pushing his hair back from his forehead. He'd taken off his shirt earlier and thrown it to one side. Now he looked around for it and found it was out of reach. It would look foolish to walk over and pick it up when he obviously didn't need it. After all, it was Kitty who had commented that he probably wouldn't need a shirt in the hot sun.

Kitty called out, 'I don't want to stop you working.'

'No, it's good to see you.' He felt unexpectedly uncomfortable standing half-naked before her. 'I haven't seen you around this way before. I'd have remembered.'

She blushed, which made him even more conscious of his naked chest. He gave in, walked a couple of paces and retrieved his shirt. As he began putting it on she started laughing.

'I don't usually tout for business, but I can mend *that* shirt for you too.'

'And leave me shirtless?'

'Only until you collect the ones I've just seen to. They're ready, that's why I've called.'

'That's quick.'

'Or I can drop them off at Herr Steiner's?'

'Thank you, but that's not necessary. I'll collect them.'

Sam took his watch from his breeches pocket then looked up at the sky, still cloudless, but not as bright as it had been. 'It's five o'clock. I'll be cleaning up in another hour, so I can collect around half past six. Will you be there?'

Kitty smiled. 'I'll be there.' She picked up her skirt and was beginning to turn when Sam had an idea which he voiced without giving a second thought.

'If you're not in a hurry, you could stay and talk to me about San Francisco a while.' He held his breath as she considered his suggestion. Guessing her thoughts, he added, 'I've a stool you can sit on.' He moved a jute sack and some tools to reveal a low three-legged stool. 'It may look rickety, but it takes my weight.' He patted the seat with the flat of his hand. 'The problem is finding a space flat enough to set it down.' He tried several positions at what he considered a polite distance from himself. Then, when he was satisfied he'd found a suitably level spot, he said, 'I think this will do just fine.'

She agreed with a slight nod and a smile and, settling herself, adjusted her hat. 'What do you want to know?'

'What it's really like in San Francisco. You've lived there, you must know.'

She thought for a few moments, looking puzzled. 'It's a big place and there's a lot happening. I'm not sure exactly what you mean.'

'I want to know the details,' he said, enjoying the slight frown she made when thinking.

'You mean the glint of the early morning sun on the water in the Bay? The unloading of the ships' cargoes? The Chinese merchants calling to each other? The fancy shops and arcades?'

Sam, noting how animated she was becoming, felt a rush of excitement. 'Aye, all those and more.'

'Why do you want to go to San Francisco? Do you know someone there?' She removed her hat and began waving it in front of her face as a fan.

'I have someone I can call on. He lives at 175 Filbert Street, if you know where that is.'

'What's his name?'

Sam hesitated, then decided it was safe enough to give the information. 'Billy Botcher. He's opened a warehouse.'

'I don't know him, but I do know where Filbert Street is. You haven't told me why you want to go to the city.'

'Because I think I'll be happy there. Weren't you?' Sam had given up all thought of digging while she was speaking. He was transfixed by the images she'd planted in his head of San Francisco's ship cargoes and its streets.

'I was there several years before we came here and,

despite what happened, it's the best place on earth. I can't wait to get back there.'

'What happened? Something bad?'

'Ma got sick with a disease in her lungs. Pa and I had to look after her. She took eighteen months to die.'

'That's dreadful.' Kitty looked so stricken, Sam wanted to take her in his arms and comfort her. 'When was this?'

'Just under a year ago. That's when Pa started having his strident days. And then he sold everything up and decided to come here.'

Sam began expressing condolences, but all the while he was thinking of how he was lying to her – right there and then, representing himself as someone he wasn't. He was ashamed of himself, but what could he do? She was going to have a poor opinion of him when the truth came out, which inevitably it would. Telling her himself was the best option, but not yet.

Kitty smiled at him. 'But, you know, despite all the sadness of losing Ma, I still love San Francisco, and I think you will too. I mean, happiness comes from the people around you. Folk can be happy in the worst of places with the person they care about by their side, can't they? And unhappy in the nicest of places without the one they love. It's the people that matter.'

Without hesitation, Sam said, 'None of that works if people carry the ghosts of the past with them.' As soon as he'd said the words he wished he hadn't. Kitty's images of ships and fancy shops were replaced by a flash of his wife Evie's body laid out on the Colville dock. He shook his head to rid himself of the image.

'I think of Ma looking down on me, enjoying all the good things and supporting me during the bad. Sometimes, in San Francisco, I visit her grave and talk to her and that brings me comfort. I don't think of her as a ghost. I don't think folk should carry ghosts around with them. They should be abandoned and forced to stay where they were created.'

'And where's that?' asked Sam.

'Where they become ghosts, of course. The place where they die.'

Sam found her naïve logic disarming. 'What about living ghosts?'

'People can't be ghosts if they haven't died.'

Sam was going to correct her. He was thinking of how often he'd thought of Grace over the previous few months, but perhaps she wouldn't understand how his definition of ghostly memories included the living as well as the dead.

'Ma loved us far too much to want to come back and haunt us. It's the way it is.' Kitty spoke quite cheerfully, picking up a stone, taking aim, then throwing it at one of the severed tree trunks. 'Have you any ghosts?'

'Let me answer your question with a prophesy,' Sam said. 'When I set foot in San Francisco it will be a fresh start and I will be very happy.'

'On your own?' she asked, not looking at him. All her concentration appeared to be channelled on taking aim at the same tree trunk with another stone.

'Most likely. Tell me more about San Francisco.'

She frowned in thought. 'What more can I tell you? You know there's earthquakes?'

'I've heard that. Have you been in one?'

'So many I've lost count.'

'Aren't you frightened?'

'No. There's a bit of a rumble. It's quite a distinctive noise, and sometimes there's a bit of a commotion in the Bay water beforehand. Things can move around a bit, and if you've a glass of water by your bed you can see the water ripple with the movement. You soon get used to them.'

'How often do they happen?'

'All the time. They're not news. They don't make the *Daily Herald* headlines.'

They chatted a little while longer until Kitty jumped up and said she'd remembered she'd to call at the store and must leave. Sam was sorry; he'd hung on her every word and she was truly lovely to look at.

As she walked home, Kitty mulled over their conversation. Sam had raised his eyebrows and smiled when he saw her, although he'd quickly looked a tad embarrassed. He wasn't the first man she'd seen naked to the waist in Harrison. Half-naked diggers were a dime a dozen, and he had nothing to be ashamed of: a straight back, wide shoulders and strong arms. It crossed Kitty's mind most women in San Francisco probably never saw a man's uncovered chest until their wedding night. Perhaps not even then, if he wore a nightshirt.

Sam had sprung to life while she was talking about San Francisco, but when she'd asked if he had any ghosts, a funny look had passed over his face. The sensible voice in her head told her something wasn't quite right. He'd been evasive about going to San Francisco on his own. What kind of an answer was 'most likely'? *Is there a wife in England? Perhaps there's a family coming out to join him in San Francisco. He's old enough, and most men his age are married.*

At home Kitty was greeted by her pa looking somewhat down in the mouth.

'Did you deliver my notice to the sawmill?'

Becky removed her bonnet. 'Yes. They're going to pin it up.' She thought her father looked tired.

Frank took out his watch. 'You've been a long time.'

'I came back by Abbot's Bar and told Sam Jenkins his shirts are ready. He's coming later to collect them. Then I stopped at the store.' She held out a paper bag. 'The raisins have finally come in from Fort Langley.'

'Be sure you take that digger's money before you hand the shirts over.' He accepted the raisin bag, opened it and peered inside.

'I don't think he's like Godfrey Bulley. He seems a decent fella to me.'

'That may be so, but it's bad enough in San Francisco. Here you never know who you're talking to, what their connections are or anything about their past. Best play safe. I learned my lesson with Bulley.'

'You're always thinking we're rubbing shoulders with rioters and murderers.'

Pa cocked an eyebrow at her. 'You may mock me, my girl, but I'm probably right.' With that, he disappeared upstairs with the raisins, saying he had a headache, but if a customer needed him he could be disturbed.

Kitty knew what Pa said was true. In San Francisco, folk were usually introduced with a brief outline of their position in society and some details of their daily life. If you wanted information about people in a place like Harrison you had to ask them for it, and even then, you couldn't be sure whether they were making it up as they went along – especially those who bragged about the grand lives they'd left behind.

She put out the mended shirts and waited for Sam to collect them. It seemed a long time since she'd left him, but when he arrived and she checked with the clock, it was only just over an hour. Even though the air was still as warm and sticky, she wasn't surprised to see he'd put his shirt back on before calling.

Handing over the repaired shirts, she said, 'If you find these satisfactory, I'll be happy to see to the one you're wearing.'

He put his hand in his breeches pocket. 'How much do I owe you?'

'Two dollars.' Kitty wanted to see him again; she wasn't going to put him off by asking for the three dollars her pa had suggested. Then, as an afterthought, she added, 'Have you made that much today?'

He smiled. 'Aye, thankfully I have, but I'd have made more if I hadn't been interrupted by a lady visitor.' He put two dollars on the table.

'How inconsiderate of her.'

'On the contrary, I'm hoping she'll call again. I very much enjoyed her company.'

Kitty felt herself blush. What was it about him that caused her to become so bothered, in a nice way, when he paid her a compliment? Lots of diggers said nice things to her – she was used to it, and always took it well, knowing they missed their wives and sweethearts – but with Sam, she felt he really meant it.

She gathered all her courage and, with what she hoped was a playful, teasing smile, she asked, 'What will your wife say?'

Sam looked taken aback. 'My wife?' His mouth gave a little twitch and he paused as if searching for the right words, during which time Kitty thought for sure he was going to confirm her suspicions.

'My wife, Evie, died.'

That was it. That was all he said, but the shock to Kitty was as if she'd received a short, sharp slap to her cheek. She couldn't believe she'd been so stupid. She knew instantly, without the need for him to confirm it, that she had disturbed his ghost and that it had to be his wife.

'I'm sorry,' she managed to say. 'I shouldn't have said that. It was meant to be...' *What was it meant to be? A jest?* No, it was her being nosy.

'It's all right. You didn't know.'

Suddenly the words she needed came to her in a torrent. 'It was wrong of me, an unwarranted intrusion. I apologise.'

'There's no need. It was a while back.'

'No, really, I'm truly sorry. I've caused you pain.'

'The truth is I'm not married now, but I was in the past.'

In her anguish Kitty was wringing her hands. She wondered how his wife had died. Was there an accident? Perhaps she had an illness?

Sam picked up the shirts and tucked them under his arm. 'Evie drowned. It was an accident,' he said.

CHAPTER THIRTEEN

Later one afternoon, Tug Tait came walking towards Sam at the claim. As soon as Sam saw him, he realised how much he'd missed seeing a friendly face.

'Tug! Grand to see you.' He put his rocker down and embraced him. 'How'd you find me?'

'I asked at the claims office.' Tug looked him up and down. 'You're looking well, lad. This digging suits you. Doing all right? Has taking that old-timer's advice paid well?'

Sam nodded. 'Let me say right away I'm glad we met him in that bar. I'm doing well, but I don't tell folk that.' He took off his hat and wiped his forehead. 'What brings you here?'

Tug perched himself on one of the taller tree stumps. 'I'm here for the day to settle a bit of business. I sold the riverboat. With the American steamer in operation, folk don't have to get off at Langley no more and that's as far as I could go.'

'Are you happy with that?'

'I've no complaints. I've made a good stash over the past few years and it's all safely in the bank. Time to slow down a bit. I got talking to a Yankee in the Colonial Bar and he's looking for an experienced riverman to watch over goods during transportation up here from New Westminster. Right away I thought, that's for me. I've been finalising things this morning.'

'You weren't tempted to take up digging, then?'

'No. I sure do envy you your strength and the youth to dig, though. My joints creak too much. What say you we two put away a couple of whiskeys before I set off back? Can you take the time off?'

'Of course. I keep out of the bars as a general rule, but today I can't think of a better way to end the day.' Sam opened his tool store and began taking the rocker apart to clean it. When all was safely locked away, they made for Main Street, where they settled themselves down in a corner of the Raging Horse. With Sam finishing earlier that day than most other diggers, the bar was quiet.

Sam was loath to ask, but he had to know. 'Did my letter get through?'

Tug wiped the beer from his moustache with a forefinger. 'No letter arrived. Was there one?'

'Aye, one for you to pass on to Victoria.'

'Nothing came through to me.' He scratched the back of his head. 'Who did you give it to?'

'One of the steamship men.' Sam shrugged. 'I guess he threw it over the side of the ship after he pocketed my money.'

'If you want to send a letter to Victoria, you can give it direct to me.'

'Thank you. I'll have a letter ready for you for next week.'

'Which steamship was it?' asked Tug.

Sam tried to remember. 'It was a couple of weeks ago. The something *Herald*.'

'The *Bright Herald*?'

'Aye, that's it. The *Bright Herald*.'

Tug sighed. 'I can tell you why the letter never arrived. She never made it back. With the river levels rising at the end of the month she struck one of the bars. They're easy to see in low water, but submerged in high. According to the inquest the captain was inexperienced and ignored advice.'

'She floundered?'

'All hands lost. It was in the papers. I'm surprised you don't know. Which reminds me.' He opened his carpetbag and took out a rolled-up newspaper. 'I think you'll enjoy looking at this.'

Sam looked at the front page. 'The *Victoria Gazette*. Victoria has its own newspaper now?' He took in the date. 'Friday June 25th. Hot off the press, almost.'

'I saw it discarded on the steamer coming up here and picked it up, thinking I know someone who'd like to read this.'

'Darn right I would. If you'd bet your bottom dollar on my interest in this, you'd have made a packet.'

'You're starting to talk like a Yankee, even if you don't sound much like one.'

Sam held his hands out. 'I can't help it. I'm surrounded by Yankees and French Canadians.'

Tug bowed. '*Oui, monsieur*. The paper will be something to while away a few hours.'

Sam bowed back. 'This shows how much Victoria is

growing. It'll soon be a proper town with paved streets. I wonder what Governor Douglas makes of it having its own newspaper?'

'Not much, I gather. It's pro-Yankee and he doesn't like that so close to the border. There's talk of the Yankees annexing British land just by being in it.'

'There's plenty of Yankees around, that's for sure, but they're here as diggers and storekeepers, not settlers.'

'Governor Douglas was up here in the Fraser Valley on an inspection tour most of June. A show of strength, I'd say.'

The two men chatted a while longer. Sam was not only happy to have someone he could talk to as a friend, but Tug's visits also meant he could now get regular news from the coast and Victoria.

After Tug had left to catch the steamer back to Fort Langley, Sam picked up the paper. Tucked away on the back page was an advertisement that caught his eye.

STAG'S STORES, QUALITY GUARANTEED.

Mining and General Supplies, Spades, Tin Goods, Blankets, Lamps, High-Leg Boots, Eagle Belts, Hosiery, Thick Gloves, Travelling Trunks, Buckets, High Quality Cooking Utensils.

Purchase here and save portage costs.
Proprietor Mr Stag Liddell.
(Adjacent to the Assay office.)

Sam smiled. A lot had happened for the better for both of them. He ordered himself a beer and was enjoying the rare luxury of half an hour's relaxation when a short, balding, middle-aged man came in and went up to the bar. A blue neckerchief with white dots was tied around his fat neck. Sam froze and quickly turned his face away. To his chagrin, he couldn't place the newcomer, but he knew it was someone from the past. Someone from Colville or Victoria. And if he recognised this man, then it figured the man would most likely recognise Sam. He left his unfinished beer on the table and departed, without looking behind him.

His first instinct was to hide in the bunkhouse. He began making his way there, but then it occurred to him if he hadn't seen the newcomer in Harrison before, it would be a good idea to hang around. Although every sinew in his body was against running the risk of being recognised, he needed, for peace of mind, to see whether the man stayed in Harrison or left on the ferry. He pulled his hat down over his eyes and, from what he judged to be a safe distance, stood and waited.

When the balding man finally left the Raging Horse, he made straight for the general store. He came out holding a baccy packet. He stopped and checked his watch, then set off frowning for the town's dock. Sam followed. It was with an enormous feeling of relief that he watched the man board the steamer for Langley. It wasn't until it had left the dock that he turned and made his way back to the store.

Inside, the storekeeper was pricing up some animal traps. 'I'd like the same twist baccy that short, balding fella who came in a short while ago bought. He sold me a pipe-fill and I like it. Do you know who I mean?'

'Blue neckerchief?'

Sam nodded. 'With dots.'

'The Langley store-runner. Comes in every couple of months to tell me what's coming in across the border.'

'Not a regular here?'

'Like I say, every couple of months.'

Sam paid for the baccy and left. He daren't ask the man's name or proffer any further questions for fear of seeming to be too interested in a man he obviously did not know. Outside the store he told himself to calm down. *This sort of thing was bound to happen. I must expect it. I've dealt with it. The threat has gone away and there's nothing to worry about. Until it's time for the next delivery.*

Later that evening, already feeling anxious after seeing the familiar face, Sam watched as a fleet of Indian canoes arrived. They set up camp amongst the tree stumps to the south of the settlement, armed with guns and axes. As he lay in his bunk that night listening to their drums and chanting, Sam was reminded of familiar sounds from Colville. Even though he was accustomed to the noises and drum rhythms, every now and then he thought he heard a loud shriek and he would sit bolt upright on his stretcher until the glow from the oil light hanging in the centre of the tent reassured him all was well.

The next morning, having hardly slept at all, the prospect of a full day's digging seemed impossible until he reminded himself of the rewards he was hoping to gain: a free life in San Francisco. The sooner he could get there the better. He smiled at the thought. That wish was something he shared with Miss Kitty Muldoon.

CHAPTER FOURTEEN

Even though he'd seen the man in the blue neckerchief board the steamer and head off to Fort Langley, Sam kept a low profile on his claim for the next few days. He used some of the baccy he'd bought to barter with two Indians for some lumber planks. He knew the Indians by sight, having occasionally traded fat smoked salmon slices from them. His tool store, about the size of a large dog's kennel, needed repairs, and he'd decided to break it up and build a better one. By pointing and gesturing he'd managed to explain to the Indians what he wanted. When the wood arrived, rougher in cut than that from the sawmill, and cheaper, he was pleased to see it was in manageable lengths. He handed over the baccy expecting the Indians to leave, but to his surprise they sat on the ground and took out their pipes. With smiles and more gestures he tried to make it clear their services were no longer required, but they proceeded to make themselves comfortable. He realised there was nothing for it but to set to work and put up with his audience.

It was off-putting concentrating under such intense scrutiny. The Indians sat in silence, drawing on their pipes. Building the new tool store posed no problem – Sam had made similar ones many times over the years. He did, however, have a problem with the nails. Not only did they keep rolling off and jumping out of the log hollow he stored them in, but his hands were sweaty in the noonday heat, and they kept slipping from between his fingers, shooting off in all directions. He was continually having to bend and search for them. They were expensive at twenty-five cents each and he couldn't afford to lose any.

The shed walls were upright and he was about to begin on the roof when the Indians began to speak to one another. The taller one disappeared, to return twenty minutes later with a small cedar box decorated on the lid with a stylised leaping salmon. He presented it to Sam with great aplomb, taking off the lid to show the interior. Sam realised they wanted him to have it. But was it a gift or were they wanting to sell it? He wasn't sure and his confusion must have shown, for the Indian picked up two nails, dropped them into the box and replaced the lid. He shook the box, making the nails rattle around inside.

Light dawned and Sam smiled. He understood now – they were organising him. He took out his baccy pouch and opened it. He was about to start bartering when he had a sudden thought. *Will they make me another one?* He pointed to the box and held up two fingers.

The Indians conferred, then the taller one pointed to the baccy pouch and held up his two fingers. Sam nodded and the taller one put his hand out, but Sam wasn't going to pay before he'd got both boxes. He pointed again at the salmon-lidded box and closed up the pouch. 'Two. Two boxes.'

The taller Indian looked as if he understood and, placing the box on the ground, gestured to his companion they should leave.

They returned after a short while with four boxes, each the same size but with a different design on the lid. Sam kept the leaping salmon and picked out a box with a large round face on it. The tall Indian pointed to the sky then put his head on one side and closed his eyes.

'The moon,' said Sam, putting his hands, palms together, to the side of his head, leaning into them as if sleeping.

The man nodded and spoke a word in his own language, which Sam assumed was their own word for moon.

After a short period of bartering, the men watched as Sam transferred his nails into the salmon box. Then, all smiles, they departed, pointing to the almost-finished tool store with approval.

It was half past seven when Sam arrived at the Muldoons', holding his third shirt and the moon box. He knew Kitty was still working because he'd walked past the window to check.

She greeted him with a broad grin. She was wearing a dark brown dress gathered in at the waist by a thick leather belt. It was a practical outfit and on anyone else it might look plain, but it suited Kitty's curves and she looked engaging in it.

'More business for me?' she asked. 'Come into the workroom.'

Sam followed her and put the shirt on her sewing table. Her eyes alighted on the Indian box.

'That's a strange face,' she said, laughing.

'Do you like it? It's a moon face. At least I think so. It's for you.' He held it out to her.

She turned it over in her hands. 'It's delightful.' She held it to her nose and breathed in. 'Ah, cedar. Where did you get it?'

He told her about the tool store and the Indians.

'They sat and watched in silence and then they brought you a box?'

'They did.'

'Why?'

'For my runaway nails.'

He explained about the difficulties he'd had with them. 'I thought you might like one for pins or similar.'

Kitty held the box in both hands in a show of taking ownership. 'Thank you, I'm sure I can find something to keep in it.' After a pause she added, 'Something special. Something worthy of being protected by the moon.'

Sam was delighted to see her eyes were sparkling. He wondered whether it was because she liked the box, or because it was something *he'd* given her. Hopefully it was a combination of both.

They discussed his shirt repair and Sam would have stayed longer, but they were interrupted by her pa, Frank, calling from upstairs.

'Time to shut up shop, Kitty. Whoever it is you're gossiping with, send them home.'

Kitty winced. 'I'm sorry. He likes his supper on time. Not that I mind. I'm happy to work to his routine. Well, most of the time.' She gave a short, embarrassed laugh. 'I don't want you to think I don't enjoy keeping house.'

Such a thought had never occurred to Sam. 'Not at all.'

An awkward moment followed.

'You're losing weight,' she said.

'It's all the exercise I'm getting working the rocker.'

'If you'd like a change from the mush and bean soup they serve in those bunkhouses, you're welcome to eat a supper with us one evening.'

A meal with Miss Kitty and some decent grub. There's a delightful thought.

He held his response back a few seconds so he wouldn't appear greedily overeager, before saying, 'I'd like that, thank you.'

'So will Pa. He's been saying he's not had anyone to thrash over the state of the country with in recent weeks. Tomorrow, six o'clock?'

It flashed through Sam's mind it would mean a short day digging. He'd have to finish early and go to the bathhouse if he was going to present himself upstairs for supper. Then he'd have to make up for today's tool store building and the early finish by earlier starts the rest of the week. No matter. 'Six o'clock it is. Thank you again.'

He gave her a big smile as he left.

CHAPTER FIFTEEN

The next day, while working his rocker, Sam wondered if he'd made a mistake accepting Miss Kitty's supper invitation so quickly. *I'm going to have to talk about myself. Will the necessary caginess about my past make me seem suspicious?* Not for the first time he felt real regret that he couldn't be himself with the Muldoons – that he would have to be Samuel Jenkins, just arrived from England, not Sam Gray, hard-working collier from Whitehaven and Colville. Kitty had indicated Frank Muldoon craved serious conversation, so he decided to do his best to show his personality through discussion and to steer away from his past as much as he was able.

The next evening, as he stood nervously on the Muldoon threshold making a last-minute adjustment to his necktie, he reminded himself to keep the conversation to the here and now.

The door was opened by Kitty, who in his eyes looked the picture of healthy beauty, and he was taken upstairs to the parlour and ushered straight to the laid table. Frank was sitting at the head with a napkin tucked neatly into his shirt collar. In front of him were three plates and a saucepan from which steam was rising, along with an appetising smell.

Kitty sat opposite her father and Sam was seated on the side of the table opposite a small square window, providing him with a splendid view of the untouched trees and mountains in the distance. The room was sparsely furnished and contained a slat-backed rocker and a velvet-covered nursing-style horse-hair chair that had seen better days. Sam wondered if it had served its time in a lady's boudoir. Logs were stacked neatly to one side of the chairs, with kindling piled high in an Indian-weave basket. A functional octagonal side-table made from the same type of wood he'd used for his tool store was strewn with some well-thumbed pamphlets and books. One of the books was about American birds. In the centre of the dining table, directly opposite Sam, was a large earthenware pitcher. It looked as if it had been placed there as a stand-in for an absent fourth diner.

Frank welcomed Sam with less reserve than previously. 'Mr Jenkins, you'll take some refreshment, won't you, sir? We're abstainers and this is a teetotal house – although we never serve tea.' He laughed at his own joke and Sam cast a quick glance at Kitty who, looking embarrassed, muttered something about letting her know if the stew needed more salt.

'We've only water, I'm afraid,' Frank continued, 'but it's brought down in barrels from upstream, so it's clean.

Were we in the city we'd serve lemonade or ginger beer as a matter of course, but here we must make do with God's wine.'

Normally when people said they were abstainers, Sam asked, out of politeness, if they had taken the public pledge to not drink liquor, but he could hardly follow that path with Frank, after seeing him inebriated. What if Frank replied with a 'yes'? However, he saw an opportunity to broaden the conversation and grasped it.

'I expect it's expensive paying for drinking-water carriage.'

'Indeed, you wouldn't believe it.'

'Yes,' Kitty chipped in. 'Just as well we can use lake water for washing and cleaning.'

'You've been here longer than I have –'

'Three months more,' Kitty said.

'So would you say prices have risen?'

'Risen?' Frank tutted and picked up the ladle beside the saucepan. After stirring the contents, he began to serve a rich-looking stew onto the plates. 'Expenses have been rising at an alarming rate.' He handed Sam his plate. 'City men coming in from San Francisco and over the border from Washington State. They think they can make a fast buck by continually upping prices, and the diggers – like you, if you'll not take offence and pardon me saying, sir – will pay them.'

'Pa,' said Kitty, taking her plate. 'The diggers have no option.'

Sam sighed. 'No offence taken. Part of the trouble is the merchants and saloon bars think all diggers have plenty of money. I've saved my takings by not frequenting the bars. I can honestly say every grain of gold is treasure to give me a new future.'

Frank looked at him thoughtfully. 'Kitty tells me you're headed for San Francisco.'

'Aye, that's my plan.'

'You came from England just in time for the gold rush. What did you do there?'

'I was a collier.'

'Used to mining then. And you've family there still?'

Sam nodded. *Here comes the questioning.*

'Whereabouts are you from?'

'The north-west coast.' To stop further probing, he added quickly, 'And where are *you* from?'

'We came from Kent in '49 in time for the Californian gold rush. Kitty was a young girl back then. Do you know Kent?'

Sam shook his head. He needed to steer the conversation away from himself. 'Have you seen the new Yankee diggers arriving?'

Frank pulled a face. 'They get off the steamer with flashing eyes and new boots. They've envisaged fields of gold and every one of them pauses to inspect the ground, as if they're looking for gold nuggets to trip over.'

Kitty laughed, playing with a button on her dress sleeve. 'You're making it up.'

'He's not,' said Sam. 'I've seen them. We've three in the bunkhouse newly arrived. One of them talks about his lust for gold as his "feverish itch" and says the more he scratches it, the stronger it rages.'

'The new Yankees are mean as hell,' Frank went on. When Kitty shuddered, he added, 'Don't look so worried. With any luck they'll move on up to Port Douglas and beyond soon enough.'

Kitty stood to collect their empty plates. 'All good reasons to get out of here and back to San Francisco, then.'

'In good time, dear daughter, in good time.'

For the remainder of the supper Sam told them about Tug and his experiences in Fort Langley. Later, he was able to sit back and enjoy listening to Frank regaling him with tales about what he called 'the old times in San Francisco, before they started filling in the Bay Area.'

When it was time to leave, Sam thanked Frank for his hospitality and complimented Kitty on her cooking.

Frank smiled at his daughter. 'She looks after me well, does my Kitty. I don't begrudge her a bit of salted ham to cook with now and then. Especially when we've a guest. We used to do a lot of entertaining in San Francisco when Caroline, my wife, was alive. God rest her soul.'

Downstairs, as he was about to step out into the street Sam paused. 'The stew really was delicious. We don't get anything like that in the bunkhouse. Thank you.'

Kitty returned his gaze with such warmth, Sam put out a hand and placed it on hers. Then he leaned forward and put his cheek gently against hers. When he drew back, she slowly drew her fingers over the spot where they had come together.

'You'll come again?' she asked.

'Aye,' he said. 'If you invite me.'

'I will. Pa likes you. I can tell.'

With a happier heart than he'd had for some time, Sam made for the bunkhouse. To match his mood, he began whistling a folk song he'd been taught by Irish neighbours in Whitehaven when he was a young lad.

Without warning, from behind him out of the gloaming light, a voice rang out. 'Learn to bloody whistle or shut up.'

Sam stopped, startled by the intrusion, and turned in the direction of the voice. He was confronted by Godfrey Bulley, dressed head to toe in black, striding towards him. Caught off guard he was unable to put together a response before the man had caught up with him.

'Your whistling's so goddamn bad, don't ever think of singing in my hearing.'

Sam was furious, and not least because he could hold a whistling tune as well as any other man and better than most. Had such a confrontation taken place in Whitehaven, he'd have gone after the man and made him eat his words. But then Cumberland folk didn't walk around with guns in holsters and saw-edged knives tucked in their belts.

CHAPTER SIXTEEN

Sam wrote to Stag describing the bunkhouse run by the French Canadian in Langley, omitting to say he'd now moved to Harrison. He felt a pang of remorse that he wasn't giving up-to-date information, but he was afraid his communication might be intercepted. He would send a true account when he was safely on American soil and out of reach of the Company.

Writing to Stag revived memories of Colville. Was the aching sadness he carried in his heart for Evie to be a constant in his life? In Harrison, at least he was not constantly reminded of her by his surroundings. He remembered the stab of pain he'd felt when he'd been at the schoolhouse in Colville one morning and seen a box full of Evie's peg-men. She'd loved painting the faces on the wooden pegs, dressing them and giving them to the collier children. Then there'd been her oatmeal biscuits. She'd loved making those too. After they were officially engaged, while still in England, his grandma had taken him to one side and said, 'She's a reet good homemaker, that little lass. She may be tiny, but I'll wager she's going to fill your home with bonnie bairns.' But it hadn't been like that. In the end it was for want of a child that everything had gone wrong, and why she became lost to him.

It had always struck Sam as peculiar that once Evie died, folk stopped talking about her. He'd never worked out whether they were embarrassed about the manner of her death, or whether they thought talking about her caused him pain, or finally whether they'd plain forgotten her. If he ever mentioned Evie, they never followed up with comments of their own. How different it had been with Grace; folk had actively encouraged them to spend time together.

And Miss Kitty? At some stage he was going to have to tell her who he really was. That he'd deceived her. That was bound to change things. The previous evening, he'd decided he would be as truthful about himself as was possible with her.

When Tug arrived back on July 15th, Sam handed him the letter addressed to Stag Liddell, at Stag's Stores, Victoria.

* * *

It was Saturday, late afternoon, when Kitty dropped by Abbot's Bar holding a small basket.

'I've brought your shirt,' she said.

'Two dollars again?'

'No, just a dollar. There's only one this time.' She pulled a small package from her basket and handed it to him.

'I guess I'll be needing new ones soon.'

'I won't lie. You will, and because of that I've also brought you this.' She held out a larger package.

Sam hesitated.

'Go on, take it.' She stepped closer.

He took the package and opened it. Inside was a new shirt. 'In my hometown in England we'd say "Ta very much".' He unfolded it and held it up. 'I can't say as I don't need one. This is most thoughtful. How much do I owe you?'

'You don't owe me anything. It's a gift. Like you gave *me* a gift.'

Sam was embarrassed. 'I can't accept this. It must have taken you a long time, and then there's the materials.'

'You have to accept it. It's a "thank you".'

'What are you thanking me for?'

'For coming to supper and talking to Pa. He's starved of interesting company and you were a delight.'

'I was more than well rewarded with the supper.' Sam was smiling inside and it was a joyous feeling. If Kitty only knew that the highlight had not been the supper, but talking to her. Being with her helped him relax and kept his ghosts at bay.

She gathered up the wrapping paper from the two packages and began folding it. 'Don't you get lonely working down here all by yourself?'

'There's plenty of folk around.'

'But I'm guessing not to talk to?'

'Everyone's digging or panning. The Indians are friendly and they come and watch me sometimes, but we have to communicate with signals.'

'That must be difficult.'

'I've been told by folk that I talk a lot with my hands. Some movements and faces are common to all.'

'It's true, you do talk with your hands sometimes. It makes you seem full of energy. I like it.'

Sam laughed. 'That's good to know.'

'One thing I've noticed here in Harrison is there are very few birds, but then there's no trees for them to nest or roost in. We've lots of birds in San Francisco. Especially when the fishing boats come in and unload their catches. Pa likes birds.'

'There's no children here, either,' said Sam. 'Just skinny dogs and mules.'

There was a short silence. Then Kitty asked, 'Do you have children?'

Sam remembered his decision to be as truthful as he could be. 'I had a son, Stephen.'

'Oh.'

He thought he detected a brief hint of disappointment in her face.

'Where is he now?'

'He's in God's hands.'

Kitty bit her bottom lip. 'I'm sorry, I just wondered...'

Sam realised he should have said, 'I had a son, Stephen, who died.' Now he'd embarrassed her again and she didn't deserve it. Especially when she was offering him the hand of friendship with such a thoughtful gift.

'It's coming up to four years ago,' he said. 'He was stillborn, but he was our son and we wanted him to have a name.'

'That must have been terrible for you both.'

'It was. Perhaps more so for Evie who had to give birth knowing our baby had died. She passed on less than a year later, so we never had the chance for any others.' This was as much as he was going to tell her. He told himself there was no need to go into the devastating circumstances of Evie's drowning, trapped under the log boom, or all the miscarriages she'd suffered and how it had affected her.

'This is tragic. I'm so sorry. I expect it's something you never get over.'

'It hasn't been an easy time. You asked me once if I had ghosts and you can perhaps understand now why I do.'

'I've upset you and I'm sorry. Perhaps I shouldn't say this, but there are times you remind me of a wounded animal. But the good thing is I think you can heal with some help.'

When she came nearer, he moved forward to meet her and took her hand. 'Are you offering me that help?'

'If you'll let me. Although by asking questions I seem to make things worse.'

'Sometimes it helps to talk things through. So, in your offer to heal me, how about if I make a space on the ground for you? Will you stay a while and talk some more about San Francisco?'

Kitty's face lit up. 'There's nothing I'd like better, but I don't want to disturb your working day.'

'I can manage the rocker and listen to you at the same time. If you make a habit of this then I'll make a stool and level a bit of ground. We can call it "Miss Kitty's Spot". How about that?'

'I'd like that just fine.'

Sam made the place for Kitty to sit, and when she was settled she began. 'Kearny Street's one of the important streets. It runs north to North Point and south into Market Street, which is one of the widest streets in the city, running east to west.'

'How do you spell it?'

'K-E-A-R-N-Y. It's named after some general. I've picked it because a lot happens there.' She closed her eyes for a brief moment. 'I'm trying to visualise it. There's always lots of expensive gigs parked outside buildings, while their horses wait patiently for their moneyed owners. Some of the buildings are three storeys high, made of stone, with balconies and arched windows. I've been told they're like Italian palaces. Whatever style they are, I can tell you they're impressive. Especially the banks.'

'What other businesses are there?'

'All kinds. I've been in some of them, but Halahan's Apothecary is my favourite.'

Sam laughed. 'I didn't think an apothecary could be such an interesting place.'

'Oh, it is,' Kitty said, her eyes alight. 'Inside there are mahogany shelves and glass cabinets full of every colour of medicine in gold-labelled flasks and bottles. There are hundreds of little drawers with circular white and brass knobs. Some of the drawers and cupboards have paper labels glued to them, and others have individual white plaques with the contents stamped in black lettering. The sort of lettering the German Protestants use. Do you know what I mean?'

'I see it stamped on Herr Steiner's boxes in the bunkhouse. Thick black letters that you sometimes see in churches in England.'

Kitty nodded. 'The store has a special medicinal smell that I love. There's menthol, eucalyptus, cinnamon, and they sell lozenges and the most wonderful cough candy which they cut into squares and pack into triangular-shaped boxes.' She grinned. 'I buy and eat it when I don't even have a sore throat.'

'That sounds like what we called "tablet" back home.' Sam was rapidly revising his idea of an apothecary store. He decided one of the first things he was going to do in San Francisco was visit Halahan's and buy some of their cough candy.

'Most of the stores have awnings that come out over the sidewalk for the rain.'

'Does it rain a lot?'

'Rain?' Kitty chuckled. 'It sure rains a lot in the winter, especially December. Does that put you off?'

'Not enough to worry about.' Sam managed to stop himself just in time from talking about the December weather on Vancouver Island. How could he know about their rain, when he was supposed to have just arrived from England?

'But only the business buildings are in the grand style. Most of the houses away from the main streets are clapboard, just like here. Talking of here, I have to go. Pa'll be wondering where I've got to.'

Sam put out his hand and, as he helped her up from the ground, her perfume rose with her. He breathed in as deeply as he could. He was caught by surprise; some feelings he thought he'd never experience again were awakening. While he was luxuriating in their closeness, she turned her face up to him, almost as if she was inviting him to kiss her fully on the lips, but he was afraid of misinterpreting her action, so he held back.

After she'd gone, he took the shirt she'd made for him and held it up to his nose. He smiled; her perfume was on it. He wondered if she'd sprayed it before she gave it to him and if that was so, he wasn't complaining.

CHAPTER SEVENTEEN

Kitty finished her household chores early and was coming down the stairs to finish off some mending when her pa came out of his workroom.

'If you've a moment to spare, Kathryn, I'd like to speak with you.'

'I'll be right with you, Pa,' she said, her heart sinking fast at his use of 'Kathryn'.

He sat behind his desk and Kitty pulled up a chair. 'I feel as if I'm being interviewed for a position,' she said. 'Is something the matter?'

'I've been going through our finances.' Her pa picked up a pencil and began rolling it between his fingers. 'We're not fulfilling our potential.'

'But we're making money, aren't we?'

He gave a dismissive wave of his hand. 'That much is a truth, but it's not enough. I had hoped by now we'd be in a more equitable situation financially.'

'You mean we're not going to have enough to return

home in October? That's our plan, isn't it? To leave before the winter sets in?'

He nodded. 'Indeed, it's a good plan.'

'You haven't answered my first question. About October.'

'Well. Here's the thing. If we could cut our expenditure a little and increase our earnings a lot then I think that goal remains in our sights…'

Kitty's first thought was *and if you don't have any more strident days*, but she loved her pa and to say such a thing would show a lack of compassion. Since they'd arrived in Harrison, she'd abandoned any thought that she could change him and now steered her efforts towards attempting to manage his periodic weakness.

'I don't think I'm a squanderer. Do you, Pa?'

'Not at all, but if you can think of any frugalities we can employ that will be helpful. Or ways we can increase business. I'll make some more advertising sheets this evening listing our services for you to take round. Folk know we're here, but it'll jog their memories.'

Kitty wondered what Pa would say if he knew she'd made the shirt for Sam and not charged him for it. She must think of a way to ask Sam not to say anything about it in her father's hearing.

'I'll do my best,' she said, getting up from her chair to give him a kiss on the cheek.

As she settled with her mending and wound the shuttle for her sewing machine, the possibility of having to spend the winter in Harrison made Kitty miserable. Talking about San Francisco with Sam was exciting for him, she could see that by his bright eyes and interest, but for her it was mildly depressing remembering the vibrant city they'd left behind. She looked at the pile of mending waiting to be seen to. Two dollars here, three dollars there – all tiny fiddly jobs. She could charge an extra twenty-five cents, but that wouldn't amount to much. *What else can I do?*

She could ask at the store about sourcing wool so she could make scarves for the diggers in preparation for the winter. This seemed a good idea until she factored in the inflated cost of buying wool in Harrison and the time spent knitting. Also, she'd have to sell the scarves in September when the weather was still quite pleasant, and that would be a problem. She gave up thinking of ways to make more money and began concentrating on finding economies. She concluded she would just have to be extra careful, perhaps to the point of miserliness. If that was going to enable them to leave in October, so be it, she could endure it. However, one thing she was not prepared to give up, and that was inviting Sam for a second meal.

The next day Kitty was busy in the Harrison General Store fixing one of their advertisement sheets to the community noticeboard when two Yankee saloon gals came in. Kitty had seen them from afar many times, but never spoken to them – not because of any disdain for their occupation, rather because they frequented different places. The gals worked in The Angel saloon, and Kitty had seen them coming and going, but never in the morning. She guessed they didn't get up until noon. Up close she could see they were older than she'd thought, most likely well into their twenties.

The taller and, Kitty thought, the prettier one, spoke. 'I hope that's a notice about something exciting going to happen in this godforsaken place.'

'Ain't nothing much happens here,' the second gal said. 'Things could certainly do with livening up a patch.'

Kitty had always thought saloon gals must lead exciting lives, but perhaps they got bored doing the same job every day, just like anyone else.

'It's an advertisement for our store,' she said.

'Which one's that?'

'Muldoon's.'

'That's the barbershop and dentist,' the prettier gal said. 'Ain't nothing for us in there.'

In what she would look back on as a flash of brilliance, Kitty seized the moment. 'You're wrong there.' She drew them close and pointed to the bottom half of the advertising sheet. 'Look.'

The shorter one began reading out loud. 'Sewing undertaken, shirts mended and made to order by talented experienced seamstress.'

'We'll have to tell the menfolk,' her companion said.

'We'd appreciate that very much,' said Kitty. 'I'm the seamstress referred to. If you're looking to have some excitement, maybe you'd like to drop by the store and I can make something for you.'

The prettier gal put out her hand. 'I'm Beth, and this here's Eliza.'

'Kitty. Pleased to meet you.'

'What kind of things can you make?' asked Beth.

'I do most things except tailoring. I've no whalebones for corsets, but you don't want fancy coats and jackets here. Why don't you drop by?'

Eliza laughed. 'Let's do this, Beth. We could have ourselves a bit of fun getting all dolled up.'

'I'm not promising excitement, but definitely fun. How long have you been here?'

'Just over a year,' Eliza said.

'So, you missed the latest fashions in San Francisco?' Kitty could see she'd planted a seed as both girls looked down at their skirts. 'Like I say, drop by and I can tell you all about them. I don't want to be thought rude in anyway whatsoever, but it wouldn't hurt to bring you up to date a bit, would it?' Buoyed by her attentive audience, she continued, 'We can mend shoes too. Think about it. There's no charge for a consultation and I've a few bits of French lace and new material better than anything you can buy here.' That wasn't strictly true, but she'd brought several dresses of her own with her that hadn't seen the light of day; she could take them apart and strip them for lace and other adornment.

After the girls had left, promising to bring their custom along 'shortly', Kitty wondered if she'd bitten off more than she could chew. For a start, she'd nowhere private for them to be measured and fitted. Her place of work was like a goldfish bowl, with diggers going past peering in all the time. But by the time she'd finished putting out their remaining advertising sheets and was on the way home, Kitty had everything fixed in her mind. She would announce to Pa she'd found a way to boost their finances and that, on occasions, she'd be needing their private quarters for ladies' dress appointments. It wasn't going to be a classy concern – they were miles from respectable society with its rules and regulations – but she'd keep her promise to the gals. They'd have fun and she'd update them. That she knew she could do.

Pa greeted her new money-making scheme with a sceptical eyebrow, but after hearing Kitty out and being told there were quite a few saloon gals in Harrison she thought she might call on, he agreed she could expand and use their upstairs parlour when necessary. Kitty spent the next morning going through her wardrobe, seeing what could be detached and salvaged. When she'd packed in San Francisco she'd thought she might have time on her hands so, unbeknown to her father, she'd put a few yards of assorted material, buttons and lace in one of their trunks. The items were still packed up, since as soon as she'd arrived she'd realised she was never going to wear anything fancy. However, it was different for saloon girls, who were dressed up every day, all hours.

* * *

The Muldoons were not the only ones thinking about money. Some days Sam brought in between five to six ounces of gold which, at sixteen dollars an ounce, was between eighty and ninety-six dollars a day. He blocked his ears to tales of hundreds of dollars a day north of Fort

Yale. Steamer and portage costs would soon eat into a poke, and besides, the Indians up there were less friendly. Some diggers had been attacked, and that also put him off.

Sam had never considered himself a greedy man, and in almost three months he'd lost count of the number of diggers who'd gone rogue, cavorting with whores and pickling themselves with liquor. He'd decided such diggers were selfish men, with no ties, no conscience and, most importantly, no self-restraint. He was on a mission to better himself financially, to provide for himself and live well.

A week had passed since Kitty introduced herself to the saloon gals. She'd put together a box of materials and made a list of the changes she could make to their clothes with the items available to her. They'd said they'd drop by 'shortly', but what did that mean? A couple of days? Weeks?

When they did arrive, unannounced, Kitty knew instantly it was them by the giggling and laughing coming from behind the door.

'We've come to be re-fashioned,' said Eliza, her blonde hair fixed into tight ringlets and her mouth all done up with scarlet lipstick. Both gals were wearing fancy bonnets with overlong ribbons tied in big bows, Eliza leant down and looked at her boots. 'Undo your laces, Beth, now. We don't want to track mud in with us.'

They removed their boots and placed them neatly side by side, just inside the door. Eliza rummaged in a large carpet-bag and produced two pairs of slippers which the girls proceeded to put on. 'We may work in the saloon but we're house-trained.' They undid the bows on each other's bonnets and took them off.

'Come in, you're very welcome,' said Kitty. 'This is my reception area, where I take orders.' She led them into her workroom. 'For ladies such as yourselves, I've arrangements upstairs.'

'Ooh,' said Beth, pushing a rogue blonde curl behind her ear. 'We're ladies now, are we? Not often we get called that.'

As they entered Kitty could see, when she looked them over in full daylight, that their clothes were quite shabby. Eliza went over to the mirror, pursed her lips as if about to kiss it, then licked a finger and ran it along both eyebrows. 'We may be out in the backwoods here,' she said, 'but that's no excuse for letting ourselves get out of date. We don't do dowdy, it ain't in our nature. You've got ideas?'

'I most certainly have. Shall we retire upstairs?'

When the gals were settled around the Muldoon dinner table, Kitty spread out some drawings.

'I've drawn what you were wearing when we met in the store, and you're wearing similar today. Let's start with the bodices. Yours are curved just here, giving a round-shouldered effect.'

The girls inspected each other's shoulders.

'The change I would make is to add some shoulder caps, giving a straighter line.' She made an addition to the drawing. 'Like this.'

'Won't that square us up?'

'Exactly, and, if you don't mind me saying, it will enhance the bosom.'

'You mean giving it more prominence?' asked Beth.

'Yes, in a discreet way.'

Eliza looked at Beth and raised her eyebrows. 'I don't think we'll be complaining about that.'

'Neither will the customers, or the boss.' Beth chuckled. 'Don't worry about the discreet bit.'

Kitty wanted them to know she was under no illusions about their employment, so she carried on. 'The other initial change I would make is to give you narrower sleeves giving a firmer outline to your arms. No one is wearing those open-ended pagoda sleeves anymore. The idea is to give prominence to the wrist, so a section of the sleeve needs to be removed and a tight cuff added.' She shaded in the areas accordingly.

Beth looked down at her wrists. 'I've got nice wrists. I'm liking this so far. Go on.'

'Waists are higher now. There's not much we can do about that without raising the hemline or making a new skirt, but we can get round it, so to speak, with a belt.'

'Hmm. "Get round it". That's very clever,' said Eliza.

'I like the sound of a belt.' Beth gave a wicked grin. 'But I don't much fancy a digger's brass eagle sheltering under my best assets.'

The three of them laughed. 'No chance of that. I can make a belt from matching or contrasting material.'

'What about the skirts?'

'Flounces are fewer now, but what we could do is rather than make new skirts we could cut the flounces down and pink the edges.'

'Pink the edges?' asked Beth.

'We make tiny "V" shapes all the way along. It looks pretty and it stops the material fraying.'

Kitty took up a pair of scissors and made several cuts in a scrap of material before handing it to them. 'What do you think?'

'I like the effect.' Eliza looked at Beth, who agreed.

'Of course, if we had access to the right sort of material, I could make clothing from new.'

'The store at Langley gets in new material for the Company wives,' said Beth.

Kitty hadn't thought of that. The Hudson's Bay Company wives had standards to maintain. Their husbands mixed with the Governor and officials. Of course, they needed to be well dressed.

'Do you think we can access a Company store?' she asked.

'I don't see why not. The boss might let us go over there and take a look. He likes us to look real pretty.'

'So, can we do business?'

'Let's discuss terms,' said Eliza.

They spent the next hour and a half looking at materials, lace and trimmings. As the girls left, Eliza put her hand on Kitty's arm. 'We sure are glad to have made your acquaintance. I think we're going to get on just fine.'

That evening, Kitty was able to tell her pa she thought she might have tapped into a goldmine of her own. She didn't tell him how sad she was going to be having to unpick two of her favourite dresses.

CHAPTER EIGHTEEN

At just past nine o'clock, Sam was enjoying a cigar, watching Herr Steiner put away his pots and pans, when his attention was diverted by voices from outside the bunkhouse tent. One was Pierre, the French Canadian he sometimes passed the time of day with. Sam recognised the second voice immediately and was up and off his stretcher in a flash. Outside he found Kitty, eyes red, cheeks burning, obviously in some distress.

She ran to Sam. 'I don't know what to do.'

Sam opened his arms and embraced her.

'Do about what?'

Her head rested briefly on his shoulder till she took a step back from him. 'It's Pa. He's having a strident day. He's playing cards with Gregory Bulley. He'll lose everything. It's a disaster.'

There was real fear in Kitty's white face. Her eyes darted from Sam to Pierre then back again. Gasping, she made a wheezing noise as she breathed in.

'Does he have gold or money with him?'

'I don't know, but he can sign a loan note and lose money that way.'

'Where is he?'

'In The Angel.'

'Who told you?'

'Eliza, one of the saloon gals I've been dressing, came and told me. If it wasn't for her, I'd have had no idea. She says Pa demanded Bulley hand over the money he owes him. It's so stupid. It's nothing, only ten dollars. I mean, I can make a shirt for that, but when he's in drink the ten dollars becomes a grand debt of long-lost honour.' She placed a palm on her chest and drew in a deep breath.

'Why on earth would your da sit down to play cards with him?' asked Sam.

'Bulley told Pa he'd play cards for it and Pa agreed. I can't think of anything more foolish. Can *you* do anything?'

It crossed Sam's mind it might already be too late, but he had to do something, even if it was only to convince Frank to go home and count his losses.

'Kitty, you go home out of harm's way. I'll go up there and see what I can do.'

'You'll not do anything foolish and get yourself hurt, will you?'

For a man who wanted to blend into the background and live a life without too many questions, this was indeed a foolish act. However, Kitty had asked him for help in her hour of need. Sam had no choice.

'You get off home and wait for your pa.'

'I'll come with you,' Pierre said.

As they raced to The Angel, Tug's words of advice about Bulley, spoken in Langley, were ringing in Sam's ears. *Take a good look at him and never sit down to a card table when he's in the room.*

Frank Muldoon was obviously drunk, but to Sam's relief he appeared not yet to have reached the point of no return, where he couldn't be reasoned with. He also appeared to be in fair humour.

He looked up and beckoned Sam over. 'Come to watch? I'm on a winning streak. I've got my ten dollars back and more. Get yourself a drink on me.'

Pierre took Sam by the elbow and deftly turned him towards the bar, away from the players. Initially Sam resisted; he didn't want to leave the card table, he wanted to see what was going on and assess the situation, but Pierre's grip was firm, so he let himself be led away.

As soon as they were out of earshot, Pierre said, 'We've got to get Frank up from the table. It's the oldest trick in the book. Let your opponent think they're on a lucky streak. They get sucked in and think they can't lose because Lady Luck's in their favour. Looks like we're at that point now, from what Frank's said. *Mon Dieu,* we are just in time. In the next game, or soon after, Bulley will go for the big time and clean him out.'

'Apart from telling him his store's on fire how can I get him away?'

'Tell him that – or something to do with his daughter. She's fallen or something.'

Bulley added to his stack of gold on the table and handed Frank a piece of paper.

'You can sign here,' he said, pointing to the bottom of the paper.

Sam leaned forward and snatched it up. Frank, caught unawares, didn't have time to react other than letting out an indignant 'No!' Sam saw immediately the paper was a loan note for $250. He crushed it in his fingers.

'Getting a drunk man to sign a note like this is akin to stealing money from a blind man,' he said.

Bulley shrugged. 'It's what he wants. I'm not forcing his hand. You can see that for yourself.'

It was true; Frank stood up and reached for the crumpled note in Sam's hand.

Sam put it in his pocket and took hold of Frank's arm. 'You have to go home. Miss Kitty's hurt herself.'

Sam watched as the drunken man, who probably felt as if his brain was floating in molasses, processed the information. Out of the corner of his eye he saw Bulley giving him the sort of look a thief gives another thief before he draws a knife.

Sam placed his hand on Frank's shoulder. 'You need to go home,' he said again. 'I don't know what's up, but something to do with the stove. Miss Kitty's hurt.'

This information seemed to resonate. 'Not my girl? Not burnt?'

'You'd better go and see. I'll come with you.'

Bulley took the deck of cards and flipped them. 'Hey, he can't back out now. I'll lose the chance to get my stake back. That's not how the game's played and I reckon you knows that.'

There was a murmur of assent from those watching. Sam didn't know what to do. He had to get Frank away from the table before he lost everything.

Pierre spoke up. '*Monsieur*,' he told Bulley, 'you must expect a father to rush to the side of his daughter when she may be burned and in pain. Is that not so?'

'This is some kind of ruse,' Bulley hissed.

A possible solution occurred to Sam. 'What if I take his place?'

Pierre leaned forward and whispered in his ear 'Are you sure you know what you're doing? Can you play cards?'

'Aye, I know how to play cards.'

'*Oui, Monsieur*, but against *him*? A professional card sharp?'

Ignoring the horrified look on Pierre's face, Sam said, 'If you take Frank home to his daughter, I'll finish here.' He turned to Bulley. 'Am I welcome in this game or not?'

Bulley looked like a man trying and failing miserably to conceal his delight – a man whose horse is three lengths ahead, approaching the winning post.

'I suppose a substitute will do on this occasion,' he said.

'First I need a whiskey.'

A stranger with a strong Yankee accent shouted out, 'I'll stand you a whiskey, in return for the show I reckon is about to git started.'

'Yeah, and I'll git the next one,' added another.

Pierre took Frank, who was unsteady on his feet, by the arm. His parting words to Sam were, 'Are you really sure you want to do this? He'll let you win two, maybe three games, then he'll increase the betting odds and go in for the big hit.'

'We played every day in steerage on the way over from England. So, yes, I know how to play.'

'All right, if you say so. I'll be right back.'

Sam thanked him and with the two gifted whiskeys lined up by his side and an imaginary pack full of misgivings sitting heavily on his shoulders, he settled himself down to play.

CHAPTER NINETEEN

After attempting to busy herself with some sewing for Beth and Eliza, Kitty went into the barbershop, where she boiled up a large kettle then put it to keep hot on the stove, draping a towel over it to warm. This she followed with some tidying up, but despite her attempts to distract herself from what was happening at The Angel, she could not settle. She began doing what she always did when her father brought them unhappiness – pacing the floor. This helped consolidate her thoughts, and so it was that evening as she waited for news. The thought foremost in her mind as she paced back and forth was how fortunate it was that, firstly, she had made the acquaintance of the saloon gals and, secondly, that Beth had been quick-witted enough to realise her pa, and their hard-earned savings, were in peril. Meeting the girls had not only boosted their finances, they were also looking out for her.

The jangling of the doorbell brought Kitty out into the hallway to greet her father, bleary-eyed, inebriated and supported by Pierre. With not a small amount of relief, despite the evidence of drink, Kitty saw her pa was not as incapable as she'd expected him to be.

'We were in time,' Pierre told her.

'Thank goodness.' She looked over his shoulder. 'Where's Sam?'

'He's taken your pa's place at the table.'

'What?' Kitty didn't like the sound of this. 'Won't it cost him money?'

'Let us hope not.'

Frank, who ever since he'd arrived home had been looking around as if to get his bearings, suddenly came alive. 'Kitty, my dear, what has become of you? Where are you hurt? Where's the fire?'

Kitty hesitated, a puzzled expression on her face.

'It seems we made a mistake,' Pierre said, answering for her. 'There must have been a fire somewhere else. Your daughter is clearly in good health.'

Kitty held out her arm. 'Come on, Pa. I'll bet you're tired.'

'No,' he said, vigorously shaking his head. 'I've a card game to finish. Lady Luck is with me tonight.' He turned towards the door to go back out, but Pierre had placed himself in front of it.

'No, that's finished Pa,' Kitty said. 'They're not playing cards anymore. Besides, it's a Sunday. Gambling at any time is bad, but it's a sin on the Lord's Day. You know that. Time for a wash and a rest.'

Frank looked at Kitty through half-closed eyes before putting his hand in his pocket and pulling out his fistful of winnings. 'Look, I told you. I'm on a winning streak.'

Kitty's eyes widened. 'I wasn't expecting this,' she said to Pierre. 'Can you help me get him into the barber's chair? I'll give him a wash down, and if I can get him seated then, with luck, he'll fall asleep. I think it's safer to keep him down here rather than struggle getting him upstairs. Once he's asleep he'll not wake until morning.'

'You're talking about me as if I'm not here,' said Frank, wearing a whiskey-induced grin.

Once he was installed in the barber's chair and partially reclined, Frank's eyelids began to droop and his head to roll. Then, just as it seemed he was going to fall asleep, he came to with a jolt. 'Frenchman, have you been to San Francisco?'

'*Non.*'

'Well, let me tell you about it. It's a wonderful city…'

Frank prattled on about San Francisco while Kitty took the kettle and poured some of the hot water into an earthenware bowl. She dipped a towel in it and began gently washing her pa's face and hands. After a few minutes, she retrieved the towel she'd put to warm earlier and, laying it over his forehead, began quietly humming an Irish melody. Frank stopped talking and joined in, but after no more than a minute he fell silent.

Kitty and Pierre retreated to her workroom. Although Kitty sensed Pierre was anxious to get back to The Angel, he related quickly what Sam had said about having played cards on the ship. 'I warned him, but he was determined.'

'He's a good man,' said Kitty.

Pierre hesitated a moment. '*Oui*, he is a good man, but perhaps I should tell you he is troubled. You are friends, are you not? Perhaps more?'

Kitty felt her cheeks redden. 'Yes, we're friends. Why do you say he's troubled?'

'He suffers pain in his sleep. We hear him calling out. We can't always make it out, but the other night he kept saying, "Save her, don't let her go." Sometimes he calls out "every". We don't think he knows he's doing it, because he doesn't wake up and he never mentions it when he's awake.'

'Could he be calling out "Evie"?' Kitty asked.

'Maybe. Who is that?'

'It's his late wife.'

'Ah, then that is possible. He has never mentioned he was married. Perhaps she had an accident.'

'I don't rightly know the details, but there was an accident and she drowned and there was a son. He's dead too.'

'*Mon Dieu*. I tell you he has this trouble because he has what we French call a "softness of heart" and, yes, he is a good man. Perhaps you can help him find some peace.'

'I'll try.' Then suddenly realising she'd divulged details of Sam's life he might not want others to know, she said, 'Perhaps I shouldn't have told you about his family.'

'I will keep what you've told me to myself, but it does explain why he might sometimes look so sad. I must hurry back and support him.'

Kitty watched him go, wishing she could go with him, but it wasn't the right thing to do, she knew that.

CHAPTER TWENTY

The back of Sam's throat felt gritty from the smoky, cigar-fuelled atmosphere, the acrid fumes from the whale-oil lamps, and his own apprehension. He and Bulley had played two games when Pierre returned, giving a thumbs-up sign. They'd begun with an ante of one dollar for the communal pot. Bulley folded on the first round without showing his cards and Sam won. On the second and third games the ante was upped to two dollars and Sam won both games. At the start of the fourth game, Bulley suggested upping the ante from two dollars to ten.

This is the beginning. He's raising the stake to make a big pot, drawing me in. On the ship Sam had played for hours, until by the time they'd arrived on Vancouver Island they were all played out with cards as entertainment. The big difference between then and now was that on the ship they'd played with dead matches; the stakes couldn't have been any lower. Gambling had been frowned upon in Colville, so since the boat four years ago, he hadn't played competitively, but he knew he'd been regarded as a very good player. He'd always played dispassionately, working out what the odds of winning might be. *I must play the same way now.*

He reached for the second whiskey. He'd been watching Bulley like a hawk, but, as far as he could tell, he'd seen no sleight of hand and no dealing from the bottom. Did Bulley have an ace or two up his sleeve? That was a possibility, but Sam thought it unlikely. If his cheating matched his finesse in cascade-shuffling then he was likely to adopt a more sophisticated method than hiding aces.

The crowd of onlookers had swelled. Sam made sure his cards couldn't be seen by anyone and conveyed to Bulley. They played and, as Sam anticipated, his pair of nines with ace high lost out to Bulley's three tens.

They played another round and this time Sam noticed that as the cards were dealt Bulley kept squinting – not casually, as if glancing at Sam's cards, but searching them with restless eyes, as if trying to bring something into focus. There was only one explanation.

As he got ready to deal the next game, Bulley raised an eyebrow. His expression held the beginnings of a smirk. 'Are you still in?'

Sam glanced towards the bar. 'Before we go on, I'd like some different cards. House ones from the bar will do.'

A twitch of irritation marred Bulley's expression. 'Why?'

'These are too sticky to riffle properly.'

'The saloon charges for new cards.'

'I'm willing to pay.' Sam watched a small bead of sweat as it followed a zig-zag path down Bulley's right temple.

'Waste of time and money,' said Bulley, making to grab their pack of cards.

Sam got there before him and, wrapping his fingers around the pack, he removed it from the table.

'Those are *my* cards, not house ones,' said Bulley, red in the face. 'Give them here.' He stretched out his hand.

Sam put the cards in his waistcoat pocket. 'You can have the new pack when we've finished. I'm keeping yours warm for you. How about that?'

'I want them back right now,' Bulley hissed.

'You seem very bothered about keeping hold of your pack.'

'Are you accusing me of having monkeyed the deck?' asked Bulley.

An old-timer smoking a pipe shouted out from the crowd, 'Yeah, I'm coming round to thinking that too, with you wanting your own cards back so badly.'

'You're fussing like a three-year-old who's had a toy taken away,' Sam told Bulley. 'Quit holding things up.'

A murmur of assent passed through the onlookers.

A saloon gal with ringlets and red lipstick brought the new cards over and handed them to Sam. 'I'm Eliza,' she told him in a soft voice. 'A friend of Kitty's. Pleased to meet you.'

Sam held her gaze for a few seconds, hoping she'd interpret his smile as more than just thanks for the cards. Eliza had saved the day as far as the Muldoons' finances were concerned, and he would thank her properly when he got the chance.

He ripped off the thick brown paper band surrounding

the new deck, crumpled it up and bent the cards a few times. Then he straightened them into a neat stack. Taking the complete deck in his right hand, he paused for a moment before using just his index and little fingers to cut it.

'These cards are much better,' he said. A ripple of approval ran round the table.

The old-timer's voice rang out again. 'I haven't seen that done in a long while – cutting the deck with one hand. That's style. Where'd you learn that?'

'On the boat coming over. It was a long trip and there were a lot of evenings to get through.' Sam allowed himself the luxury of a satisfied smile. 'Your turn to deal, Mr Bulley, I think, sir.'

Bulley attempted his usual cascade shuffle, but the new cards were stiff and didn't respond well to his handling. Several cards fell from his grasp and, after waltzing across the table, dropped to the floor. Sam watched Frank's awkward fumbling with satisfaction. Here was further proof he'd rattled his opponent. Bulley, annoyance all over his face, began gathering the dropped cards, watched carefully by the onlookers as he groped around on the floor. Sam guessed it was not only he who had detected something false.

After another cascade attempt, slightly better than the previous one but still not completely satisfactory, Bulley said, 'These cards are too stiff. Give me back my cards. I'd rather sticky than stiff.'

'Sir, I'd rather "clean" cards, whichever way you want to interpret that.'

There was laughter from several of the onlookers.

Bulley's face was now one big scowl. 'I'll have those cards back, even if I have to draw my gun to get them.' He put his hand on his holster.

'You're not going to shoot me in here over a pack of cards with all these folk looking on,' said Sam, trying to mask his unease. 'It's citizens' law here. At best they'll tar and feather you and put you in a canoe with no paddles. At worst, they'll lynch you for murder – especially when they examine the pack I've got for safe-keeping. Like I said, I'm keeping your cards warm for you. Now let's play on.'

Bulley gave Sam what could only be described as a death stare. 'I don't like your tone. You force yourself into the game, call for new cards, accuse me of playing dirty and now you won't give me my own cards back.'

'You seemed happy enough to take me on when we were playing with *your* cards.'

The room fell silent as, one by one, folk became aware of the change in atmosphere.

'Like you say, *my* cards.' Bulley stood and extended his hand. 'I'll have them back. Right now.'

Sam sighed theatrically. 'I don't know why you're carrying on so. I get the sticky cards and you get the new pack. Or you could say, I've got the dirty cards and you've got the clean ones.'

Bulley stood stock still, his hands fisted, his black eyes ablaze.

'What your opponent is saying,' Pierre told him, 'is if he were you he'd quick-tail out of here and hire a ride to Fort Langley pretty damn sharp, before all the folk you've been playing cards with over the past few days find out your cards are…' He paused and looked around. 'How do you Yankee card players call it?'

'Monkeyed,' came a voice.

'*Oui*, monkeyed.'

One of the onlookers stretched his hand out and helped himself to a fistful of the pot piled up in the middle of the table. Looking directly at Bulley, he said, 'I reckon I've been diddled and I oughta git some of this, if you've been monkeying the cards. I'm only taking my fair share, mind. What I've been cheated out of.'

Another man also leaned forward and helped himself, expressing the same motivation.

Several of the onlookers began murmuring amongst themselves and it became clear they too were feeling hard done by. There was no denying that, even without definite evidence, the room was turning against Bulley. He stood up abruptly and shoved the table away from him. Cursing crudely and loudly, he was forced to elbow his way through the onlookers. A few separated half-heartedly to let him pass, while others stood their ground with sneering faces, making him work round them.

With the saloon doors still swinging on their hinges in the wake of Bulley's hurried departure, Sam took the suspect cards from his pocket and laid them out face down on the table. He, Pierre and the onlookers found themselves looking at 104 bald eagles, a pair top-and-tailing each other on each card.

Despite the absolute certainty he was right, Sam now had to prove it, and do so in front of an excited, expectant audience. He picked up two cards, looking for differences. Spotting nothing, he kept picking up, until he was holding five cards.

I'm going to have to admit defeat, he told himself. He was making to replace them when a man standing behind him pulled on his cigar, casting an orange glow on two of the cards.

Sam smiled. 'It's in the wings,' he shouted. 'If you look closely at the feathers on the eagle's outstretched wings you'll see a small dot. A dot that's not in the same place on each card.'

Men began pushing each other out of the way to reach out and pick up a card so they could see for themselves.

'I can't see nothing,' said a voice at Sam's elbow.

'Turn the card into the light. Gently,' said Sam, looking at the back of the card. 'Don't show me, but that's an eight, isn't it?'

The man turned the card over for everyone to see.

'He's right,' he said. 'How'd ya know that?'

'Looking from left to right, the dot is on the eighth feather.'

'What's this one?' asked another man.

'A queen,' said Sam. 'It's on the twelfth feather.'

The card was turned over to reveal the queen of hearts.

There was an almost palpable intake of breath in the room. Then everyone wanted a turn.

'I'll be doggone,' said one of the barmen, scratching his forehead. 'Who'd a believed it? Right in front of our noses all week. That's downright slick.'

'This is all fine and dandy,' said the old-timer, 'but what about the suits? I'll bet they're marked somewhere too. I'd have a look meself, but my eyes ain't what they used to be.'

It was Eliza who had the sharpest eyes. 'I've got it. Beth, try me out, see if I gets it right.'

Eliza held up a card.

'Ace of spades.'

'That's right. Here's another.'

'Six of diamonds.'

'Right again.'

'Aren't you going to share it with the rest of us?' asked one of the barmen, putting his arm around Beth's waist.

Beth shrugged his arm off and pulled up a chair. 'Let's have two strong fellas hoist me up so's you can all see me,' she said, raising her elbows. 'One on either side.' There was no shortage of volunteers and she was soon standing on the chair. 'The card suits are in the eight tail-feathers. Working left to right, spades is feather one, hearts is the third, diamonds the fifth and clubs the seventh. You have to look really carefully. The dots are very tiny, but you can see them when you know they're there.'

Sam was congratulated with back-slapping and hand-shaking, but inwardly he had mixed feelings about the evening's events. By unmasking a card sharp and saving the Muldoons from what could have been financial ruin he was being fêted as a hero, but being a celebrity was the last thing he wanted. Shunning offers of free drinks, he made his way to the door and slipped out of the bar.

CHAPTER TWENTY-ONE

The next morning Kitty hoped Sam would call in at Muldoon's, not just so she could thank him, but to find out what had happened. When he hadn't appeared by noon, and she judged her pa sufficiently recovered to reliably open the barbershop for trade, she made her way to Abbot's Bar to seek him out. She stopped first at the general store to enquire about the material the saloon gals had ordered from Fort Langley.

The storekeeper looked at the calendar hanging on his wall. 'I'm awaiting Gus with the order in the next week or so.'

'I hope he's not too long coming. I could use that order.'

At his claim, Sam was replacing the rope handles on a wooden bucket when Kitty arrived. She called out and he looked up with a smile, putting the bucket down.

Kitty felt a warm glow as the memory of the previous evening, and her head nestling on his shoulder, came back to her.

'I've come to thank you for saving us from ruin,' she said.

'It was a close call. We have Eliza to thank for being so quick to warn you.'

'Word is Bulley avoided waiting for the steamer and took off in a huge fury in an Indian canoe late last night. I can't say I'm surprised. There were a lot of angry people looking for him after I called him out.'

'He really was a cheat then? Have you still got the cards?'

Sam shook his head. 'I gave them to the bartender. Pierre told me later they were burned in an iron bucket, for all to see.'

'I'd have liked to have seen them.'

'If you don't tell anybody I can show you.' He put his hand in his trouser pocket and pulled out a card. 'Here you are. I kept one back.'

Kitty took the card and scrutinised it. 'You'll have to show me.'

'Here,' he said, moving close enough for Kitty to smell the rich masculine sweat rising from his body as he explained about the dots.

'Oh, yes, I see them now, but they're so small. How could Bulley see the dots across the width of the table?'

'The table's not that wide, but it's by knowing exactly where to look, and being sober while your opponent is drunk. The first deck will be unmarked, then, when sharp eyes become bleary through drink, the first deck is exchanged for the marked one. It's easily done under the table while your opponent is talking to someone or ordering a drink.'

'Pa's eyes were all bleary last night.'

'I could see he'd had a few drinks, so he was an easy target right from the start. When we got there it was clear Bulley had let him win a few hands to draw him in.'

'He'd never have sat down to play had he been sober.'

Sam held out his hand to retrieve the card. 'I'll walk away. Tell me when you can't see the dots.'

He began walking backwards. After three steps, he said, 'Can you still see them?'

'Yes, I can.' Kitty laughed. 'I wouldn't have believed it if we hadn't done this. I really wouldn't.'

'Fraudsters like Bulley are calculating thieves who prey on the innocent and the inebriated.'

'I can't thank you enough.' She lifted her head and smiled. 'I'd like to kiss you if I may, as a thank you. If you won't think that too forward?'

Sam bent down and she kissed him on the cheek. It was a brief kiss, but when he stepped back she could see her own delight mirrored by his wide smile.

* * *

A week passed and Sam fell happily and easily into the routine of calling on Kitty and Frank at the end of the day. When Kitty had tentatively suggested inviting Sam to share their supper table again, Frank had acquiesced straight away and even suggested they order a chop to roast despite their economies. Although Frank never referred directly to Sam's intervention to save their finances, he was always so pleased to see him these days, Kitty told Sam she was sure he remembered everything and that his sober self was grateful.

It was after supper one evening, when Kitty was clearing away, that Frank was called upon to deal with an emergency dental patient in the barbershop. Kitty and Sam found themselves alone. Sam, well fed, happy and more content than he had been for some time, felt secure enough to outline his future plans.

'I'm thinking of staying until mid-October. According to Tug, the river becomes much more hazardous in November. He says he can drop me at New Westminster and from there I can easily get to San Francisco, but it must be on an American ship.'

'Tug's the boatman you travelled to Fort Langley with, isn't he?'

'Aye.'

'Why not get the boat to Victoria and then to the city? It's cheaper.'

Sam realised he'd made a mistake. Travelling via Victoria was the obvious route, but he couldn't tell Miss Kitty he daren't set foot on Vancouver Island for fear of being recognised.

'Tug's advised me to take that route,' he said, thinking fast. 'He says it's quicker and not so crowded.' That much was true – Tug had said that, but he'd meant it as a way to avoid the Company officials who would still be keeping a sharp look out for him.

'It would be good if we could travel back together,' Kitty said. 'I'm thinking this recent scare may turn Pa's attention towards getting out of here. With the money to restart a business in the city, he might be able to control his impulses.'

Sam's heart leapt. He'd envisioned upsetting goodbyes on the quay and perhaps a long wait in San Francisco for their arrival, but with Kitty's suggestion there would be none of that. He would be able to spend the whole journey with her, instead of alone. As an additional gain, he would be travelling as one of a group and would stand out less than a single man travelling solo.

Kitty's next question caught Sam by surprise.

'Do you dream about Evie?'

Seeing no reason to lie, he said, 'Sometimes, but I don't think that's odd. She was my wife.'

'I'm not saying it's odd at all. I'd be surprised if you didn't.'

Then, in a burst of openness, he added, 'And I dream of Grace Williams too. There have been two women in my life. Evie married me and Grace turned me down.'

'Are you sad Grace turned you down? Is that why you left England.'

Of course, she will think Grace was in England too. Qualms about lying to Kitty flooded Sam's brain, but were he to tell her all, he would be putting her in an impossible situation. She'd either have to alert the authorities or be complicit in his subterfuge. He would put everything to rights as soon as he possibly could.

'Grace has a contract with the Missionary Society. Am I sad? Maybe not as much as I was, but at the time it cut me to the quick.'

'And you loved them both?'

'It's enough to say they're in my past.' He hoped this would shut down the conversation because he knew he was on the cusp of reddening, and that would make him look guilty of something, which in truth he was. However, Kitty didn't pick up on the cue.

'How do you see your future?' she asked.

Sam was about to say he saw his future in San Francisco, when Frank reappeared looking worn out, but amused.

'I've just had a real bleeder,' he said. 'He cursed louder than a shipwrecked whaler on a raft with no baccy. I almost called for you to come and help me hold him down. I'm surprised you didn't hear him. These tough men can be real babies sometimes.'

The conversation turned to how business had been that week. Sam learned several militia men had passed through on their way to Port Douglas wanting their beards trimmed. This had been good business for Frank, but it reminded Sam there was a world outside Harrison, and with the route to Port Douglas becoming more and more popular, he needed to keep his head down.

CHAPTER TWENTY-TWO

On Monday morning, a big-bellied man arrived at Muldoon's, to deliver the material from Fort Langley. The man introduced himself as Gus Boston. A blue neckerchief with white dots was fastened around his thick neck.

He looked round Kitty's workroom in a nosy way. 'Shall I leave these on your table?' he asked.

'I'd like to see the materials before you leave. Check they're in good condition.' Kitty found his presence intrusive. Having such a large belly he seemed to take up a lot of space and he stank of stale tobacco. She expected the smell would linger when he'd gone.

Gus gave a sneering laugh. 'It'll have to be suitable as there's none other. Leastwise not until we get another shipment, and that could be a couple of months. I don't think you'll be disappointed. I got these in especially for the British Columbia celebrations at Fort Langley.'

'I'd still like to see them. The ladies I sew for are very particular and they'll be paying.'

Gus shrugged and opened the first parcel, holding the material out for her to inspect.

'If your customers are that particular make sure you charge them well. Quality always costs, and out this way everything is at a premium. But you don't need me to tell you that.'

'So far so good,' said Kitty.

The next parcel drew an excited 'ooh' from her lips. 'This *is* nice. Blue velvet.' She put her hand out and touched it. 'The loom width is a bit narrow, but no matter.'

They were just about to open the last parcel when the doorbell jangled and Sam came in, smiling widely. As soon as he set eyes on Gus the smile fled from his face. He mumbled something about being early and turned to leave, but it was too late. Gus took two steps forward and placed his hand on Sam's arm.

'I know you, don't I?'

Sam had retreated halfway into the hall. Shaking his head vigorously and snatching his arm from Gus's grasp, he said, 'No,' and turned away again.

There was a funny look on Sam's face from which all colour had drained.

Gus peered at him. 'Aye, I do know you. Come back in here. You're from Colville, aren't you?'

Sam had no choice but to step back into the workroom. It was obvious to Kitty something was terribly wrong.

'You're from Colville on the island. It was your wife lost me my job complaining I was robbing folk at the Company store. Remember me? Gus Boston?'

Kitty was sure Gus must be mistaken. Sam's wife had

died in England, but with Sam looking and behaving so oddly she was bewildered. *What on earth is going on?*

'I don't know what you're talking about,' Sam said, his voice firm.

'Your wife...What was her name? You'd think I'd remember straightaway since she got me in so much trouble with the Company.'

Kitty looked at Sam, waiting for him to answer, but he remained silent.

'I might not remember her name but I do remember yours, because I've been recently reminded. It's Sam Gray, isn't it?'

Still Sam said nothing.

'I've seen the Company poster about you at the fort.' Gus took a rolled cud of tobacco from his pocket, put it in his mouth and began chewing.

Kitty looked from one man to the other. Sam was completely rigid, like a statue, as if frozen in time.

Gus punched the air with his fist. 'I remember,' he said, 'Evie, that was her name.'

Kitty drew in a sharp breath. Both men turned to look at her.

'I'm right, aren't I?' said Gus triumphantly, transferring his gaze from Kitty to stare at Sam with leering satisfaction. 'You're Sam Gray.'

'No, he's Sam Jenkins,' said Kitty. Even though the man might know something she didn't – and Sam's dead wife's name wasn't that common – she leapt to his defence.

'He might be that now, but he used to be Sam Gray in Colville when I last saw him over three years back. Are you aware he's a wanted man?'

Kitty didn't know what to do or think. All she could manage to say by way of an answer was, 'Wanted for what?' She couldn't believe Sam was a criminal. What could he have done? But, more importantly, if he really was this Sam Gray, then who was Sam Jenkins?

Gus, with an ugly twisted face, pointed a finger at Sam. 'I bet you don't know he's a Company deserter. Signed a five-year contract and not finished it. The Company don't like that. They're looking for him and…' He gave a satisfied laugh. 'I can't believe my good luck.'

Sam seemed to pull himself together. 'Is your father in?' he asked Kitty.

'Yes, he's upstairs.'

'Would he mind if this man…What's your name again?'

'Gus. Gus Boston. As if you've really forgotten.'

'Would your pa mind if this man and I used the barbershop to speak in privacy?'

'I don't see why not,' Kitty said. Her father had finished for the day.

'Follow me,' Sam told Gus. 'We've things to discuss.'

* * *

As soon as Sam had closed the door behind them and they heard the latch click, Gus said, 'I reckon you don't want to be going to Fort Langley much these days, what with the fort plastered with notices looking for you. It seems you've upset the Company a great deal. Looks like the officers want to make an example of you.'

'What business is it of yours where I go or what I do?'

'Some might say it's very much my business since your Evie shopped me. What goes around comes around.'

'Aye, shopped you for deliberately overcharging decent womenfolk in the Company store. Women freshly arrived from England not knowing how to buy in bulk. You took advantage of their confusion.'

'So, you *do* remember me. I knew it. It wasn't my fault those women couldn't add up. Your Evie caused me a great deal of disruption and lost me my job.'

'I'm proud of Evie for exposing you. It's not as if you weren't guilty as charged.'

'Talking of which, so are you – guilty as charged of absconding and breaking your contract. You've set a very bad example for all the hard-working folk you've left in Colville.'

Sam flinched inside. That part was true. He knew he was guilty of that, but he assuaged his guilt with the thought that the folk he'd left behind were happy in Colville, whereas he never had been.

We're wasting time. 'Let's cut to the quick. What we're chewing over is long past. You've unmasked me, so now what?'

'How long have you been here?' Gus rolled the cud of tobacco against his teeth, causing a dribble of brown liquid to escape from the side of his mouth and roll down his chin. He brushed it away with a forefinger.

'Three months and more.'

'I'll bet you've a decent poke by now. I hear diggers've been picking gold up here as it's just lying on the ground.'

'It's not like that now and you know it. That was the early days.'

'Let's not argue over how you've made your money. The truth is we both know you've got some and with all that inconvenience causing me to lose my job, making me have to work for Yankees – well, I reckon you owe me.'

'I owe you nothing.'

'Oh, but you don't have any choice.'

'I don't?' Sam scratched a non-existent itch on his elbow.

'Now I think on it, you've two choices. You can keep me sweet, so I forget I've seen you, or I can report you to the Company bosses like your missus did to me. A tit for tat situation, except I'd be able to claim a reward.'

Within the short space of time Sam had been able to think clearly through all the confusion and shock, he knew Gus spoke truthfully. He either had to pay up or be arrested for desertion. His first thought, that he would certainly lose Kitty's affections, was almost too painful to contemplate. That all dreams of a new life in San Francisco would go up in smoke were of little consequence compared to the loss of Kitty. There was, however, a third option – to cut and run.

'I can see you're thinking,' said Gus. 'What have you decided?'

'Neither of us have had time to think this through, but I expect we can reach a clear financial understanding.'

Seeing the broad smile break out on Gus's face, Sam was tempted to strike him, but what would be the use? All he wanted right then was to be rid, so he said, 'I'll be in The Angel tomorrow morning at half-past ten.'

'Bring your poke with you. I don't give credit.'

* * *

After their private discussion, Sam escorted Gus out onto the boardwalk. Returning to Muldoon's he paused on the threshold, feeling himself almost unable to stand, but he must return and face Kitty. She was exactly where he had left her, sitting at her work table. Her face was ashen.

'It's true, isn't it? You're not Sam Jenkins?'

Sam shook his head. 'No, I'm not.'

He pulled up a chair and sat beside her. He glanced at her hands, thinking he would take one in his, but she was keeping them tightly clasped in her lap. He imagined how she must have been sitting, waiting for him to return, and all the things that must have been rushing round her head.

'Then who are you?' she asked.

'I'm Sam Gray.'

'You're married, aren't you?'

'No, I'm a widower. I have no wife and no romantic understanding with anyone. I've told the truth about that.'

After a slight pause Kitty spoke in a voice swollen with wretchedness. 'In that case, what haven't you told the truth about?'

Her eyes were sad and reproachful. If only he could make her understand that the pain he was causing her was breaking his heart too.

'I'm sorry, it's true. I've told lies, but I've tried only to do so when absolutely necessary. Please understand I've only done so to protect myself, not to be deceitful to those who know me. Also to protect you and your da.'

'Protect *us*?'

'Aye, so you couldn't be accused of harbouring a deserter. It's just seemed better you didn't know until it was safe to tell you.'

Kitty, staring at the floor, seemed to consider this point. 'Now that I know, you may as well tell me the whole truth.'

'I came to Colville almost four years ago as a collier to help open up the mines. My son, Stephen, was stillborn on the journey over and my wife Evie drowned under a log boon in tragic circumstances because she wanted another child. I've tried to carry on as best I can, but in Colville Evie was everywhere in spirit. She is my dead ghost.'

'What about the Grace you mentioned?'

'Grace is my living ghost. I asked her to leave Colville in the hope we could find a life together, but as a contracted missionary it was too difficult for her. She's made friends in Colville and is a valued member of the community. It's a community that, no matter how hard I tried, I couldn't feel a part of, and one day I realised I never could. I would always be the sad man whose wife drowned.'

'You're sitting in front of me looking the same, sounding the same, but you're not the same because I don't know who you are anymore. I never, for a single second, took you for a liar.'

Sam shuddered inside. He knew she hadn't chosen the word 'liar' lightly; it was probably one of the most derogatory comments anyone could make about someone.

'I want you to know I appreciate the kindnesses you and your pa have shown me, and that it must seem as if I'm repaying you with falsehoods, but truly it's never been my intention to take all and give nothing in return.' He wanted to say he had love to give her, but it was too late.

Kitty shrugged.

'Do you want me to leave?' He tried to smile, but he was dying inside.

'Yes, I do. You're a stranger to me now, despite all you've done for us, and when I think about it you've always been furtive. I put it down to your being shy, but all the while you were concocting a tower of lies.'

'If I'm unlucky then soon everyone will know. That man wants to blackmail me. He's nothing if not persistent and he's been quick to appreciate my situation is in his favour. Either I pay and he informs on me, or I disappear. I've agreed to pay him off to gain some time, but the temptation will be too much for him. He'll bleed me of brass then hand me over to the Company. I've an appointment with him at The Angel at half past ten tomorrow. If I run before then he'll report me to the authorities and they'll soon catch up with me.'

There was an awkward silence during which Sam knew he should leave. He stood up.

'Before I go I want to say again that I'm truly sorry for all the hurt I'm causing and, that you, your pa and Tug have all touched my heart in different ways. I want you to know that.'

Kitty followed him out into the hall. It felt as if he was being escorted from the premises.

She put a hand on his arm. 'Have you ever killed a man?' she asked, looking him right in the eye.

Sam was shocked by her question and did not answer immediately.

'You have. I can see it in your eyes.'

He shook his head. 'No. What you see is doubt in

how to answer. A Yankee attacked Grace, I fought with the man and he fell on my knife and died. There was an inquest and I was exonerated.'

'You could have told me you hadn't killed anyone.'

'I've had to tell you enough lies already and I'll tell you no more.'

'Why don't you talk to your friend Tug? When is he coming back? He may be able to help you. We certainly can't.'

Kitty's suggestion appeared to Sam to be a hopeful sign. Even if she wasn't going to associate with him anymore, at least she was suggesting he seek support from others. She cared enough for that. He smiled, but she remained expressionless and he guessed he'd been wrong; she just wanted to see the back of him.

'Tug's here, now,' he said.

'You'll have to tell him who you really are.'

'He knows. He knew when we were at Fort Langley.'

Kitty looked surprised. 'He could have turned you in for a reward.'

'I know, but he says I remind him of someone he cared about. That's why he's looked out for me over the past few months.'

'There's nothing more to say.' Kitty stood up and straightened the creases in her skirt, as if she was physically brushing Sam out of her life. 'I'd like you to leave.'

On the threshold, Sam turned to say goodbye, but Kitty was quick to close the door behind him and he was left staring at the paint peeling on the door.

On his way back to the bunkhouse, Sam felt sick. That

which he'd dreaded and feared had caught up with him: he'd lost Kitty, and most likely his San Francisco dreams were in tatters. Kitty was right, he must speak with Tug, if only to put his own thoughts in order.

CHAPTER TWENTY-THREE

After Sam left, Kitty sat stock still looking through the window, oblivious to the folk passing by. She didn't know what to think, because she couldn't collect her thoughts. She couldn't see a way past the deception. There was the niggling doubt that Sam might never have told her. *What if they'd married?* she asked herself. She'd have married Sam Jenkins. Would that have made their marriage illegal? Surely such dishonesty would invalidate everything, and if so, their children would be...The word to describe them was too awful.

Then there was Grace. Kitty had thought she was in England. Why did it upset her so that she was on Vancouver Island? She didn't have to look far into her heart to know the answer. The living ghost she had thought thousands of miles away was almost within touching distance, alive and well. A boat ride away. A rival, certainly in thought if not in body. Kitty was adult and level-minded enough to realise that if she was experiencing jealousy, it had to be because she cared – otherwise, why would Grace's proximity matter? But if Sam cared enough, wouldn't he have told her the whole truth to avoid the hurt she was now feeling?

She felt an unexpected stab of pity for Sam and his travelling ghosts. *Is he a good or a bad man?* she asked herself. Whichever way she looked at it, he had good reason to lie to protect her and her pa.

She decided she wouldn't tell Pa; she needed to think about it all first. Yet in this moment of crisis came the thought that she wished she'd made Sam promise not to leave Harrison without saying goodbye. It occurred to her she might never see him again, and such a thought, despite all she now knew, was unbearable.

After supper Kitty pleaded a headache to be able to retire early. She woke in the early hours wondering whether Sam had been using their friendship only to enjoy her cooking and whether he'd just been dallying with her all along.

Sam, in search of Tug, went first to the ferry dock. He saw with relief that the steamer was still there and it didn't look as if preparations were being made to sail that evening. The watchman directed him to the general store, but he was too late; Tug had moved on. Finally, after almost an hour of frustration, Sam tracked him down to the sawmill where he was negotiating a lumber transaction. He saw Sam and raised his hat.

'What brings you up here?'

'I'm looking for you.'

'Well, you've found me, and by the look on your face it's too important to wait.' He turned to the man he was speaking with. 'You know my terms, they're commercially sound for us both. Consider them overnight. I'll drop by in the morning.' He put his arm around Sam's shoulders. 'I've a few things to see to before we leave tomorrow. Walk with me.'

Sam waited until they were out of earshot of the workmen, and the working sounds of the sawmill had quietened.

'I've been recognised.'

'Who by?'

Sam told him all that had happened and some brief details of how he knew Gus. 'He could at this moment be sending a message to Fort Langley. There's bound to be a reward.'

'There is. I've seen the poster.'

As if feeling himself being observed Sam cast a glance around. 'How much am I worth?'

'A hundred dollars.'

Sam gave a sour laugh. 'This may sound strange, but with some folk making that in a day here, that's not a great deal. However, I still think he'll try and string me along before he tells the authorities. On the other hand, he could get drunk this evening and decide to tell all to anyone who'll listen.'

'I don't think he'll do that. He'll want all the reward money for himself. My thoughts are he'll drain you, then head straight back to the fort and inform on you.'

'Whatever happens I'm in deep trouble.' Sam shrugged, then, after a short pause added, 'With everyone.' He was thinking of Kitty.

'Not with me, you're not. What does this Gus look like?'

'Overweight, grubby, heavy jowls, lopsided moustache. Blue-and-white spotted neckerchief.'

'Sounds like a rum-looking fella, but that makes him easy to find. You're meeting him at ten?'

'Half-past.'

'Pay him something tomorrow. I'm just wondering if we can get him on my steamer.'

'What good would that do?'

'You want your gold back, don't you?'

'Of course.'

'That steamer's my kingdom. If we get him onboard, I can guarantee you'll get your gold back, because I'll take it off him.'

'But then he'll report me.'

'Only if he gets back to Fort Langley.'

'What do you mean?'

'No need to look at me askance,' said Tug, laughing. 'He can be delayed until you get yourself onto US soil. You need to think about moving over the border, or taking a ship.'

'I've no choice now, have I?'

'Do you really need to dig anymore? Haven't you enough to set yourself up in Frisco?'

'I'd have liked another month's worth.'

'A true digger is never satisfied with their poke. Better

a bit short on brass than locked up in Fort Langley jail waiting to be shipped back to Victoria. Much as I hate to see you leave, I suggest you start thinking about hightailing it out of range of the Hudson's Bay Company.'

'You said once I reminded you of someone. Who is that?'

Even though Tug was smiling there was a sadness in his eyes. 'My nephew. My sister had a boy, Mason, a grand lad. I thought of him as my own.'

'What happened to him?'

'He got himself involved in a logging deal. His job was to cut the lower branches – they called it "hooking" – to bring them down before the main trunk. There was an accident when one whipped round and caught him. He fell and died. He was like you in many ways. Lots of plans for his future. And I see the same spirit in you. You've got a bit of a look of him.'

'I'm sorry. A young life lost.' Sam put his hand on Tug's arm. 'Can I say thank you for all your help?'

'No need. You can thank me by living a long life.'

CHAPTER TWENTY-FOUR

The next morning Pierre arrived at Muldoon's with some mending. Kitty took his order and expected him to leave, but he hovered, fiddling with his shirt sleeve.

'Can I help you with something else?' she asked.

'I don't want to interfere, but I'm not wrong in thinking you and Sam have an affection for each other, am I?'

Kitty couldn't help it. Having been awake most of the night tossing and turning, she broke down in tears.

Pierre's face crumpled in sympathetic alarm. He took a small step forward. 'I ask forgiveness. I have said something to upset you. A thousand pardons.'

Kitty fumbled for the handkerchief she always kept in her sleeve, found it, and wiped her eyes. 'There's been an upset.'

'Again, forgive me, but I see you are unhappy and I can tell you that Sam is unhappy too. May I ask, have you had a disagreement?'

Kitty was at a loss as to how to respond. There was so much more to recent events than a simple 'disagreement'.

'There has been an upset between us, that much is true, but a lot more has happened. How do you know Sam is upset?'

'He has the face on him of a dead porpoise. His eyes are dull and strained, he is inward, he woke early, there is something very wrong. I am thinking perhaps I can help to mend things between you.'

'Ah! So, you came to help under the guise of needing trousers mended.' She managed a smile to show she was not cross with him.

Pierre looked sheepish. 'You see right through me – although I do need those trousers mending. I have both your interests at heart. He is a good, if troubled, man. Am I right?'

Kitty was in a quandary. *How much can I tell without revealing Sam's background? How much do I trust Pierre? Would it be wrong to refer obliquely to Sam's predicament?*

'Allow me a moment to collect my thoughts,' she said.

Pierre looked out of the window while she tried to decide her best course of action. After a short interval she said, 'I take you at your word, Pierre. You helped us with my pa and I think you too are a good man, so I will tell you enough for you to decide what, if anything, you want to do.' She indicated to him to sit down. 'A trader, Gus Boston, called here yesterday and recognised Sam. I cannot tell you more, but I understand he's attempting to blackmail him. They have a meeting at half past ten in The Angel.'

Pierre pulled out his pocket watch. 'That's in half an hour.'

'I can't tell you why he's blackmailing him, because that's for Sam to say, but I can tell you Sam hasn't killed anyone, and no one has been physically hurt.'

'*Mon Dieu*, I was expecting a matter of the heart, not this.'

'Do you think you can help him?'

'There is no reason why I should not be in The Angel at half past ten too.'

'That would be a relief to me. If Sam is sitting with a man who has a blue neckerchief with white dots, it's the same man. Take care. I don't know this man, he may be dangerous.'

She stood and put her hand out. Pierre took it and performed a little bow. 'If we were in France, I would kiss you on both cheeks in friendship, but we are not, so a kiss on the hand must do.'

After he had gone, Kitty was overcome with misgivings. *I've said too much. I should have said nothing. Now I've probably put Pierre in danger too.*

❋ ❋ ❋

When he arrived at The Angel just before half past ten, Sam was surprised to see Pierre sitting tucked away in a corner reading an old newspaper. Pierre acknowledged him with a quick nod then returned to his reading.

At just gone half past, Gus Boston arrived. He settled himself at Sam's table.

'I don't suppose you had much sleep last night?'

Sam ignored the question. 'Shall we commence with the business?'

'If we must. I thought you might like to observe the niceties of a financial transaction. A little small talk before we get down to business.'

'I don't find that necessary. What are your terms?'

Gus pulled a soiled scrap of paper from his waistcoat pocket and passed it across the table. 'Here you are. I've been making a few calculations.'

Sam took the paper and, after smoothing it out, he began reading.

Loss of HBC wages – $150

Damages – $150

Interest – $ 75

Total – $375

He gave a brittle laugh. 'Interest?'

'Payable on my loss of earnings. Calculated from when your wife got me fired to today's date – August 20th.'

Sam passed the paper back. 'You're making a big miscalculation. I don't have that kind of money.'

'You don't have to pay me all at once. A down payment of a hundred dollars will do nicely for now. I've checked with the assay office and the going rate is sixteen dollars per ounce, so I calculate that around six ounces. You've been here long enough to have made that much without it being a burden.'

Despite his calm exterior, Sam's insides were churning. It didn't matter what the ridiculous list totalled, the claims on his purse were going to be persistent to the point of never-ending. He shook his head.

'Now, don't be like that,' said Gus, his fatty jowls wobbling.

Remembering Tug had told him to pay up, and feeling he had no option, Sam called the barman over and asked for his gold balance scales. After weighing out some small gold nuggets and adjusting with dust, he looked up to find Pierre had put down his newspaper and was watching him intently. It crossed his mind that should Pierre ask, he would have to think up some excuse as to why he was settling a debt in broad daylight.

As soon as the scales balanced, Gus stretched his hand out. 'That looks about right.' He scooped the weighed gold into a small red leather purse and put it in his pocket. 'I'll be back more regularly now and we can settle up again. If you're not here when I return then, as you'd expect, I'll be straight to the Company office. I'll be disappointed, but I'll have the hundred dollars in reward money to console me.'

Gus rose and extended his arm for a handshake. Sam snubbed the approach.

'There's no need to be unfriendly. Think of this as paying off an overdue debt,' said Gus.

Watching as his hard-earned gold went out through the door in the red leather purse, Sam felt he really had hit rock bottom. He thought of ordering a stiff whiskey, then cautioned himself – he didn't want to end up like Kitty's pa, drowning his sorrows to ease his pain. While he was thinking these thoughts Pierre came over.

'My friend, forgive me for intruding, but –'

Sam cut him off. 'Just a gambling debt. Lady Luck

appears to have abandoned me these days.' *And that's not a lie about luck.*

Pierre put an elbow on the table and rested his chin on his fist. 'I spoke with Miss Kitty earlier. She was very distressed.'

'We've had words.'

'I know there's more to it than that.'

Sam was suddenly anxious. 'What has she told you?'

'Very little, except that you are being blackmailed over something unnecessarily.'

Sam would have denied it, but knew his face would give him away.

'I just want to know if I can aid you,' Pierre went on. 'It is your own business, I know that, but seeing the man you were with, I do not think he is a gentleman. My money is with you.'

'He's someone my wife caused trouble for years ago and he holds a grudge.'

'As I say, I know it is not my business, but can you not report him?'

Sam gave a hollow laugh. 'It is *he* who wants to report *me*. I have a previous life that has caught up with me.'

'You will not be alone in that here.' Pierre chuckled. 'I expect most of us are running away from someone or something.'

An idea began to form in Sam's mind. All morning he'd been wondering how he could ensure Gus boarded Tug's steamer. He'd come up with nothing he thought would work, but now he could see a way.

'Pierre, there *is* something you can do to help me.'

'Tell me and I will try.'

'I have a friend, Tug Tait, who pilots a steamer between here, Fort Langley and New Westminster. He's agreed to help me by delaying Gus Boston, with a view to getting my gold back. I imagine by picking his pocket or getting him drunk on board.'

'Or throwing him overboard?'

Sam frowned and shook his head. 'I don't think he'd do that, although it would certainly solve things for me. I just need to make sure Gus gets on the correct steamer this evening.'

'There is business I can see to in Langley. I will strike up a jovial conversation, offer him a free drink and a card game on board. Then I can watch over things.'

'That sounds like a good plan. Gus won't know *you*, but *you* will know him. Can you do this for me?'

'But of course.'

'May I ask why?'

'I don't like the way he is treating you or the way he looks at you, my friend. He is nothing but a cheap peddler. You, you are a decent man with true grit. You proved that in your dealings with the card sharp. That is a good enough reason, is it not?'

Sam laughed. 'If you say so. Where I come from you get grit in your eye, but I know what you mean.'

CHAPTER TWENTY-FIVE

From the raised vantage point of the sawmill, Sam watched the steamer depart for Langley with Tug at her helm. It was too dark to make out the passengers clearly, but as Pierre was not at the bunkhouse when Sam returned, he assumed all had gone to plan. When he woke the next morning and saw Pierre's stretcher had not been slept in, Sam also assumed Pierre had left with Gus. He would have been happier knowing for sure.

He spent the day working on his claim. He had a good day digging, but his mind kept jumping from the steamer to Kitty. Neither topic held any comfort for him, except for the thought that Kitty had got Pierre involved. This might indicate she cared. But then what did that matter now, if he had to make a run for it? He knew he should call and apologise to her, but what to say? How could he expect her to believe anything he said?

On his return to the bunkhouse, Herr Steiner handed him a note.

Dear Sam,

I think we should speak before you leave. There are things unsaid and questions that need answering. If you agree, perhaps you will call and see me.

Kitty.

Sam dumped his gear, washed, and changed his shirt. He was going to put on the one she'd made especially for him, then decided against it, since it might look like he was trying to ingratiate himself. He told himself her note did not imply any intimacy, yet his heart had hope.

Kitty was in her usual place, sitting at her workbench as if she hadn't moved at all. They greeted each other somewhat formally. The atmosphere in the room was exactly as it had been the last time they'd been together – heavy with difficulty, and loaded with regret and emotional pain. Sam felt stifled, and from the look on Kitty's face, and the way she was fidgeting, he thought she was probably experiencing the same.

'Will you walk with me?' he asked. 'It's a sunny evening. A shame to waste it, with the ground being so dry and easy underfoot.'

Kitty thought for a moment then nodded. 'I'll just tell Pa I'll be out for a while.' She called upstairs and Frank gave his approval. 'He likes to know where I am. Not in a nosy way, you understand, more to keep me safe.'

'There's something going on at the Indian encampment. Lots of dancing and singing. Shall we walk along the lakeside and take a look? Or will it be too noisy for you?'

'I'd like that,' she said.

Sam watched as she put on her favourite light cotton jacket. It fitted her trim body perfectly. If he never saw her again, this was how he would always picture her.

They set off along the boardwalk. Sam offered Kitty his arm, which she accepted. He allowed himself the luxury of thinking this might be a good sign. As they passed The Angel, one of the saloon gals caught sight of them and hurried out with loud greetings, the scarlet feather she'd entwined in her hair bobbing up and down wildly.

'Nice to see you walking out with a gentleman.'

'This is Sam. We're just friends,' said Kitty, sounding defensive to Sam's ears.

'I'm Beth,' the girl told him. After studying him for a few seconds, she added, 'I remember you. You and that card sharp. You did well there, mister. Looks like you've got yourself a good 'un, Kitty dear, and what's more, I can tell you he ain't no regular here.'

Kitty's cheeks reddened. It was clear she knew what Beth was referring to. She recovered quickly. 'I'll see you and Eliza on Friday for your fitting. Half past three.'

'Don't you worry. We'll be there.' Beth smiled conspiratorially. 'We can't wait to see the new materials.'

They left Beth and walked on a little way. 'Sam would have been delighted if Kitty had told Beth 'we're friends', but she'd added the 'just'. Was this good or bad? They were passing the doctor's office when Sam decided it was easier to ask a difficult question walking along, than face to face.

'Did you mean it when you told Beth we're friends?' he asked.

'I did. That's why I wanted to see you. I've been thinking about everything you've told me.'

'And?'

'I was too quick to chastise you and I'm sorry.'

The distant hope Sam had felt on receipt of her note began to bud. Perhaps not all was completely lost.

'You'd suffered a shock,' he said. 'You've every right to feel angry.'

'What I'm trying to say is, the last two days I've missed not having you to talk to.'

'I've felt the same way.' It was true, he really had missed her, and if he was honest with himself, Kitty was the reason he hadn't yet made any practical arrangements about leaving. He'd told himself he was just waiting until Tug and Pierre got back, hopefully having retrieved his gold, but there was more to it than that. He couldn't leave before he'd sorted things with her. His heart wouldn't let him.

Kitty brushed away a small tear. 'Despite my feelings at being lied to, I want to get to know the real Sam. Does he want to know me?'

They stopped walking and faced each other.

'You have to ask that? Of course he does. Sam Gray is standing here right in front of you. He'll find it a relief to be able to talk honestly about the things he's done, the people he's known, the life he's led. Everyone has regrets in their lives and, I promise you, I truly regret not taking you into my confidence. I've decided I'll only find happiness when I've a definite future, with plans made under my real name.'

'A future that overshadows your past and your ghosts? A future in San Francisco?'

'That's my waking dream.'

Kitty tightened her grip on Sam's arm. 'If I may say so, I think that's a very sound waking dream.'

Sam moved closer. 'If you get to know me better, will you be in that dream of the future?'

'I'd like that...'

'But...?'

'But I still need time to think things through.'

'I understand,' said Sam. And it was true, he did understand.

They walked on a little way in silence, until Kitty asked, 'And Pa, what about him? Can you be friends with him?'

'Of course. Have you told him?'

'No. It's as you said, if he doesn't know then he can't be accused of harbouring you. It would put him in a dreadful quandary. It's better that way. For now.'

Sam was relieved, while at the same time feeling guilty for forcing Kitty to withhold the truth. He would face that conversation later, in the expectation it would be a difficult one.

They carried on, passing some tied-up mules which Kitty stopped to pet, and proceeding to the quay. Sam told her about Pierre and Tug hoping to retrieve his gold from Gus on the steamer. They watched the Indians for a while and Kitty bought some smoked deer meat from them and a small woven basket to carry it in.

On the way home, Kitty asked, 'Do you think Evie and Grace should be angry with you because you've deserted?'

Sam was brought up short. 'It's not something I've ever considered.'

'Perhaps you need to ask yourself why you can't let them go. I don't think either of them would want you to be forever miserable, do you?'

'No. Evie's anger was with God for not giving her a child that lived, not with me. Grace didn't feel about me the way I felt about her. So no, I can't see that Grace is angry with me, either. More likely I felt upset with her in a selfish way, because when I asked for devotion she spurned me.'

'That's understandable. Since Evie's drowning was an accident, she was taken from you, she didn't want to leave *you*. Grace, you tell me, didn't want to break her missionary contract and as you say, perhaps didn't love you as much as you did her.'

Sam shrugged and looked away from her questioning gaze.

'Don't be sad forever.'

As they approached the barbershop, Sam thought about how things had changed since the morning. He had felt at a complete loss, but now there was hope. After saying goodbye, he was walking away with a lighter heart, when Kitty called out, 'Pa wants to speak with you.'

Sam's first thought was that Frank had got wind of his false name. 'What about?' he asked.

'I don't know, except he's got the fresh water out and he just called me Kathryn.'

A summons to the parlour was not an invitation Sam felt he could refuse. He drew in a deep breath and went upstairs to face whatever music was about to be played.

Frank was sitting in the horse-hair chair like a manager in an office, smoking a small cigar. A half-empty tumbler of water stood on the small table beside him. He indicated to Sam to sit.

Sam took off his hat and accepted the glass of water Frank poured and handed to him.

'Are you from a large family?' Frank asked.

Sam was surprised by the question. He shook his head. 'My ma died and I was raised by her ma. My father, a collier, worked down the pit in England.'

'Brothers? Sisters?'

'A sister and a brother.'

'Nephews and nieces, then, too?'

'Possibly by now.'

'All in England?'

'Aye, all in Whitehaven in Cumberland.'

'Then you are blessed. You have people in England to call on. I expect they will welcome you back when you return.'

The questioning had the air of preliminary chat. It was obviously leading somewhere, but where? Sam didn't think for one minute Frank could be interested in his family.

'I expect they would be pleased to see me if I had plans to return,' he said.

'Can I take it your use of "would" and "if" are indicative that you have no immediate plans for returning to England?'

'My plans when I leave here are to live and work in San Francisco.'

'And your future?'

'My future? I'm not sure what you mean.'

'Where do you see yourself in, say, ten years' time?'

Sam hesitated then he thought he saw the light. *This isn't about my future; it's about Kitty's.* 'I see myself living and working in San Francisco. Hopefully I'll be rewarded for hard work and will have a nice house, a wife and a family.'

Frank nodded slowly, almost sagely. 'I ask because you understand that Kathryn is the only family I have. We all have our faults, and in my eyes she is not perfect, but she is more important to me than anything else in this world.'

'You are her pa, that's only natural.' Their conversation was not a man-to-man exchange of views, which was how it had felt on previous occasions; this was more like an employer interviewing a job applicant. But what was the position Sam was supposed to be applying for? He wasn't sure whether he was being warned off, or wooed.

'You have a friendship with Kathryn. I am correct in that?'

'We are friends, that is true.'

'In that case, what are your intentions towards her?'

Sam didn't know how to answer. Frank was staring at him intently, making him feel as if he was searching for his inner soul. He had to say something, he realised that.

'My intentions are honourable. By that, I mean I regard Kitty as a friend, a very good friend who I hope to get to know better. Whether our friendship will lead to a permanent association –'

Frank butted in. 'You mean matrimony, for which you would ask me for her hand?'

'Aye, marriage. I think it fair to say it's early days.'

'Early days it may well be, but I will only give her hand to someone I trust. Also, it may seem self-centred of me, but I would be unhappy for you to take her away to a foreign place, or even an American city such as New York or Boston. The decision would be hers, but I'd like to think she would not want me to be left alone in San Francisco. We have very few acquaintances and no relatives.'

'Were I in the same situation, with a daughter, I would probably feel the same way.' As he spoke, Sam was reminded how when he and Evie had left England, he'd turned a deaf ear to her agonised declarations of leaving her family, and even more so to her family's loudly expressed grief. He wasn't proud of the recollection.

'We are of similar minds, then,' said Frank. He drew on his cigar until the end glowed red. 'I would add that I take it as a given you are an honest man.'

Sam knew that if he was truly an honest man it was at this point he would own up to his false identity. He could have mustered up the courage to do so, but he would be putting Frank in danger of being accused of harbouring him. There were also his drinking bouts. How could Sam be sure Frank, on a strident day, might not share his secret with all and sundry? No, he couldn't divulge his past to him. It was impossible for him under any circumstances until they were on American soil.

'Kitty knows what I am,' he said.

'How long are you staying?'

This was another question he had hoped Frank wouldn't ask. 'I don't know exactly, but I may leave soon. And you? Shall you stay for the winter?'

'We'll be gone before the bad weather sets in. Perhaps we can travel together. There's safety in numbers. Take the boat to Victoria to see the place and maybe pull a few teeth, make some money and then home.'

If that was to be the Muldoons' route home, Sam wouldn't be accompanying them, but he didn't say so.

When the interview was over Kitty was waiting downstairs. 'What did he want?' she asked.

'He wanted to know about me and whether I am an honest man.'

'What did you say?'

'I said you knew what I was and he accepted that. My conscience is pricking me that he doesn't know my story. And now it's as if you're aiding and abetting me. I'm sorry, but my true identity will have to wait, as far as your da is concerned.'

'You're right. We can't tell him yet.'

CHAPTER TWENTY-SIX

Beth and Eliza were late for their dress fittings. At four o'clock Kitty was beginning to wonder if they'd forgotten, when with the momentum of a whirlwind, they bounced into her workroom.

'We've been so-o-o-o busy,' said Eliza, fanning herself melodramatically with a large black fan decorated with a pair of entwined white swans.

'We have indeed,' said Beth, pulling out her own fan. 'A party of geologists and map makers have arrived. I thought we might not get away, until their boss suggested they might like to do a bit of surveying, since that's what they'd come for.'

'I said to Eliza, any boundary lines they pace out this afternoon will be twisted as a shepherd's crook, the amount they've had to drink since they got off the steamer.'

Kitty took their bonnets with the overlong ribbons. 'Well, I'm very glad you're here now. Shall we retire to the parlour upstairs? I've everything laid out for you.'

The girls were soon looking over Gus's material, holding pieces by the window to check the colours in full daylight and testing the fabric between their fingers.

'I can't believe there's blue velvet. It's glorious.' Beth held up a piece for Eliza to admire. 'Those ladies at the fort must fuss themselves real fancy for all the dinners and balls they have to dress up for.'

'It's very nice,' said Eliza, 'but red would have been better for us.'

Kitty picked up some taffeta. 'This is a vibrant red. I can make a nice skirt from it and bond the sides with the blue velvet. What do you think? Would you like that?'

'Will the taffeta be strong enough to match the weight of the velvet?' asked Eliza.

'I think it'll be swanky and just fine for you,' said Beth.

'You don't think it'll be too much?'

'It'll be striking. Folk'll certainly notice you.'

Beth sniggered. 'She means men,' she said, addressing Kitty.

Kitty chuckled. 'I rather thought that. To make it really classy you could have matching ribbon bracelets around the wrists.'

'As a rule we don't go in for sleeves with the fancy working dresses. They cover us up too much.'

'No, of course not,' said Kitty, feeling foolish.

The girls undressed down to their corsets and cotton pantaloons. Beth admired herself in the full-length mirror Kitty had carried through from her bedroom, running her fingers along the top edge of her corset. 'You know, a new chemisette inset would go very nicely here.' She placed two fingers on her cleavage. 'What have you got?'

'I've a nice piece of lawn linen somewhere.' Kitty rummaged in a small trunk and found the fabric she was looking for. Beth slipped it in the top of the corset before checking in the mirror.

'It's nice material, but there's too much of it. I don't want to hide the goods on display.'

Eliza giggled and Kitty, irritatingly, felt herself blush. She knew how the girls made their living, so the comment shouldn't have shocked her, but long-learnt social mores were difficult to shed.

'Shall I adjust it?' asked Eliza, putting down the piece of poplin she'd been arranging around her neck.

'Better Kitty does it, don't you think? That's what we're here for, a fitting.'

Kitty studied the chemisette, moving her head from side to side as she contemplated it from different angles. 'I don't want to cut the material, but if I make a little seam along the top, that'll work.'

'We'll do that, then,' said Beth.

The next hour was spent drawing up patterns and deciding on details until, as things began to grind to a halt, Kitty thought she had better broach the subject of costs.

'I've a list here with the material prices,' she said.

Eliza picked up the piece of paper and looked at the letter heading at the top of the page. 'Oh, it's from Gus Boston?'

'Yes,' said Kitty. 'Do you know him?'

'He comes in The Angel now and then, when he's over from Fort Langley.'

'Yes, it was him. He brought everything on Monday.'

'You must have paid him handsomely.'

Kitty was puzzled. 'He said we could buy what we wanted and the store could take the rest. He left the list of prices I've just shown you. He didn't ask for a deposit.' She'd only realised after he'd gone he hadn't asked for one. But then he'd seen Sam, and that had definitely sent him off track. She'd half-expected him to call the next day, but he hadn't.

'Well, that's most odd, because on Tuesday he was fair putting liquor away in The Angel and buying drinks for other diggers. Ain't that so, Eliza?'

'Sure. Kept saying he'd done a great deal.'

'He didn't get anything from *me*.' Kitty's heart was sinking fast. If it wasn't payment from the general store, then it was probably Sam's gold that had financed Gus's generosity. She wondered whether his tongue had been loosened enough to brag about the source of his newfound wealth. Even an indirect comment could be enough.

✳ ✳ ✳

Sam looked up to see Kitty striding towards him. Her brow was furrowed and her lips clamped together.

'What's happened?' he asked. She was breathless and looking serious. 'Something wrong with your pa?'

'It's Gus Boston,' she said, putting a hand on her chest.

Sam groaned inwardly. 'What about him?' Whatever it was about Gus, he didn't really want to know. That man could rot in hell, for all he cared.

'He was drinking in The Angel on Tuesday night, buying

drinks and throwing his money around. Beth and Eliza just told me.'

'On my money no doubt.'

'Are you all right?' asked Kitty. 'You suddenly look really peculiar. You'd better sit down.'

Sam put his hand up to his forehead and pushed his hair back from his eyes. 'I'm all right. I've tried over the last couple of days to forget about Gus Boston. Just thinking about him makes me agitated.'

'I thought you said he was on the steamer with your friend Tug.'

'What I said was I watched the ferry leave on Wednesday from up on the sawmill. I only assumed he was on it.'

'Have you seen him around since then?'

Sam frowned. 'No.'

'If he was still here he'd be doing more drinking in The Angel and the girls would have seen him,' Kitty said. 'Don't fret. He'll have got on that steamer, you just couldn't see clearly enough.'

'You're probably right. I hope so.'

CHAPTER TWENTY-SEVEN

On Sunday 22nd August, while working on his claim, Sam saw Tug's steamer arrive and tie up. He locked his tools away and made straight for the dock. Tug was standing by the gangway when he arrived, overseeing the unloading of several crates of what looked like hard liquor. Sam waited impatiently while goods were checked and signed for. The unloading seemed to go on forever. In reality only an hour passed between the steamer's docking and Sam and Tug being able to sit down together and share a tot of rum on board.

'What happened about Gus?' Sam asked, when they were finally alone.

'I wondered when he didn't board the steamer what had happened to him.' Tug took his baccy tin out of his pocket and put it on the table. 'I guess he got another ride. Sorry I couldn't do anything.'

'You mean he didn't board?' Sam wasn't prepared for this and a wave of nervousness washed over him.

'I watched every passenger walk up that gangway with Pierre by my side. We both concluded he'd changed his mind. Is he still here? We should have sent you a note, but the situation took us by surprise. By the time we realised what had happened, we were away from the dock.'

Sam was now in a panic, so much so it was proving an effort to breathe evenly. He'd thought Gus Boston was well away. Surely he couldn't be hiding out somewhere still in Harrison?

'Did Pierre come back from Fort Langley with you?' he asked.

'He was first off the boat to look for you. You just missed each other. But he knows as much, or as little, as I do. What will you do now? Will you stay or are you minded to flit?'

'I don't know.' Sam had a horrible taste in his mouth and he thought he might be sick. He swallowed several times, but it didn't help.

'Wherever Gus is, you don't want to be here for the winter. The boats can't navigate the river and you'll be stuck here, unable to dig in the hard earth, with nothing much else to do. It can drive an industrious man mad. If I was you, I wouldn't tarry longer than the first week in October.'

'That's five weeks. He'll come looking for me sooner rather than later. I've been unlucky, him recognising me, but what's to say there won't be someone else?' The nausea he'd felt earlier was still there, combined with a pulsating in his temples that he knew to be the prelude to a pounding headache.

'Whenever you decide you want to leave, I can get you to New Westminster. Then you'll have to board another vessel for San Francisco. Once you're on that ship, the Company can't touch you. It's the same as standing on American soil. You'll be home free.'

*** * ***

When Sam and Pierre finally got together, back at the bunkhouse, Pierre duplicated Tug's account.

'Gus never arrived. Your friend Tug and I watched closely.'

'He hasn't been seen here.'

'He's a travelling salesman, is he not?'

'Aye, that's what I've been told.'

'Then perhaps business here was not as he expected. Perhaps he changed his mind and took one of the steamers up to Port Douglas. I could understand that. It's a new place, he could find fresh custom there, then return on a direct steamer to Fort Langley to fulfil his orders.'

Sam hadn't thought of that. It was a possibility. It was the not knowing that unsettled him. He never wanted to see Gus Boston again, but that didn't mean he didn't want to know where he was and what he was doing. At the very least, if he knew Gus was away from Harrison it would be a small comfort.

Later, hoping the drowsiness he was feeling would lead to sound sleep, Sam pushed his feet down into his bedding. As he did so he felt something. He pulled his feet back quickly, thinking it must be an animal, but the object didn't move. He put his hand down and felt leather.

He wriggled the object free from the covers. It was the red leather purse Gus had used to hold Sam's gold. It felt promisingly heavy. As unobtrusively as he could, he opened the purse's drawstrings and, to his overwhelming relief, he saw it contained gold. He propped himself up on one elbow to look at Pierre. If, as Sam suspected, his friend had put it there, he would surely be watching, enjoying seeing Sam reunited with his lawful diggings. They would exchange glances and Sam could thank him properly in the morning. But Sam was wrong. Pierre appeared to be fast asleep, with his back to him.

If it wasn't Pierre or Tug, then who was it? Who else knew he was being blackmailed, apart from Kitty? And where did that put Gus Boston now? He would hardly have returned to Fort Langley or set off for Port Douglas without his red leather purse. By whatever deed Gus Boston lost his ill-gotten gains, he'd not waste time demanding more. He could be back any day.

CHAPTER TWENTY-EIGHT

The dresses, belts and re-stylings were ready for Beth and Eliza. Kitty had worked steadfastly to finish them. She was anxious to find new custom and the girls were excellent advertisements for her dressmaking prowess. She was about to ask a passer-by to drop a note into the saloon, asking them to come and collect their items, then thought she might as well venture down to The Angel herself. It wasn't very ladylike to be seen in a saloon bar, but she could put her head in the doorway and leave a message.

She waited outside the bar for a few moments for someone to come out so she could ask them to deliver her message, before deciding it was cowardly not to enter. After all, she was there on business, not to play cards or drink whiskey. Inside, she was surprised to find it quite dark. She'd thought saloons were lively places, but perhaps that was only at night.

The barman regarded her with interest. He was running a cloth over the counter.

'A large whiskey?' he asked in a jovial tone, looking her up and down.

Kitty matched his mood. 'Not just now. I don't drink until gone midday.'

He chuckled. 'In that case, how can I help you?'

'I've a message for Beth and Eliza. Can you give it to them, please?'

'I can, but why don't you tell them yourself? They're out back, pegging out washing.'

Kitty hesitated. Being in the saloon was one thing, being seen disappearing into its bowels was another – no matter how interesting it might prove to be.

'Thank you, but I'm in a hurry and I'm expecting someone. Please tell them Kitty Muldoon called and their orders are ready to collect. I'll be in for the rest of the day.'

The barman, looking disappointed, shrugged. 'As you wish.'

Less than an hour later the girls were upstairs in the Muldoons' parlour. When everything had been tried on and admired, the question of payment came up.

Kitty produced a list of materials and hours worked and handed it to Eliza.

'I guess things are different now?' said Beth.

'Different? Why?'

'Gus Boston sold you these, didn't he?'

Kitty nodded. 'Yes, we were lucky. He'd put in a big order, what with the Inauguration Ball for the British Columbia celebrations next month, and the ladies at the fort all wanting new dresses. That's why we've got the blue velvet. He put it on one side for us.'

There was a pause while the girls looked at each other. 'She doesn't know,' said Beth.

'I don't know what?'

'They fished him out of the lake this morning. Drowned. Been in there a while, by all accounts.'

Kitty heard the words, and knew what they meant, but she was unable to deal immediately with the repercussions, apart from knowing that this changed everything for Sam.

'You look shocked,' said Eliza. 'I'm sorry. I didn't mean to upset you. This being such a small place I thought you'd know. Word always travels fast, especially bad news. Was he a friend of yours?'

'No,' Kitty managed to say. 'He was no friend of mine. Are you sure it was him?'

'Sure as sure. The storekeeper was called to identify him.'

'And he'd drowned?'

'No one saw him drowning, so probably more truthful to say he was washed up dead. No gunshot or knife wound. The talk in the saloon is he probably had too much to drink and fell overboard from a steamer. Folk heard him say earlier that he'd done a special deal and was going back to Langley to celebrate.'

All Kitty wanted at that moment was to be rid of the girls and to speak with Sam. She needed to look him in the eyes. Had he lied when he said he'd never killed a man? Or was it that when she asked him he hadn't yet done so, but was about to?

'Looks like you got yourself a host of free materials, Kitty dear, so you'll be able to do us a real good deal.'

Kitty was only half listening. Her mind was on who could be responsible. Sam, Tug, or Pierre? One thing she knew for certain was that Gus wasn't taken by God's hand. And if Sam wasn't responsible, it was likely he didn't yet know. She had to find him and tell him.

'I'll sort a good deal for you,' she said. 'Let me think about it.'

* * *

Kitty tracked Sam down in the claims office. When he saw her beckoning, he stepped out of the line.

'What are you doing here?' she asked.

Aware people might be able to hear, he spoke softly, almost in a whisper. 'I was going to tell you this evening. I'm giving up my claim and leaving. I can't wait for Gus Boston to track me down again.' He was on the point of telling her he'd got most of his gold back, but Kitty began speaking very quickly.

At first, he couldn't grasp what she was saying, her speech was so garbled, but he did make out, 'They fished him out of the lake.'

'Who? Let's go outside.'

On the boardwalk, Kitty took two deep breaths. 'They've fished Gus out of the lake.' She corrected herself. 'No, he was washed ashore. Oh, I can't remember exactly what they said, but he's dead.'

If this is true, I have a reprieve. This was a wicked thought. The man, however distasteful, had lost his life, but the relief was overwhelming. Sam couldn't believe it could be true. 'Who said?'

'Beth and Eliza.'

For a moment, confused, Sam couldn't remember who these girls were.

'You know, the saloon gals,' Kitty said. 'They think he fell off the steamer when he was drunk.'

Gus must have been on Tug's steamer, after all. Was it Tug or Pierre who pushed him overboard? Or had he ever boarded the steamer? Perhaps someone had drowned him at the lakeside in the dark, to make it look as if he'd fallen overboard. His killer had to be whoever left the pouch in Sam's stretcher. As far as he knew, Tug had been nowhere near his bunkhouse, so it must be Pierre. Unless, of course, Tug had taken the purse and given it to Pierre to put back. That was a possibility, but more likely Tug would have just handed the gold back to Sam face to face.

Another thought struck him. Did Kitty think he was the one who'd gone after Gus?

'I didn't kill Gus. As the ferry left the dock I was speaking to the sawmill foreman. He will remember me. You have to believe me. I swear on my dead son Stephen's memory. It was not me.'

Kitty's eyes swept Sam's face and he thought for an agonising moment she was doubting his words until she touched his cheek. 'I believe you,' she said.

He reached for her hand. 'Thank you for trusting me. It means a lot, although I fear others may suspect me.'

'Why would others suspect you? Apart from myself, Tug and Pierre, who else knows your situation with Gus? He's hardly likely to have told people he was blackmailing you. Your secret was his golden egg; he wasn't going to crack it open and spread the valuable yolk around.'

Sam squeezed her hand. 'You can't honestly say the thought hasn't crossed your mind I did it?'

'I won't lie, but your surprised reaction to the news and the honesty in your eyes proves to me you didn't kill him.'

'Then it must have been Tug or Pierre. If so, I'm shocked. Much as I'm relieved to be spared his presence, I never wanted to see him dead.'

'Perhaps it's as Beth and Eliza suggested, that he was so drunk he fell overboard and there's been no murder.'

Sam didn't want to say anything, but with the red leather purse finding its way to his stretcher, it couldn't possibly be the case that Gus had simply fallen overboard, as the gold would have gone overboard with him. However, a stronger voice in his head spoke up, reminding him he'd promised her he would tell the truth, so he pressed on, even though he was incriminating himself.

'I've got most of my gold back.'

Kitty's eyes widened and a flash of uncertainty crossed her face. 'How? Who from?'

'It was put into my stretcher. I know it sounds ridiculous that it suddenly appeared, but you believe me, don't you?'

Kitty nodded. 'I believe you, but I admit it looks convenient. It must have been taken from Gus at some stage, either before or after his death.'

'I know, so to my thinking it can only be Gus or Pierre. Anyone else would have kept it.'

'You've no need to rush away to San Francisco now, have you?'

'I haven't had time to think properly, but I'm still a

wanted man. I'll most likely stay until the beginning of October.'

'If we can persuade Pa to leave then, perhaps we can all travel back together.'

Sam nodded, not trusting himself to speak. He was still lying to Frank. *Must I forever live a life of lies? It won't be like this in San Francisco; this is one thing I'm sure of. I intend to walk down every street like a bastion of honesty.*

CHAPTER TWENTY-NINE

Early September brought unexpected heat and the news that James Douglas, as of September 2nd, was officially Governor of British Columbia and Vancouver Island, and as a result had to resign from his position with the Hudson's Bay Company. It wasn't long before copies of another new publication, the *B C Colonist*, arrived on one of the steamers, but Sam wasn't paying much attention to what was happening in other places. His long days were filled with his rocker and shovels, and his nights with sleep. The episode with Gus had shattered his confidence and he sought solace and safety in his digging. Pierre claimed no knowledge of Gus's demise or the return of the gold, leaving Sam none the wiser. He decided to leave well alone.

A young, tall, good-looking officer, with a well-trimmed beard, came from Fort Langley and interviewed the sawmill worker who had found the body, the doctor who had declared the cause of death as drowning, and the barman in The Angel, who gave a statement about Gus's demeanour and drunkenness on the night he disappeared. Beth and Eliza offered their statements, but the officer, either nervous in their presence or anxious to leave Harrison and return to livelier Fort Langley, told them their testimonies were unnecessary, and that he had all he needed. Before he left he declared officially that 'accidental death by drowning' was the result of his enquiries.

Sam continued toiling on his claim and Kitty elicited more custom from other saloons' gals. Since Gus had never delivered any of the materials to the general store, they couldn't claim ownership. As a result, just as the girls had suggested, Kitty found herself with a windfall of free material. Her days were spent sewing and refashioning dresses. Every evening at half past six she went to sit with Sam before returning for supper with her pa at eight.

While Sam and Kitty appeared to have settled into an easy routine, as each week passed, the prize of living in San Francisco crept nearer. As a result, each day it seemed there was more to lose should he be recognised. In the second week of September, seeing Tug's steamer at the quay, Sam sought him out.

Tug poured them both generous whiskeys and they sat on deck, watching the commercial activity along Front Street. Sam raised the subject of Gus's death.

'He must have fallen over the side,' said Tug. 'I'll bet he was on the Port Douglas steamer and he was drunk. If the ship lurched when it left the quay, which I've seen it do many times, he'd be over the side in a flash if he was unsteady. The captain of that steamer is often the worse for wear with drink himself.'

'You're probably right,' said Sam.

However, that didn't explain the gold. Tug showed no indication of guilt in the affair and Sam decided to let things lie.

'I've made my mind up,' he said. 'I want to leave, as you suggested, the first week of October. Can you book me a passage?'

'I can always squeeze you in, but after New Westminster you're on your own. I can't book a passage through to San Francisco for you, as you'll have to go through the border checks.'

'Like the ones on the way here?'

'Exactly that, but now British Columbia's been officially recognised by British charter, you'll find the system is much more ordered and official. I'm not saying they haven't got tired of looking out for you, it's that the people running the border are government officials now, new in their jobs and keen. It's not like when the Company was in charge and they just gave you a look up and down.'

'What do they do now?'

'I've heard tell they question folk, and if they suspect you of anything, they take you aside. I hate to say it, but with your accent, they might cotton on to who you really are.'

'I guess that's the last hurdle. Getting onto an American boat.'

'Indeed.'

'Do you think it would make a difference if I wasn't on my own?'

'It might. They'll be looking for a single Britisher.

What are you thinking? Travelling with your friends the Muldoons?'

'I know Kitty would love to return to San Francisco, but her father may take some persuading to leave so early, and he'll also likely want to shut down his business. You can't do that overnight.'

'It's not his premises, is it?'

'No, he rents.'

'Well, in that case, I'd say he travels with his business. He's no premises, no goods to sell. I'd think he can get up and leave at the drop of a hat.'

Sam hadn't thought of this. It made sense. 'The only other problem is he wants to travel back by way of Victoria. Thinks there'll be a lot of folk needing their teeth pulling and a host of beards trimming.'

'I've news will stop Mr Muldoon wanting to visit Victoria.'

Sam leaned forward to listen with interest, and stored away the information.

✳ ✳ ✳

More and more Company men were being billeted in Harrison, and there was now an even greater risk of Sam's being exposed. By the Saturday after his discussion with Tug, he'd formulated a plan he thought workable enough to suggest to Kitty.

He broached the subject as they were taking a stroll past the Chinese laundry to the livery stables. One of the mares had dropped a foal, and Sam thought Kitty might like to see it. They found the foal angelically asleep, but Kitty was enchanted, despite not being able to pet it.

On their return, having decided they would speak with Frank, they found him bidding goodbye to an unhappy-looking digger holding a bloody handkerchief to his mouth.

'If it starts bleeding like a tap, roll up a piece of cotton, jam it into the hole and bite down on it as hard as you can. That'll stop it. And keep your tongue out of it. No probing.'

Sam winced and ran his own tongue over his top teeth. He'd been lucky with them so far.

He and Kitty went upstairs and waited for Frank to clean up and join them. When he did so, he was in a cheerful mood.

'That last one was a hard twist and pull, I can tell you, but it didn't get the better of me.' He looked at Kitty and Sam and lost his jokiness. 'You two look as if you're about to interrogate me.'

'Mr Muldoon sir,' Sam began, 'I've been speaking with the steamer captain, Tug Tait, who works between here, Fort Langley and New Westminster. He's of a mind that anyone thinking of leaving for the winter should do so before the middle of October.'

'Why?'

'There are only so many steamers working the route. It's not like we can just walk down to the dock and get on one. We need to buy tickets. My friend Tug can organise this for us.'

'You say "us". Are we travelling as a trio?'

'Will that not work for you, sir?' asked Sam. 'I can help with your boxes and cases.'

Frank bit his bottom lip. 'I was planning on a couple more weeks and then seeking business in Victoria until the end of November.'

'I don't think Victoria's a good idea. My friend Tug tells me there are fever cases and conditions there are far from wholesome. In fact, he used the word "unsanitary". Too many folk living in tents.' Sam waited for his words to sink in before adding, 'Don't you think we'd be better off heading straight for San Francisco? It would be safer.'

'Pa, don't you think we should take this advice?'

Sam held his breath.

'I suppose if the diggers know I'm leaving, there's a chance they'll come rushing to the door before I go. I'll think about it.'

'What you could do, Pa, is say you're cutting your prices for a couple of weeks. That'll definitely bring people to your door – the ones who've a niggly tooth they're thinking of having seen to. If they think they can get it cheaper then they'll come.'

'That might work very well,' said Sam, wishing he'd thought of the suggestion.

'I'll sleep on it. I'll not be rushed into something like this.'

CHAPTER THIRTY

Frank kept Kitty and Sam waiting four days before summoning them to the parlour. Kitty thought she would almost die if he made them stay longer in Harrison and Sam had to leave before them. San Francisco had been calling to her even before Sam had told her he wanted to travel with them. Going home was all she could think about.

Frank rubbed his hands together. 'I've thought through what you said last week. We've made a good living and perhaps it *is* time to move on.'

Kitty was so relieved she ran forward and, putting her arms around her pa, gave him an enthusiastic kiss. 'Thank you, thank you.' She stepped back, picked up the sides of her skirt and did a little dance, before rushing to Sam and giving him a hug. 'Home to San Francisco. At last. I can see it all in my mind's eye. We're getting off the quay at Pacific Wharf. All the carriage carts are lined up, our luggage is coming off the ship and –'

Frank cut in, laughing. 'And is it raining in this mind's eye of yours?'

'Of course it is, it's San Francisco,' said Kitty. 'It's raining like billy-o.'

Frank pointed to some papers on the nearby table. 'I've made notes. Can I leave you to make the arrangements with your friend Tug to transport us to New Westminster? Then we can pick up an American ship to San Francisco. I think we'll give Victoria a miss with that fever.'

'Thank you, sir. I'm sure we're making the correct decision,' said Sam. 'I'll see to the arrangements.'

'There you are, Pa. Sam'll take charge and you don't have to worry about a thing – just getting on the ship on time. It'll be my job to make sure you're not late.'

'I'll not deny you're going to be a great help to us, Sam. Suffice to say I'll be able to repay you with local knowledge when we reach the city.' Frank put his hand out to him. 'You're going to arrive with two seasoned San Franciscans, so you'll never feel a stranger.'

Kitty felt a burst of joy in her heart seeing Sam and her pa shake hands, but the emotion was quickly displaced by an awareness that Pa had no idea who Sam really was. He was technically shaking hands with a stranger. This thought was going to be an unwelcome companion for her as they travelled together. But in happier vein, once she got Sam on American territory, be it ship or land, she just knew she could rid him of his ghosts.

The rest of the morning was spent making notices for Frank to nail up at the sawmill, the general store and other public places, offering reduced rates before they left.

Later that afternoon, when Sam left to check the steamer timetable at the quay, Kitty made a list of all the things she wanted to show him in the city. It was going to be so exciting seeing San Francisco through his eyes; she was certain he was going to find it as wonderful a place as she did.

* * *

Exactly two weeks after Frank had agreed they could leave, Sam met up with Tug at The Angel and arranged passage to New Westminster.

He reported back to Frank. 'I've booked two men to carry everything downstairs and then on to the quay and they'll be here at nine, on Wednesday October 6th. The steamer leaves at midday. We'll be at New Westminster by evening.'

'Then the final leg onward to the city.' Frank raised his glass of water. 'A toast, to a safe journey for us all.'

CHAPTER THIRTY-ONE

As dawn broke on October 6th, Kitty was up and awake. She'd already laid out her clothes and was preparing a travelling bag for the rest of their journey. Shoes and boots were at the bottom, underwear next, followed by accessories wrapped in her skirts and blouses. Everything else would be inaccessible to her until they reached San Francisco.

Kitty saw to her toilette, taking especial care with her hair. After washing it, she twisted it into a thick plait that she wound round at the back of her head, fixing it with long pins. Her pa was whistling to himself and she was relieved he was in a good mood. His travelling clothes had been laid out by her the previous evening, and so it was a surprise when he appeared for breakfast in different attire.

'You're wearing your Sunday best,' she said. 'I thought we agreed to pack our better clothes away.'

'I've changed my mind. I want folk to see us for the gentlefolk we are. We may have been surrounded by diggers for the last seven months and we may even be travelling with one as a companion, but we haven't lost our sense of occasion.'

Kitty didn't think folk would give them much thought, and that by wearing his best buttoned waistcoat, seamed trousers and top hat, Pa was drawing attention to himself. But she didn't want to say anything that might lead to an upset. She set about tidying up the breakfast things. She was anxious; it was the first day of what could prove to be a difficult journey. The fact they were leaving had only come home to her when she'd had the saloon gals for their final fitting. They'd given her a brass locket to keep her safe on her journey. Although she'd had other saloon gal customers in the last month, it was Beth and Eliza she'd had the most rapport with. From the start, even though they were from different worlds, they'd shared the same sense of humour. She would miss their laughter and candour.

When Sam arrived, Kitty thought he too was looking neat and tidy and she told him so.

'I've dressed up. My least-darned trousers and the new shirt you made for me. Thank you again. I'll begin stacking the cases and boxes in readiness for the two carriers.' Sam inspected the luggage. 'I sold my kit on the quay last night to a greenhorn. I gave him lots of encouragement and recommended Herr Steiner's bunkhouse.'

'Did you get to the claims office?'

'Aye. My claim is surrendered. Everything's seen to, but I won't relax until we're in Tug's safe hands.'

✳ ✳ ✳

The carriers were loading up their cart when, as agreed, Pierre appeared.

'Thank you for coming, Pierre,' Sam said. 'I couldn't have left without a fitting farewell.'

'You're all packed up, I see,' said Pierre.

'We leave at noon.'

'Safe journey, my friend. We've shared some interesting times.'

Sam put his hand on Pierre's arm. He'd never been happy about their conversation over Gus's disappearance, and this was his only opportunity to ask his friend the one question he might never get the answer to.

'Did Gus Boston really not board the steamer?'

Pierre's smile was enigmatic. 'If you're asking did he fall overboard, the answer is *non*, my friend.'

'How can you be so sure?' Sam held his breath. Whatever Pierre said wouldn't please him, but he had to know.

'As he never boarded the steamer, he cannot have fallen from it.'

'He may have slipped past you.'

'It is enough for you to know he never set foot on the dock.'

'And you know that?'

Pierre nodded and the enigmatic smile reappeared on his face.

Sam dropped his voice. 'You killed him? You drowned him?'

Pierre looked shocked. 'I did not say that.'

'No, but that's what you're hinting at, isn't it?'

'If that were so, I wouldn't tell you, my friend. Such knowledge would be a burden to you.'

'Perhaps you wouldn't tell me, but why would you do such a thing?'

'If I had, it would be a matter of Frenchman's honour. Blackmail is the most heinous of crimes.'

'And you happened to come across my gold just lying on the ground by the dock?'

'I expect if I had found your gold, my explanation would be something like that.'

Sam didn't know what to say. Should he now thank Pierre for returning his gold? Pierre had turned out to be a good friend, someone he felt he could trust, but now it seemed he was letting Sam into the secret that he was a murderer and it had been done for his benefit. The thought was too shocking to contemplate, and yet it seemed the most likely – perhaps the only – explanation for all that had occurred.

Pierre put his hand on Sam's arm. 'I don't know what it is you are running from and what Gus Boston had on you, but with Miss Kitty I think you have found a companion. A life companion perhaps. Keep her safe.'

Without waiting for a response, Pierre wished him well, then turned and strode off. Sam stood stock still, watching Pierre's retreating back. He was roused by the sound of Kitty berating one of the carriers for putting a box down too roughly. She came up to him.

'Pierre's gone?'

'Aye.'

'You were deep in conversation. What did he say? Anything interesting?'

'Just a prolonged farewell, that's all.' And that, thought Sam, would be what it always was. He could never tell Kitty that Pierre had more or less admitted to the murder of Gus Boston. It was his burden to carry, alone, forever.

CHAPTER THIRTY-TWO

Sam, desperate to board the steamer, was with Kitty at the quayside by half past ten, ahead of the luggage which Frank had volunteered to accompany. The dock was a scene of bustling activity. Goods were being hoisted on deck, and men, impatient to board, were clustered in groups talking amongst themselves, surrounded by bedrolls and small, cobbled-together wooden crates. Some were transporting their possessions in hessian sacks with drawstring ties. Beneath every shirt was a thick leather belt to which they'd attached a leather purse containing their poke. The contents were either still in their raw state as nuggets and dust, or had already been converted to gold dollars at the Harrison assay office.

The carriers had been engaged to stay and help load the Muldoons' bags and boxes onto the steamer. As they came in view, Kitty tugged Sam's arm.

'Where's Pa?'

Sam saw the carriers' cart and the two men with the luggage, but there was no Frank. He ran to meet them.

'Where's Mr Muldoon?' he asked.

'We dropped him off at the general store. He wanted to refill his baccy pouch. Said he'd follow on.'

Sam looked behind the cart, hoping beyond all hope he would spot Frank's top hat in the distance, but there was no sign of him.

Kitty paled.

'You don't have to tell me what you're thinking,' Sam said to her. 'I'll go and find him.'

He checked his pocket watch; it was almost eleven. They would be boarding any moment, and even though Tug was in charge, he couldn't delay more than ten minutes at the most. He turned to the carriers. 'If they start boarding, escort Miss Kitty to that man with the black cap standing on the deck at the top of the gangway. His name's Tug Tait. He's expecting us. And see the luggage safely stowed. I'll settle up with you when I get back.' He pointed out Tug to Kitty. 'Tell him who you are.'

'Where will you go?'

'I'll check the general store, then the saloons.'

He took off at speed. It didn't take him long to eliminate the general store and he scanned the first saloon with no result. Next he tried The Angel. Beth and Eliza were just beginning work.

'What are you doing here?' asked Beth.

'Isn't the steamer about to leave?' said Eliza.

Sam explained his predicament.

Beth frowned. 'Try next door. If he isn't in there, he might be down at the livery stable. The Scot that runs it sometimes has whiskey to sell.'

Sam was relieved to find Frank sitting on a stool in a corner of the livery stable. An open bottle of whiskey was on the floor beside him. But how to get him to the steamer in time? Already it was twenty to twelve. He pulled up a chair and sat down.

'It's time we left for the steamer, Frank,' he began.

Frank looked at him with glassy eyes and a wobbly head. He'd obviously managed to down a great deal of whiskey in the short time he'd been supposed to be buying baccy. Sam was annoyed with the Scottish livery man, but on reflection, he didn't know there was a steamer to catch and must have thought Frank, in his Sunday best, was having one of his 'strident' days.

Frank smiled. 'I'll be along.'

'We need to go now. If we don't leave in the next five minutes, we won't make it in time.' Sam calculated they'd about fifteen minutes if they walked quickly.

Frank put his hand out for the bottle but Sam got to it first and put it out of reach. He couldn't afford Frank to be too unsteady on his feet: he needed him to walk to the quay.

Frank, who so far had been peacefully drunk, became annoyed. 'That's my bottle. Give it to me,' he said, stretching out an arm.

'Indeed it is and we'll take it with us.' Sam stood up, hoping Frank would do the same, but he remained sitting.

There were choice words Sam wanted to utter, but he kept them to himself, not wanting to inflame the situation. Frank was putting his own departure at risk.

'Last month you said to me that Kitty was the most

important thing in your life,' Sam said, 'and that if I took her to a foreign place or an American city such as New York or Boston, you would refuse me her hand in marriage. Do you remember?' Frank ought to be sober enough to remember, although he gave no outward sign of doing so.

'Well, there's a steamer waiting at the quay,' Sam went on. 'Kitty and all your worldly goods are loaded on it. I'm taking her to San Francisco. You can stay here and finish this bottle, and several other bottles, for all I care, but you could also come down to the quay, get on the steamer and keep Kitty close. Your choice is to stay here alone in Harrison or be with Kitty in San Francisco. What's it to be?'

✳ ✳ ✳

Kitty had been pacing up and down since half past eleven. The carriers were crossing and uncrossing their arms and muttering to themselves.

'You've got to board, Miss Kitty,' one of them said.

'But what if Pa doesn't come in time?'

'We've instructions to load the luggage and escort you on board.'

'Can't you wait just a little longer?'

'We need to start moving nearer the gangway or they'll close up.'

Kitty was about to forbid them to move a single item when the younger man said, 'Miss, if we don't load up now and get you on board, we don't get paid. You can always get off before she steams away.'

Kitty didn't want the men to lose payment, so she nodded and began walking to the gangway. They were right, she could always jump off at the last minute. With that in mind, she insisted their luggage be kept on deck and was not to be stowed below until her pa and Sam appeared.

On board, Kitty stayed by the gangway, looking out, while the carriers exchanged a few words with Tug.

'Miss Muldoon,' Tug said, when the carriers had returned to the quay. 'I understand there's a problem.'

Kitty, having fought against tears on the dock, seeing Tug's friendly face began sobbing. 'We've lost Pa, Mr Tait.'

Tug took her hand in his and patted it, as her pa might have done. 'Now, now. Tears won't help. I can hold the ship for fifteen minutes, so we've a little extra time.'

Fifteen minutes is a long time when you're kept waiting for something you want, and a fleeting moment when you don't want that thing to come to pass.

'What if Sam can't find Pa and returns on his own? What shall I do?'

'I don't think that will happen, but if it does, we can unload everything quickly. There are other steamers.'

'But this is the one Sam wants to take, isn't it?'

'I'll not lie, this one connects well with the ships to San Francisco at New Westminster, but his wanting to leave today is in your favour. He'll put every effort into bringing your pa on board.'

The angst Kitty was experiencing was physical as much as mental. She couldn't remember having felt so agitated since her ma passed away. That had been expected, this situation was not. She was short of breath, and when she swallowed, her throat seemed narrower. The smells from the waterfront and the oil from the steamer's engines were combining to make her feel queasy. She wished the other passengers would be quiet and keep still; they were chattering, laughing and jostling her against the rail.

Tug left her to sign some papers, while the two carriers sat on the quay on an old trunk. They were looking expectantly along Front Street, just as she was.

Three diggers with no luggage ambled up the gangway. One of them smiled at Kitty, to be rewarded with an icy stare.

'Not very friendly, miss, are ya?'

Kitty turned her back on him. At that very moment, the man beside her chose to release cigar smoke from deep in his lungs. It hit her full on, and she began coughing and beating her chest with the flat of her hand. To his credit, the man was quick to apologise.

When the engines started, Kitty panicked and the two carriers looked up at her, waiting to learn whether they were to unload her luggage or not.

Kitty turned to the cigar man. 'Excuse me, sir, what time is it?'

The man consulted his pocket watch. 'Five minutes past twelve. We're late.'

Kitty didn't need telling that. She looked around for Tug, but she couldn't see him anywhere. She let a few minutes go by, then, with a reluctant acceptance that things were not going to resolve themselves, she motioned to the carriers to come forward.

With everything taken off except for their two leather bags, Kitty was halfway down the gangway when there was a shout from one of the carriers. 'They're coming!'

She lifted her skirts and ran back up as fast as she could. From the deck she could see Sam waving and shouting, propelling her pa down the road. She began jumping up and down, waving back. When everyone began cheering the latecomers along, she relaxed. She knew then for sure that Tug would wait for them.

The carriers loaded everything back on board, and, after pushing Frank onto the gangway, Sam paid them off. Everyone cheered again, providing the casting-off with a festive air.

Face to face with her pa, Kitty couldn't contain her anger, even though she knew folk were looking at them.

'Have you any idea what you've put us through?' she said. 'Me especially, waiting here for you? What on earth possessed you to lead us such a merry dance. I'm so cross –'

'Don't,' said Sam, in a calm, quiet voice. 'He's here now. That's the main thing.'

Frank gave her a liquor-fuelled smile. 'Now then, Kathryn, that's no way to speak to your pa.'

'Don't call me Kathryn,' she said. 'My name's Kitty.'

They settled Frank in a corner to sober up and moved away, keeping him within sight. Sam had handed the remains of the whiskey to the carriers.

'I should have stayed with the luggage and sent your pa on ahead with you,' he said.

Kitty shook her head. 'I don't think it would have made

any difference. He would have slipped away from me, too. I blame myself. I should have known when he put on his best clothes that either he planned to drink, or else the clothes would set him off anyway.'

'Don't blame yourself. We are where we are. Once he sobers up, everything will be back to normal.'

'I used to think there must be something I could do to help him or to stop him, but I know now it's part of the way he is since Ma died. It could be worse – he could drink all the time, he could be violent. He's none of these things. He drinks to forget, then he forgets he's been drinking.'

CHAPTER THIRTY-THREE

There was a chill in the air when Sam, Frank and Kitty disembarked in New Westminster. It had been an uneventful journey, apart from the usual upsets caused by rough loafers, idlers, and gamblers intent on livening things up and making a fast buck. At Fort Langley, where they'd picked up additional passengers, Sam had stayed on board in Tug's cabin, well out of sight so as not to run the risk of being recognised. Kitty had gone ashore and bought some food supplies. Frank, somewhat chastened in sobriety, had refused to accompany her.

'I fear temptation,' he'd said. 'Best I stay on board.' It was the nearest either Sam or Kitty had ever heard him refer to his one weakness.

New Westminster had grown considerably since Sam had passed through almost five months earlier, and the creation of British Columbia meant there were more British officials in evidence. Kitty knew this was Sam's final hurdle. All he needed to do was board an American vessel and he was home and dry. Part of the problem they both faced was that Frank didn't know Sam needed to keep a low profile.

Tickets for San Francisco, for the 6 pm early-evening departure, were twenty-five dollars each. Sam held back at the ticket booth, leaving Frank and Kitty to do the talking and see to the luggage. Kitty joked about how excited they were to get back to their home country with their fellow Yankees, and it seemed the man in the ticket booth assumed she was speaking for all three of them. Besides, he was only interested in taking their money and getting a smile from Kitty, so he hardly gave Sam a glance. Even so, Sam was pleased he'd had the sense to let his beard grow free, and he kept his hat pulled down over his forehead.

After they'd bought their tickets, Tug sat with them for a farewell meal. He extracted a promise from Sam to write to him care of the Colonial Bar, to let him know how he was getting on. After they'd eaten, Tug had to leave to take the steamer back up-river. It was a poignant parting, both men having to face the reality they were unlikely ever to meet again. Sam followed Tug's back as he walked away. When he turned back to Kitty, she saw his eyes were moist.

With Tug gone, Frank said he needed a walk after being cooped up on the steamer. Sam was reluctant to wander around. Being so much closer to Victoria and Vancouver Island meant he was much more likely to be identified. He was happy to sit in the Colonial Bar, but Frank was insistent.

The only thing Sam could think of was to lie about the

state of his health, so he said to Frank, 'I think it best you and Kitty go for a stroll without me. I've a bad stomach. I'll wait here.'

Frank's eyes widened. 'Do you think it's the fever?'

'Oh, no, I've no headache and I'm not shivery. More likely that fish I ate last night. A good job neither of you had it.'

Frank appeared satisfied. He and Kitty had been gone for half an hour, and Sam was passing the time reading out-of-date newspapers, when three men came and sat at the table next to him. It soon became apparent they were Hudson's Bay Company men waiting to return to Victoria. Sam broke out in a cold sweat. If he got up and left it would seem strange, with his glass only half empty. Yet if he stayed, they might speak to him and, realising he was British, think he deserved their attention. He closed his eyes. It was all he could think of to do. He soon found pretending to be asleep when not only wide awake but on full alert was almost impossible. He tried to think himself in another place, back home in Whitehaven, standing on the cliffs looking out to sea, the landmark candlestick chimney behind him, but that didn't work.

He began to panic. He realised he had to move, because when Kitty and Frank came back, they would wake him and begin talking to him. He thought the best thing to do was to appear tipsy. He opened his eyes, gave them a good rub, ran his fingers through his hair and walked out, with swaying legs that were shaking so much, he thought his breeches must be flapping from side to side, like unfurled sails at sea. Outside, feeling like the fugitive from justice he was, he found a niche between two riverboats commanding a view to the entrance to the bar, so he could keep watch for Kitty and Frank.

When they finally appeared, he stepped out. To his surprise, Kitty immediately steered them all to a low stone wall, telling them they could sit and watch the sea-going ships. She began a conversation about how much bigger some of the sailing ships were 'these days' and how there were more steamers than there had been. Sam was mystified. It wasn't Kitty's usual topic of conversation, and she hadn't commented on the ships and steamers they'd passed on their way downriver.

'Pa, can you see the name of that big sailing ship?' She pointed to where several ships were moored.

'Which one?'

'The one where they're furling and unfurling their sails.'

Frank squinted in the direction she was indicating. 'No.'

'That's a shame, it looks like a beauty. I'd love to know where it's going.'

As Sam was beginning to suspect, Kitty had something to say to him she didn't want her pa to hear. To her obvious relief, Frank took the bait and stood up. 'I'll stretch my legs and wander down and have a look.'

As soon as he was out of earshot, Kitty said, 'There are Company men everywhere.'

'I know.' Sam told her about feigning sleep and why he was outside. 'Perhaps I'm being too cautious. The Company's probably forgotten about me and moved on to more recent murderers and vagabonds.'

Kitty shook her head. 'They haven't. There's a poster in the general store window naming you and two others from Victoria. It seems you're not the only one who's fallen for the lure of the goldfield and broken their contracts.'

'What does it say?' Sam felt sick. He'd been anxious about being found out many times, but his nerves had never jangled this much before.

'There's a description of you, minus your beard, saying you have a distinctive north-western British accent.'

'Damn it,' said Sam.

'You'll just not have to speak.'

'That's easier said than done if I'm questioned directly.'

'When we bought the tickets and left the luggage, we kept you well in the background. When we board this time we can do the same. Hopefully that'll be enough.'

Frank returned with the name of the ship, the *Gloria*, and the news she was bound for Shanghai.

* * *

As they approached the *SS Norcost*, Sam saw the way ahead was lined with Company and government men checking and questioning folk as they passed. Beyond them, Yankee boatmen were inspecting tickets and waving people on board. He had a sudden desire to slink away and disappear back up the Fraser River Valley, as far east as he could. But if he did that, he would remain a fugitive, whereas if he could get through the departure checks and board the American vessel not thirty yards in front of him, he would be a free man. He'd never thought of himself as a gambling man, but he was prepared to take this chance.

Kitty whispered in his ear, 'Take my hand. It'll make you look less like a man on his own. And try to smile. You're going home.'

Sam took her hand, even though he knew his was horribly sticky and sweaty. He swallowed, but his mouth was dry, and he began coughing.

Kitty patted him on the back. 'Too much baccy,' she said, in a loud voice for everyone to hear. 'I've told you before. If you'd given up smoking that damned pipe three years ago when that Frisco doctor told you to, you wouldn't be spluttering over everyone.'

Sam put his hand to his mouth to stifle another cough.

They reached the first official, a middle-aged man with hollow cheeks who smelt of the unlikely combination of soap and cinnamon.

'Name?' he asked Kitty.

'Kitty Muldoon.'

'Where you headed?'

'We're going home to San Francisco.' She smiled.

The officer looked at Frank and then at Sam.

'This here's my pa, Frank Muldoon, and my beau, Sam Jenkins.'

'All born in Frisco?' asked the official.

'Do we look that young? Ain't nobody born in the city older than ten.'

'Well, where *were* you born?'

'We're Irish Yankees,' said Frank.' And he's –'

Kitty butted in, 'From the west coast. Never thought I'd get myself hitched to a west-coast man. My mammy kept telling me to "go get yourself a good Dubliner" and –' Stopping mid-sentence, Kitty stared at the officer as if suddenly mesmerised. 'You've the Irish in you, haven't you? Don't deny it, I can see it.'

The officer grinned. 'How'd you know that?'

'It's obvious. You've green in your eyes and there's an inherited lilt in your voice. Where were you born?'

'Boston, Massachusetts, but my family comes from –'

'I knew it.' Kitty turned round to include Sam and Frank. 'We've found a friend from the Emerald Isle.'

Sam did his best to produce an enthusiastic smile, while Frank put his hand forward to shake the official's hand. Beaming from ear to ear, he said, 'Well, you'll be going o'er to the green country one day, won't you?'

The official glanced behind them at the queue. 'Perhaps. Now let me see your papers.' He checked Kitty's and Frank's papers and waved them through. Sam took out his digging licence and handed it over. The official glanced at it, then looked at him. 'We're looking for an English deserter called Sam. Is that you?'

Sam never knew where it came from or how he managed it, but in a clear Irish voice he said, 'Sure now, do I look like an English eejit?'

The man laughed. 'No, you don't. On your way.' He folded the licence and returned it.

Sam didn't look back or waste any time catching up with Kitty and Frank. His heart was pounding in his chest and his hands were shaking. The gangway was in sight and as he stepped onto it he felt an explosion of liberation pass through his body.

After they'd boarded and were looking out at the quay,

and while the seamen were casting off the ropes, Kitty took Sam by the hand. 'Can you see them?' she asked.

Sam scanned the crowd. 'See who?' He couldn't see anyone or anything out of the ordinary.

Kitty pointed. 'Over there. Evie and Grace.'

Sam looked at her in disbelief.

She leaned up and kissed him on the cheek. 'Don't you think this is a good place to say goodbye to their ghosts, forever?'

After taking a moment, Sam turned towards the quay and waved. 'Evie, Grace, I'm not taking you with me this time,' he said quietly. 'You must remain here. Stay here with Sam Jenkins. Because Sam Gray is headed for San Francisco.'

He turned to Kitty, and with tears of relief and joy in his heart, he kissed her for the first time on the lips.

Frank made a loud tut-tut sound. 'In broad daylight?'

'Yes, Pa,' said Kitty. 'On board, in broad daylight.'

PART TWO

CHAPTER THIRTY-FOUR

San Francisco, California
Monday October 11th 1858

It had been blowing hard all night, and by the time they were tied up at 6 am at the Pacific Street Wharf, most of the passengers, including Sam, Kitty and Frank, were boat weary. Despite rough-weather-induced nausea, headaches and an overwhelming desire for sleep, the passengers began scrambling to get off.

Standing at the rail in the rain, looking out over the city, Kitty, her voice full of excitement, pointed out various landmarks she'd spoken of during the journey. 'Over there is Filbert Street where your friend Billy Botcher lives. I bet he'll be surprised to see you.'

'It's been four years.'

'Yes, but you spent six months cooped up on the boat with him. He'll remember you.'

And Evie, thought Sam. Then he reprimanded himself. He'd left Evie on the quay in New Westminster.

'What number Filbert Street?'

'175,' said Sam.

'I think that'll be towards the northern end. It'll be a bit of a climb getting up there.'

The view was overwhelming. Sam had never seen so many tall brick buildings, which looked like fortresses, nor had he seen such big glass panes in the windows. There was nothing small or reserved about San Francisco. For a start, there must have been fifty or more ships in the harbour with furled sails: sailing ships, Pacific Mail steamships, brigs and riverboats rubbing up against each other on either side of the city's many wharves.

Grey, thick industrial smoke belched out from some of the tall chimneys towering over the dock warehouses. On the quayside goods and boxes were being sorted and loaded onto flat-back carts, ready to be sent on their way.

The fresh sights and sounds were almost too much for Sam to absorb – a veritable flood of people and things to comprehend. He stared open-mouthed like the country boy he was, finding himself in the big bad city. He'd spent one day before leaving England in Liverpool, but it had been nothing like this. He was fascinated by everyone and everything around him. There was, however, one disappointment, and he did his best to shrug it off. He couldn't help remembering the first day he'd arrived at Fort Langley. The odour that had accosted his nostrils then was evident in San Francisco, even more so – human detritus and harbour smells. He could taste it on his lips and was about to say something to Kitty, but she was obviously wildly happy to be back home, and her eyes were shining so brightly, he didn't want to risk spoiling her moment by saying something negative.

Frank recommended Sam go straight to a bank to deposit his poke, and then to Chapin & Company's accommodation and employment office at the corner of Kearny and Clay Street.

'They'll find you somewhere to stay and then you can start looking for work.'

'He'll not be starting work before I've had time to walk him round town and show him off,' said Kitty, taking hold of Sam's arm.

'If you must, Kitty dear, if you must. Sam, we'll drop you off at the bank opposite Chapin's. We've to find a guest house since we've no longer a home here. I'll leave a note for you at Chapin's with our address.'

Kitty squeezed Sam's arm. 'I'm thinking the day after tomorrow we can go to Halahan's Apothecary in the morning and buy you some of their renowned cough candy. I told you about it early on when we talked about San Francisco.'

'Sam might wish to discover the city independently,' suggested Frank.

'And get himself lost?'

'I'm sure he can find his way around with a good map, and be quite safe.'

Looking out at the buildings, carts and carriages, Sam wasn't sure that was true. 'It's a strange city. I'm obviously from out of town and I must be careful when walking around on my own.' He took Kitty's hand. 'In the meantime, I'll be happy to let you chaperone me until I get my bearings.'

Then as an afterthought, forgetting Frank didn't know

his true identity, he said, 'Don't forget when you leave the note at Chapin's that I'm Sam Gray again now. You'll never find me if you ask for Sam Jenkins.'

As soon as the words left his mouth, Sam knew he'd made a monumental error. From the look on Frank's face, the timbers supporting the roof of his newfound happiness with Kitty were about to come crashing down.

'Who's Sam Gray?'

'It's our Sam here. Don't worry, I can explain.' Kitty dropped Sam's hand to grasp hold of Frank's. 'There's something we have to tell you, Pa.'

'Will someone tell me what's going on?'

Sam and Kitty began speaking at once.

Sam raised his hand. 'I think it's *my* place to explain.' He gave Kitty a glance for permission to continue.

'All right,' she said. 'But you can't go into everything now, we haven't time. Save it for over a cigar later.'

'Go into what?' asked Frank.

'My name is Sam Gray, not Sam Jenkins. As you know, I'm a collier from Whitehaven, in Cumberland. What you don't know is that I've been living on Vancouver Island for four years as a Hudson's Bay Company collier.'

Frank looked at Kitty. 'Did *you* know all this?'

'Yes, Pa, only recently, but it's nothing to worry about.'

'I'll be the judge of that, Kathryn.' Frank drew himself up to his full height. 'And until I know who you really are, sir, and what your business is about, I'll ask you to leave my daughter well alone.'

Still holding Kitty's hand, he took two steps back. They were only small steps, but the symbolism of distancing himself and his daughter from the old Sam Jenkins were not lost on the new Sam Gray.

'Pa, don't make a rash decision. We would have told you earlier, but we couldn't until we were on American soil because –'

Frank placed himself between Kitty and Sam. 'Because you're a criminal, that's why, isn't it?'

'Not in the way you mean,' said Sam. How stupid he'd been to be so strict about waiting until they were in San Francisco before using his real name. He'd been afraid Frank might get drunk and let his secret out. On reflection, it probably wouldn't have mattered if he had done, as the Company had no jurisdiction over him on the ship. When he'd imagined telling Frank the truth, Sam had thought he'd come round, as Kitty had done, but now the deception was out it was clear he had every right to be angry and protective towards his daughter.

Frank raised his chin. 'Let me be completely clear. Why were you using an assumed name?'

'Because he wants to make something of himself in San Francisco,' Kitty said. 'To better himself.'

'Kathryn, I'm not addressing you.' Frank spoke to Sam. 'What is wrong with the name your parents bequeathed you?'

'I was tied to a five-year contract with the Company in a place I didn't belong. I'm a Hudson's Bay Company deserter.'

Sam looked at Kitty's pale face, pursed lips and crossed arms. All her excitement at returning to San Francisco had evaporated.

'I haven't fulfilled my contract,' he went on. 'To the Company this means I'm a thief. That's what I have on my conscience.'

'There's a lot more to it, Pa. He's suffered much tragedy along the way. Please don't make a hasty decision. I want him to be a part of our lives here. Really, I...' Her words drifted away.

Frank pulled his waistcoat down and straightened his cuffs. 'Now is not the time for this conversation except to say my disappointment in you, Mr Gray sir, at this moment in time, knows no bounds. You can put your case to me tomorrow. I shall be at the entrance to St Mary's Cathedral at six o'clock tomorrow evening. Meet me there.'

Maintaining his frosty air, Frank hailed a porter to see to their luggage and find transportation. It soon became clear Sam was to organise his own conveyance to the bank and on to Chapin's.

With her father's back turned, Kitty, eyes full of despair, leaned forward and whispered, 'I'll bring him round. He'll understand when he knows the full story.'

Sam smiled at Kitty, but he didn't share her optimism. Would he ever see her again?

* * *

The Miners' Exchange Bank took Sam's gold deposit with no fuss about needing a residential address, and for the first time in months he was able to walk around without carrying every penny he owned in the poke purse tied around his waist. He hadn't made a huge fortune by some people's standards, but he'd taken the equivalent of four years' Company wages in five months, and he was more than happy with that. He'd plans to use his nest egg setting up a general repair and maintenance business, but he needed to make sense of the city, to decide what it could offer him and see what he could offer its residents in return.

Frank's having taken against him so strongly had muted the excitement of exploring, but he was pragmatic enough to realise he should find work and leave his nest egg to grow until absolutely certain of the way ahead.

Chapin's offices were in one of the impressive tall red-brick buildings Sam had noticed earlier. He climbed the stairs to the first floor. These opened out onto a landing waiting area, with straight-back chairs around two walls and doors leading off.

A young lad with a bright smile looked up from his desk as Sam approached.

'Just back from the Fraser River, are you?' he asked.

'Aye. How did you know?'

'It's your kit,' said the lad. 'You all look the same: weather-beaten, weary and dressed in diggers' clothing. What is it you're wanting?'

'Somewhere to stay.'

'You're in the right place. We run alongside the Young Men's Christian Association's hostel. You're a Britisher, aren't you?'

'I'm English.'

'We get a lot of you Britishers passing through. Did you make your fortune or do you need employment as well as somewhere to bed down?'

Sam had already made the decision he would play down the value of his poke and let everyone think he had no money. That was the best course of action until he knew what he wanted to do with it and whom he could trust.

'Aye, I'll be looking for work seriously in a day or two.'

'We've vacancies for servants, grooms, coachmen, farmhands, road diggers, mechanics and clerks.' The lad was obviously used to reeling off the list several times a day. 'Some diggers enjoy being out in all weathers, others not a bit. Which are you?'

'I'm good with my hands, I can make and mend things, but I'm not looking to be a farmhand or lay roads.'

The lad took Sam's details, handed him an information sheet about the YMCA hostel, the addresses of some workplaces to approach, and a city map to peruse while he waited. He pointed to a green door with a shiny brass handle that looked as if it was polished every day. 'That's the accommodation booking room. Take a seat. There's two in front of you.'

By the time Sam's turn came, he'd studied the information and was happy to take a room, supper included, at the hostel. His billet ticket was handed to him by a middle-aged lady who smiled at him in a kindly way, but not warmly enough to indicate she wanted to exchange pleasantries.

On his way out, Sam quizzed the young lad about the city's newspapers.

'The *Trinity Journal* has advertisements for labourers on long contracts and the *Mirror of the Times* also sometimes has them. There's one piece of advice I can give you to help you on your way.'

'What's that?'

'If you're thinking of staying, you oughta get yourself a bath and out of your diggers' kit. No one'll employ you in a permanent position if they think you're going to rush off back to the goldfields in the spring. You need to look the part of a worker, and take it from me, you sure don't. There's a good, cheap Chinese bathhouse, the Tong Yan Gai, two blocks up from the hostel.'

The young man marked the bathhouse on the map with a big black cross.

Sam thought some men might take offence at such personal advice, but he could see the sense. He'd book in at the hostel, deposit his small bag and buy some new clothes.

On arrival late-afternoon at the hostel close by St Mary's Roman Catholic Cathedral, Sam was billeted in a dormitory with seven other men straight off the boats. The dormitory was clean and the room smelt of soap, which was encouraging. He found the Tong Yan Gai bathhouse situated conveniently next door to a gentlemen's outfitters which was run by the same family. The men all had Manchu-style shaved heads and long black 'queue' pigtails that fell halfway down their backs, like the Chinese he'd seen working in the goldfields. When a curtain was pulled aside he caught a glimpse of a young Chinese lass in a pretty pale blue silk dress with embroidered sleeves.

She was sitting on a wide Chinese chair having her hair brushed by an old lady in black trousers and top. *A different world*, he thought.

The outfitters suggested he decide what clothing he wanted from their stock. They would then take his measurements and deliver the items to the bathhouse where, if the clothes were satisfactory, settlement would be required. When Sam commented they ran a profitable arrangement, they politely explained it was something they did all the time for returning diggers.

Two hours later, with the hour for supper at the hostel drawing near, Sam walked back to his lodgings with a heavy heart, thinking of Kitty. After a lacklustre meal of warm potato pie and gravy, he put his head on the pillow and fell into a deep sleep.

CHAPTER THIRTY-FIVE

The next morning Sam, depressed by the scene on the ship with Frank and feeling very much at a loose end, decided he would take a stroll and found himself walking along Battery Street towards the Coal Yard. He crossed the street and quickened his pace. The next building was the Merchants' Exchange. It was an impressive construction with a statue of Britannia, complete with Neptune's trident and shield, sitting in state over the entrance. On the pavement outside, clusters of well-dressed men had gathered, talking softly, their heads close together. It seemed as much negotiation was taking place outside the exchange as within its hallowed walls. Sam walked on and bought a cigar and some matches from a shop with a large 'TOBACCO' sign swinging in the wind on sturdy iron brackets.

After turning right onto Pacific Wharf, where they'd docked the previous day, he paused, perched himself on a mooring bollard, and watched the ships being serviced and loaded. He lit his cigar and rested for another twenty minutes. He should be enjoying the hustle and bustle of city life, but in his flat mood he was finding it brash and noisy. Everywhere was so busy. Or perhaps it was that he'd already had enough excitement in his life. It was true to say the thing he most craved – a loving wife and family – had seemed there for the asking on the ship, only to be stolen from him the moment he landed in what he thought was going to be the city of his dreams. He'd made a bad decision not to come clean to Frank earlier and was paying for it dearly.

* * *

At exactly six o'clock, Sam arrived at St Mary's Cathedral. He was nervous at having to face Frank and fervently hoped Kitty had been able to put forward his side of the story to good effect. If Frank couldn't be won over, then Kitty would, to all intents and purposes, be lost to him.

Frank was waiting. There was no smile upon greeting and he didn't offer his hand.

'Walk with me,' ordered Frank.

After a few paces, to break what felt to Sam to be a stony silence, he said, 'I assume Kitty has told you all there is to know about my past circumstances. I hope you can find yourself in a position to understand and forgive my deception.'

Frank didn't answer and, for what seemed forever, all Sam could hear was the dull thud of their footsteps, in unison, on the sidewalk. When Frank did eventually speak, there was not one speck of warmth in his voice.

'You have been false with me, sir.'

Sam swallowed. 'I have been false, as you call it, with everyone since I left Vancouver Island. My subterfuge was not personal to you, to Kitty, or to anyone else. My actions were solely to forge a better path in life and to leave behind some of the misfortunes that befell me in Colville.'

'You are referring to the loss of your wife and your son?'

'Aye.' *And all the other lost babies, and Grace's rebuttal.*

'There must have been others who suffered similar losses?'

Sam's thoughts went straight to the tragic death of Mr McAvoy, the schoolteacher on their outward journey. 'It's a truth not everyone who made the journey from England arrived safely.'

'Others who suffered personal loss remain in Colville?'

Sam nodded.

'What then turned you into a deserter and not them?'

Sam thought for a moment. 'I guess I had more than my fair share of struggle because I lost the only true family I had. Friends did help me, but for all intents and purposes I was on my own, and after Evie died, I was not at ease within the community.'

'Yet you formed another attachment with a missionary?'

'That is hardly fair.' Sam hadn't thought Kitty would disclose Grace to her father, but perhaps she had done so in the context of his 'living ghost'.

'Fair or not, it is the truth, is it not?'

'Aye, I formed an attachment that was not shared and the eventual loss upset me.'

'I will concur your circumstances have been somewhat irregular and unfortunate, but I have to say, Samuel Gray, or whatever you are calling yourself, that in my opinion trust is proven and earned by deeds and actions.'

Sam opened his mouth to defend himself, but Frank continued in full flow.

'Words from your mouth will not now suffice. You have sorely vexed me. So much so that I have asked Kitty to forgo your company. She is an honest girl who will heed her father's wishes. You will understand I cannot possibly condone an association between my daughter and someone who does not share the same moral code we do.'

Sam's thoughts went straight to Frank's strident days, but he knew it would not help his cause to refer to them.

'Mr Muldoon, I am at heart an honest man, a hard worker and a reliable friend.'

Frank ignored his entreaty. 'Kathryn and I have discussed your behaviour at length. During these conversations, she has declared a formal attachment to you. There is no confusion between right and wrong, or truth and deception in my mind, but she remains muddled. You express regret over your deceit, but what appears to me sadly lacking in your character, sir, is responsibility and honesty. Perhaps you will dwell on my words and find yourself gainful employment and a purpose in your life.'

With that, Frank stopped walking, directed a curt nod

at Sam, and turned on his heel. As he retraced their steps Sam realised two things: he had no way of contacting Kitty and he had carried his past with him. He might have left his personal ghosts on the quay in New Westminster, but as surely as if he'd folded it and placed it in a Gladstone bag to travel in the ship's hold, his past was travelling with him.

CHAPTER THIRTY-SIX

The next day Sam went in search of Halahan's Apothecary on Kearny Street. Kitty had talked about the store with such enthusiasm, he wanted to see it. In his imaginings of his first visit Kitty had been by his side, but now that was not to be.

Halahan's was as interesting as Kitty had promised. The glass bottles, brass knobs and labelled drawers were a treat. Sam bought the cough candy and allowed himself a small smile. It was tasty in a mouth-cleansing way, which was unsurprising, since it was officially being offered for medicinal relief. In some ways, though, he wished he hadn't entered Halahan's portals. It unsettled him not being able to share the experience with Kitty.

After leaving Halahan's, Sam began checking the 'Help Wanted' notices in the store windows. He soon realised decorating and carpentry works were commandeered by big firms, and he couldn't compete with them as a newly arrived sole trader with no connections. These lines of work needed word-of-mouth recommendations; since he knew no one, how would he find his customers? The reality of building a life in San Francisco was proving to be more complicated than he'd anticipated and, as hard as he tried to be optimistic, he became less sure of his plans. He bolstered his mood by telling himself he'd feel better after he'd spoken with Billy Botcher, which he hoped to do that afternoon.

Sam was also learning that walking in the city required concentration. A passer-by had to put his arm out to stop him stepping into the road when his attention was caught by an interesting store-window display. Later he was cursed by a carriage driver who raised a fist and swore at him.

'Get out the way, damned halfwit. Don't they have streets where you come from?'

Sam told himself he must pay more attention. He hadn't arrived in the city to be mown down in the first week by a trader's wagon. He was feeling very much the country boy in the big city and, strangely, he was more anxious walking around in San Francisco than he had been in the goldfields, where everyone carried a gun. At least he didn't have to worry about exposure anymore, which was a definite advantage of being in San Francisco. He was beginning to think it might be the only benefit.

At two o'clock, Sam was at 175 Filbert Street in search of Billy. He was surprised to find Billy's dwelling was a house rather than a commercial building. Kitty had been right, it had been a bit of a climb, but it would be downhill on the way back. He rang the bell and looked out over the city while he waited.

The door was opened by a young lass.

'Aye?'

'I'm looking for Billy Botcher. Is he here?'

The lass viewed him suspiciously, but said nothing. Sam felt he needed to fill the silence.

'I travelled with him on the ship from England.'

The lass half-turned and shouted over her shoulder. 'Ma, there's a man 'ere wants Uncle Billy. Knows 'im from some ship.'

A woman's voice with the same accent came from inside. 'Tell 'im I'll be there in a jiffy.'

'She'll be 'ere in a jiffy,' repeated the lass, continuing to stare at Sam with undisguised wariness.

The woman appeared with an infant boy perched on her hip. He was clutching a small wooden dog.

'You're wantin' our Billy?'

'Aye,' said Sam.

'He ain't 'ere. What you want 'im for?' she asked guardedly.

'Stag Liddell gave me his address. We were all on the *Princess Rose* four years ago.'

'Oh, I see. I'm 'is sister Rosie, and you are?'

'Sam Gray.'

'He's never mentioned you.'

Sam was beginning to think they thought he was a debt-collector or some official they'd been instructed to turn away.

'I'll take a wager you've heard of Stag Liddell?'

'Maybe,' said Rosie, still giving no ground.

Sam turned his attention to the infant and spoke directly to him. 'I'll also wager your Uncle Billy made that dog and gave it to you.' The boy held it out for Sam to take.

'He made *me* an elephant,' said the lass, brightening up.

Sam looked down at her. 'I'm not surprised. He made animals for all the bairns on the ship. Another crewman told me he'd once made a Noah's Ark for his bairns, because the crossing was so uneventful, he'd nothing else to do.'

Rosie smiled. 'Aye, that's reet, I was wanting one for mine, but being so busy these days, Billy says there's only time for single beasts.'

'Is there somewhere else I can find him?' Sam wondered if this setback was showing in his voice or on his face.

'He's a warehouse near Long Wharf, but you'll not find him there today. He's out o' town, buying.'

'When will he be back?'

'He don't tell me everything he's up to, even though I'm his sister and he lives here, but I expect he'll be back afore too long.'

Although Sam was disappointed not to connect with Billy himself, at least now he knew Billy was still around.

'A few days away, maybe?'

'Happen it'll be more than a few days, but not two weeks, 'cos he'd say if it were that long. Like when he disappears to New Zealand to see his bairns. Then he's gone for months and months, but he always comes back to see me and for his business here.'

'He's his own family in New Zealand?'

'Aye. His wife and bairns.'

'If he wants to find me, I'll be at the Christian hostel for now. Ask for Sam Gray. Otherwise, I'll call at his warehouse. Where exactly is it?'

'It's on 32 Commercial Street, down a "ten foot" between Sacramento and Clay. You can walk right past it if you're not lookin' out for it. At the end you'll see Botcher's Stores in big letters on the door. Are you lookin' for work?'

Sam nodded.

'You can try the auction houses down by the wharves as a porter, but you've to be quick. A lot take a fella on then don't take the notice down. There's always jobs at the fish merchants, but it's smelly labour. Depends how desperate you get.'

'Talking of smells, what's that street-light smell?'

Rosie wrinkled her nose. 'Horrible, isn't it? Whale oil and kerosene. You'll get used to it.'

Sam doubted it. He would have liked to have lingered and asked Billy's sister about San Francisco and whether she liked it, and how long she'd been in the city. Then he reckoned he'd been lucky she'd deigned to tell him all she had done, and in any case, the infant on her hip was beginning to fret.

✳ ✳ ✳

The early morning sun shone so brightly on the gleaming brass plaque affixed to the door, Kitty had to shade her eyes to read it. 'Chapin & Company – upstairs.' She hoped it wasn't going to be the fourth floor. It was warm for an October day and one flight of stairs was more than enough.

Arriving at the first landing she approached a middle-aged man sitting behind a desk.

'Can I help you?' he asked, in a voice that belied interest.

'I'm looking for someone who called here recently in search of accommodation and employment.'

'You'll have to be a bit more specific, although I have to tell you we don't divulge our clients' details.'

Kitty's heart sank. It had occurred to her this might be the case, but she'd hoped against reason she was wrong.

'His name's Samuel Gray. He's recently arrived and I just want to make sure he's settled. We travelled together on the same boat from Canada.'

The man looked at her oddly. 'If he called here I'm sure we did for him amicably and professionally.'

Kitty gave the man what she hoped was her sweetest smile. 'Could you just look through your records and check?'

The man sighed. 'You seem like a nice lady, miss, but I've to tell you we get all sorts in here – jilted brides, girls who've fallen into trouble, if you know what I mean, deserted wives, all with tales to tell, some true, some false. Every one of them asking after some gentleman, and often it's someone they met on one of the boats. You understand?'

'But I'm nothing like that. He's a friend.' Kitty felt tears prick her eyes and blinked.

In a kinder voice, the man said, 'Why don't you write a note and leave it with us? Then if he *is* a client, I'll see he receives your note. Then it's up to him if he contacts you.'

'Yes,' said Kitty, thinking this a wonderful idea and a genuine lifeline. 'He will contact me, I know he will.' Her heart was suddenly pumping fiercely, in a good way.

He handed her a pencil and a sheet of paper. 'Take a seat,' he said, pointing to a row of straight-backed chairs.

Kitty sat down and began to write.

Dearest Sam,

I trust this finds you safe and well. As you know, Pa will not entertain you under our roof and I have promised we will not speak. However, I know in his heart he wants me to be happy and I believe, in time, when you are settled with good prospects, as I am sure you soon will be, he will come round to our friendship. In the meantime, I will attend early Mass in the cathedral every Sunday, and even though we cannot engage in conversation, if you attend too, our eyes can meet, and we will know we still care and each of us is in good health.

Your Kitty

She didn't add their temporary boarding house address because she didn't want Sam turning up unannounced with Pa feeling as he did. There might be a scene and then they could get thrown out. She read the note through twice, folded the paper and wrote 'Mr Samuel Gray c/o Chapin & Company' before handing it to the man behind the counter. He gave a sad smile as if he felt sorry for her, which she thought a bit odd, since he'd just gone out of his way to help her.

'I'll deal with it for you personally,' he said. 'Since

you're newly arrived, are *you* looking for employment? We've vacancies for women.'

Kitty shook her head. 'No, thank you. I'm going to set up my own business as a seamstress. I do alterations and theatre costumes.' She made no reference to 'saloon gals', thinking he might get the wrong impression.

'There's plenty of theatres here,' he said. 'But if you change your mind, we've vacancies in dress stores that need filling.'

When she was gone, he read the note. Then, with a wry smile and a sceptical shake of his head, he opened the bottom drawer of his desk and dropped it in, where it became lost in a pile of similar notes and messages.

* * *

While Sam was actively seeking employment, Kitty and Frank began negotiating for a barbershop business with accommodation above, but Kitty's mind was elsewhere. She couldn't stop going over Sam and Pa's terse exchange, and she kept wondering if Sam had received her note. All the while, she was searching for a way to bring her father round to seeing Sam as she did. Her father had been reticent about his meeting with Sam at the cathedral, saying only, 'I instructed him he needs to find gainful employment and a purpose in life, in order to prove himself to me.'

The salesman who showed them round the barbershop was wildly enthusiastic, as real-estate sellers can sometimes be, and he was soon in full flow, extolling the opportunities the premises offered both as a business and a home.

'It's well situated, being close to several banking houses,

so you'll attract a steady stream of business from the men, young and old, who work there. Bankers need to keep themselves neat; it inspires confidence.'

As they looked around the upstairs accommodation Kitty thought the premises had potential, but she was wary. 'If it's such a good buy, why is it up for sale now?'

'The previous owner was knocked down by a bolting horse and passed away. The sale is to raise money for his widow and four lasses.'

Frank took out his handkerchief and rubbed some grime from the window-glass, so he could look out on the street below. 'They want a quick sale?'

'Indeed, so they can go back East where they came from. The furniture's included.'

Kitty felt a twinge of guilt that she and Pa would be gaining from another family's bereavement, but the premises were just what they were looking for, and the furniture, although not exactly to her taste, was serviceable enough.

'You'll be able to brighten it up considerably.' The salesman had a gleam in his eye, suggesting he thought he was on the cusp of finalising a deal.

Frank wasn't going to decide on so important a matter in haste and, after some financial negotiating with the salesman, he and Kitty retired to a nearby coffee-house to consider the purchase.

Kitty opened their conversation with, 'It's suitable, but it needs fixing up.'

'Yes, we're not talking about a few scuff marks. It needs more than a lick of paint.' Frank signalled to a waitress they were ready to order.

'The barbershop equipment looks serviceable. Is it?'

'The chair needs some oil, but I can work with it.'

'It's upstairs that needs the work. One of the bedroom windows is terribly rattly.'

The coffee arrived. Frank added sugar and stirred it in. 'We should leave that bedroom window like it is, then we'll always know if we're having a quake, because believe me, that bedroom window'll rattle like a can of hot nails in Hades when we do.'

'No, Pa! That's exactly why we need to fix it.'

'If you insist we can get someone in.'

Kitty's immediate thought was if Pa hadn't fallen out with Sam, they could have asked him for help putting the place in order.

It was Sunday October 17th, and Kitty and Sam had been separated in San Francisco for almost a week. It seemed like a month to Kitty as she sat quietly in the cathedral, rubbing shoulders with the great and the good. She'd made a special effort with her appearance and was wearing a pale blue dress with a wide ruffled skirt that she knew Sam hadn't seen before. She'd gone to a lot of trouble with her hair too, fixing a wide tartan ribbon to her loose bun.

Arriving early, she'd chosen a seat near the back so she could see and, more importantly, be seen. However, attendance was excellent, and the spaces around her were soon filled. Hemmed in as she was, she thought it likely Sam hadn't been able to see her, so when the service finished, she made her way quickly out onto the street. She took up a vantage point a little way along and watched as the congregation chatted in groups before leaving to go their separate ways.

After half an hour, Kitty realised Sam hadn't been there. Feeling bereft and empty, she didn't want to go home, so she began walking down Dupont Street and found herself on Market Street. This was the widest thoroughfare in the city, and on Sundays the well-to-do paraded up and down in their carriages. With tears of disappointment rolling down her face, Kitty made her way to the wharf to watch the ships.

A passing lady put a gentle hand on her arm. 'Are you in need of assistance?'

Kitty wiped the tears from her cheeks with her fingers. 'No, thank you. I've had an upset, that's all. It's nothing to worry about.'

The lady looked at her with doubt in her eyes. 'Are you sure?'

Kitty nodded. 'I'll be all right in a moment.'

The lady, still with concern on her face, went on her way. Kitty found her handkerchief and blew her nose. *It's not as if someone's died*, she told herself, but in her heart it felt just like that.

CHAPTER THIRTY-SEVEN

Monday was the start of a new week, and Sam approached Botcher's Stores to find a great commotion in progress. Goods in boxes and barrels were being unloaded from carts by lean Chinese labourers in sleeveless shirts and black trousers. The men had wound their queues round their heads and pinned them out of the way. A pile of boxes stood by the entrance and, to the right of them, Billy was overseeing the proceedings. He was older and rounder than Sam remembered, but it was Billy all right. He recognised him straightaway. He was obviously fully occupied. Sam decided to call back later. He was walking away when a distinctive voice rang out. Billy's early Orcadian burr had long ago picked up a Liverpudlian twang from the ships making his accent unmistakable.

'Sam! Sam Gray! I see you, don't you go wanderin' off now.'

He turned to see Billy hurrying towards him, arms outstretched for a reunion hug.

'Well, I'm blowed,' said Billy. 'Our Rosie was right. She said Sam Gray had called and I thought, that can't be. He's apprenticed in Colville. Then her being my sister and me growing up alongside her, I know she's truthful, but like I say, I did wonder.'

'I was apprenticed, but I'm not now. Well, I still am, but I left.'

'Ooh, I can tell by your face there's a sad tale there, but you're here now and I'll not let you go until I've heard every last tale you've got t'entertain me with.'

'It's good to see you, but you're in the thick of things. Shall we settle on a time and place?'

'My friend, I'm not too busy for an old marra, as they say in Cumberland. Especially one I haven't seen for... how long?'

'Four years, coming up.'

'That long, my, it seems no more 'n two.' Billy took hold of Sam's arm and pointed to a narrow alleyway. 'At the bottom there you'll find the Dog and Monkey. Ask for Billy's table. I'll be there within the quarter. Just got to set my foreman on and free myself up.'

Sam felt he'd been caught up in a tornado. He'd forgotten how exhilarating it was to be in Billy's orbit and how difficult it was to get a word in edgeways. He felt his mood lift.

The Dog and Monkey was busy, but not crowded. A roaring fire in a well-filled grate warmed the room and the oil lamps cast a yellow glow. It reminded Sam of some of the ale houses in Whitehaven; a place for working men to relax, play dominoes and fix the troubles of the world. He felt at ease right away.

Sam was shown to Billy's table in the corner and he ordered an ale. He didn't usually drink in the early afternoon, but today he'd make an exception. He'd been boosted by Billy's warm welcome. Even though he was busy, he'd downed tools, and Sam took that as a great compliment.

Billy arrived, all smiles, and waved and nodded to the men who called out to him. Sam felt the whole room's mood lift and he remembered how Billy had had the same effect on the ship. Always cheerful, always ready with a joke or a sympathetic ear. He'd done the right thing seeking Billy out.

Billy ordered 'my usual', which turned out to be a double measure of Irish whiskey and a jug of water.

'If I'm havin' a drink, it's gotta be a stiff one.' He added a tiny measure of water to the whiskey. 'You'll join me in a drop of the hard stuff, won't you?'

Sam knew then they were in for a merry afternoon, and if he got a little tipsy for once, it was going to be in safe hands and good company.

'I'll be happy to join you.'

Billy leaned forward conspiratorially. 'Now, tell me what you're doin' out of Colville. You must have done a runner.'

Sam told Billy about his escape from Colville and his flight to the Fraser River, and about the Muldoons, making a brief reference to his friendship with Kitty. It took an hour, and by then Billy was on his third whiskey and Sam halfway down his second.

'And here you are in San Francisco. What do you think of it?'

Sam hesitated.

'Let me answer for you. It's not quite what you expected?'

'Well...' Still Sam hesitated.

'Your reluctance tells me you're in two minds. You've made it to the city, it's an exciting place, but the magic's not here. Am I right?'

Sam was stunned. 'How did you know?'

'Because you're not the only new arrival who's felt that way. It's a common reaction. When folk dream of somethin' and want it really badly, life is such that after all the effort, the dream can't hope to live up to the expectation.'

Sam was surprised at such worldliness from Billy. This was a serious side to him he hadn't experienced before. He was right, though – the dream wasn't living up to his expectations. He'd put it down to his sadness over Kitty, but perhaps there was more to it than that.

'There's truth in what you say,' he said. 'I thought the city would welcome and embrace me, but it's almost as if I'm a nuisance.'

'I haven't heard it put like that afore.' Billy laughed so loudly, others turned their heads to share the joke. 'What is it you don't like?'

'Apart from the smells and the noise, it's that no one seems to have time for anyone else. People push into you on the streets without a second thought. They don't look you in the eye, there's no conversation. No exchange between folk passing greetings. It's exciting in that there's a lot happening, but it's an alien place to me.'

'You're right about the smells, but you get used to 'em after a while. Folk are in a hurry. It's all about business, there's no time to raise hats as they pass you by. They're caught up in their own thoughts. What's coming in, what's going out, how much can be made on it, who's got the best credit.'

'I guess that's why folk don't engage; they're too intent on depositing their brass in the bank.'

'And some are counting their losses. You've got to be sharp. Folk don't look you in the eye 'cos there's so many tricksters about, but take my sister Rosie, she loves it. Can't get out onto the streets for a look round often enough. Mind you, since she were widowed, she's become quite feisty. Not one of those types that wears black and sits in a darkened room for six months. I tell you, he was dead barely three months when she begged me to take her and her eldest to the Adelphi for a concert evening.'

'I'm sorry she's been widowed. Must be difficult for her with bairns.'

'Don't be sorry. He were a drunk and I see she's all right for brass.'

'You seem to have done well.'

'I'll not complain. After we dropped you all off on Vancouver Island, we arrived here and I thought, this place is booming. In them days you just had to set up shop and folk queued up to buy. We made a lot o' brass from diggers like you passing through. It's the same in Victoria right now, and that's why Stag Liddell's doin' so well. I see him from time to time. Said nowt about you doing a bunk, though.'

'I asked him not to in case the Company tracked me down. He told me you helped set him up in business.'

'All I did was give him saleable stock and marras' credit when he couldn't get any. Main thing is, Stag's proved he's a head for business. Some folk are too soft for it.'

'I saw his advertisement in the newspaper.'

'Everything's changed here now the boys from the Eastern States've moved in. In my opinion, San Francisco's golden days are over. New Zealand's where the future lies. There's hundreds of Britishers going out there, all needing supplies and support when they get there, and I've tapped into that vein.'

Sam thought of their steerage voyage and how difficult it had been in all aspects, and it had to be a much longer voyage to New Zealand. 'Why are they travelling all that way?'

'The Auckland government's giving settlers forty-acre farms for a payment of ten shillings, and twenty acres for five shillings. They can get extra land if they take bairns with them over five and under eighteen years old.'

'Rosie says your family's there?'

'I brought them and Rosie, and her husband and family, over here two years ago. Then the opportunity came up to visit Auckland, so I went to take a look around, taking merchandise with me. I tell you, I knows a profitable market when I sees one, so I came back, told the missus all about it. She was like you, found the city too big and dirty, and that was that. They've been there over a year now and staying put.'

'You're giving up your business?'

'I can't give up the sea, so keeping things running here gives me an excuse to sail.'

'How long does it take to get there?'

'Around ten weeks. I went out last year to settle the family and got back mid-March. I've set up a reliable manager and I'm leaving again this January.'

'For good?' *Just when I've found someone I feel at home with here and he's upping and leaving.*

'No. I'll manage the Auckland end and when the urge to smell brine out of sight of the shore accosts me, I'll come back. By then the missus'll be glad to see the back o' me for a while. She says she's not used to having me underfoot for months on end.'

'And your sister?'

'Rosie's another reason to return. To my despair and eternal upset, she won't move further west. Says she's never stepping on board a sail ship again. Whereas me, I'm looking forward to the voyage and not just to see the family. I can afford to pay for a proper passage, thanks to my good customers, and I don't have to clamber barefoot up the ratlines seeing to the sails no longer.'

They talked some more about the Muldoons and Kitty, and Sam asked whether Billy had any ideas on how he could look for them.

'I'd suggest you start looking round barbershops.'

'I've been doing that.'

'Did you go in them? Likely even if he's got his own business, the billboard won't be in his name yet.'

'No, I haven't, but do you realise how many barbershops there are here?'

'You're telling me there's more than a few?'

Sam sighed. 'Aye, seems there's one on every street corner and several in every block.'

'San Franciscan businessmen like to look smart. I wish you luck with tracking them down. I'll keep my eyes open and tell the men, but I've to get back now.'

'Thank you.'

'We'll meet again a week on Sunday, shall we? Find a job where they don't make you work the Sabbath.'

'I'll try.'

'Come for some dinner. I'll speak with Rosie. I'm sure she can accommodate another at her overflowing table. I'll drop a note by the Christian hostel confirming.'

Sam was at the door when Billy shouted out, 'Didn't you say the daughter did dress alterations for dancers or something?'

'Aye.'

'Then you could ask around some of the saloons, see if anyone's been round offering alterations. Just a thought, mind you.'

It might have been just a thought to Billy, but for Sam it was an excellent idea, and one he could act upon immediately.

After calling in at several saloon bars and two theatres on his way back to the YMCA, it occurred to Sam that it was probably too soon to be seeking out Kitty in this way. He thought idly about putting an advertisement for dress alterations in a couple of shop windows himself, then rejected the idea as too haphazard. No, he would do a round of the entertainment establishments later, but he would still look keenly at every barbershop he came across.

CHAPTER THIRTY-EIGHT

Muller's Fine Felt Hat Emporium on Chatham Street was Sam's fifth employment interview. It was becoming clear to him there were few openings for out-of-work colliers, or any folk who used the strength of their bodies to earn a living, other than lifting and shifting. He'd considered taking dock work, but soon decided that would be a choice of last resort, since it was dangerous and unreliable, and the hours erratic. He was realising quickly that San Francisco was a city of warehouses, banks, merchants, auctioneers and ship repairers. Goods were bought in, sold, and then moved on to the interior, as far as the Rockies, or else overseas to Europe and the Far East. The goods sent from New York, Boston, Baltimore and other established ports arrived already made. The closest the city came to manufacturing was importing the raw materials for clothing and millinery.

He was shown into a mezzanine office from which the management could look down, through dusty windows, onto their employees in the workshop below. The man who was interviewing him, alone in the room, was sitting behind a desk covered with ledgers and scraps of paper. He was so pale, Sam wondered if he'd seen daylight over the last ten years. He motioned to Sam to take a seat.

'And you are?'

'Samuel Gray. Just arrived here, sir.' He added the 'sir' on a sudden whim, thinking it better to be overpolite than appear surly or entitled.

'And you're looking for employment as a clerk?'

'Yes, sir.'

'Experience?'

'I've a good head for figures, I'm not workshy and I'm never late.'

The interviewer yawned and rubbed his chin with a thumb. 'Where have you been doing all these good things?'

'I worked for the Hudson's Bay Company on Vancouver Island.' This was true enough. No need to say he'd been down the mines. If the man thought he'd worked in the office, then that was *his* assumption and good luck to him. 'I've just come back from the Fraser River goldfields and I'm looking to settle here.'

'If you stay, you'll be different to most folk. They tend to come here, make their money, then return to where they came from. Going by your accent, in your case I guess that's England?'

Sam nodded, 'Aye, sir, but I'm not returning there. My life's here now.'

'We expect our clerks to begin their days at 8 am. Our hat-makers start at 6 am, and sometimes we boil and dye at night, but that won't affect you. Your duties include making and accepting deliveries, keeping invoice records, making up the books, copying letters and seeing to accurate billing. I expect that's what you were used to in Canada?'

'More or less.' It made him uncomfortable that the city was turning him into a liar again.

'We don't want any of that educated English writing that you can't read for all the curlicues and embellishments. Just make sure we can understand what you've written.'

Sam couldn't do the 'curlicue writing' to save his life, so it was a relief he wasn't expected to.

'I'm Edward Bradden, the company manager. You will see the founder of our company, Mr Muller – or Herr Muller, as he is known within these walls – from time to time. He runs a tight ship and likes to keep an eagle eye on things. He'll rarely converse with you, because his English is somewhat limited. He arrived from Berlin via New York eight years ago and has built up a good business with judicious foresight. Being a grand milliner, there's nothing he doesn't know about hats, from washing and drying the wool to selling and skinning rabbits. We supply all California, Portland, Oregon, Denver, Colorado and up the coast in British Columbia. If you need anything you come to me. Do you understand?'

'Aye, I do, sir.'

'We pay one ounce of gold a day, which is the equivalent of eighteen dollars at the moment. Non-negotiable, take it or leave it.'

'I'll take it.'

Mr Bradden handed Sam a piece of paper. 'Write your address on here.'

When Sam handed back his address, Mr Bradden glanced at it. 'Just checking I can read your writing. I don't expect you'll stay long at the Christian hostel, so make sure you tell me when you get a permanent address.'

Sam knew his handwriting wasn't that of an educated man, but in San Francisco the rules of class and status seemed all over the place. At least he was fluent in English, which it sounded as if his new boss was not.

Mr Bradden put the piece of paper to one side and looked Sam up and down, before glancing at the office wall-clock. 'I like the look of you and you're polite. If you were good enough for the Hudson's Bay Company, I expect you'll be good enough for us. You can start on Monday and if you work hard, after training, there are prospects for increased responsibility.'

'Thank you, and I accept your offer, sir.'

CHAPTER THIRTY-NINE

Kitty was anxious for Sunday to arrive with the prospect of seeing Sam. The days dragged. She was relieved Pa had found the motivation to purchase the barbershop premises. Now she could divert her energies to herself and her mission to find Sam.

'You know, Pa, I'm still thinking I can set myself up like I did in Harrison. I learned so much from the two saloon gals, it seems a waste to not capitalise on it here. What do you think?' She held her breath. Dressing saloon gals in San Francisco, where there were social values to uphold, was not the same as in Harrison, where everyone more or less did what they pleased.

Frank lowered his copy of the *Trinity Journal*. 'You're looking for my approval to dress the saloon and dance gals here?'

'Yes. I'm good at it. The bosses pay for the dresses and they want the best for their girls. It's an easy way to bring in money.'

Frank pursed his lips. 'That is as may be, but I don't think it proper for us to have saloon gals coming in and out of the barbershop.'

'I understand that, but they don't have to. I can visit them.'

Frank's eyes widened. 'But then people will see *you* coming and going from saloons and bars, and that's even worse in my eyes. I've no trouble with you setting up a business – in fact, I'll welcome it – but why can't you set your sights higher? I'm sure there's plenty of respectable ladies who would welcome your services.'

Kitty sighed. She'd liked saloon gals because they were down to earth and friendly. Respectable ladies would have airs and graces and she would have to pander to their whims. She wished she could talk it over with Sam. She wouldn't allow herself to think he'd received her note and was deliberately not responding. It was more likely he had yet to receive it.

The next morning, Kitty was certain Sam would definitely be at the cathedral, and with the excitement of anticipation, had dressed herself once more with care. When he didn't show she buoyed herself with the thought she could probably find him by going to Billy Botcher's at Filbert Street and leaving a second note there. She had no guilt over that, because it was not like meeting up and talking.

* * *

Sam arrived for Sunday lunch at Rosie's to find Billy settled on one side of the fireplace in the parlour, a glass of ale by his side. He was bouncing a small boy on his knee.

'This is the way the ladies ride,' he sang, 'clip clop, clip clop....' The boy was giggling and laughing. As the maid showed Sam in, Billy finished the rhyme at breakneck speed before giving the boy a kiss on the forehead and setting him down.

'Welcome,' said Rosie. 'I hope you're hungry. I've a mountain of edibles.'

'Aye, I am, very,' Sam said, with a little bow of his head. The aroma of pork crackling was increasing his anticipation of a good home-cooked meal by the minute.

With smiles aplenty on everyone's faces, and the three children coming in and out interrupting, the atmosphere in the home was light-hearted and friendly. Sam had a moment of pain that such familial happiness had so far been denied him.

They sat down to the pork, which was served with thick, flavoursome gravy, crusty bread and parsley-flavoured butter. The children ate quickly and were excused from the table, with the eldest offering to read to the other two. The conversation turned from keeping the children entertained with jokes and stories to New Zealand.

Billy leaned back in his chair with the satisfied expression of a man who has just eaten an excellent meal. 'I'm definitely not going for good,' he said. 'I've business interests here to see to.' After a 'look' from Rosie, he added, 'And family here.'

Rosie picked up the story. 'When Billy's wife Elsie told me that after sailing around the world several times, settling here, starting a thriving business, and shipping his family over from England, our Billy was wanting them all to go and live in Auckland – well, I was knocked speechless.'

'And that takes some doin', I can tell you,' said Billy.

Rosie made as if to throw her napkin at him.

'And your wife hasn't regretted it?' asked Sam.

Rosie laughed. 'Regretted it? She writes me letters praising it all the time. I reckon she's just lonely and wants me out there for company. That's a chorus I'm not ready to sing along with.'

''Tis true, she loves it,' said Billy.

'Is there nothing she dislikes?' asked Sam.

'She's mentioned some quakes in her letters –'

Billy butted in, 'There was some when I were there, but nothing like we get here.'

'You're just sayin' that,' said Rosie, sticking out her lips with a teasing face.

Sam was thinking again how much fun a family could be, when he was stirred from his thoughts by Billy reminiscing about their trip over from England on the *Princess Rose*.

'On the Company pioneer ships, especially when going round the Horn in winter, you know, us mariners really felt the pain of you steerage folk.'

'It was tough sometimes,' said Sam. 'But we were on a journey to a new life, so we put up with it.'

'They had to work part of their passage,' Billy explained to Rosie. 'And although Sam's group were seasoned miners and used to hard work, they weren't mariners, but they all coped well and did their bit.'

'I can still tie some good knots,' said Sam with a grin.

'Billy told me some folk lost babies on the way over. Is that true?'

'Aye, that's true. Our son Stephen was conceived not to live.' Sam smiled at Rosie, to show he wasn't upset with her. After all, had she known they'd lost Stephen he was sure she'd never have brought the subject up.

'Rosie, I should have mentioned that Sam were married when he travelled over. Sadly, his wife passed away the next year.'

After a short pause, Rosie asked, 'May I ask what your wife were called?'

'Evie. She was called Evie.'

'Then I'll remember her and your son Stephen in my special Sunday prayers this evening.'

Sam was touched and thanked her.

They chatted for a while about Sam's gold-digging in the Fraser Valley, and the subject turned to the Muldoons. He couldn't be sure, but with Rosie being no fool, from the warm expression on her face he guessed she knew there was more to Kitty than he was saying.

'It's good to know you've other folk in the city,' Rosie said. 'Where do they live?'

'They were hoping to set up another barbershop. They're in lodgings until then, but I don't know where.'

'San Francisco's not that big a place,' she said. 'You'll run into them somewhere along the line, although maybe not for a while.'

'It's a big place when you've lost someone and are hoping to find them again,' said Sam. He was feeling particularly low at that point. *If things don't work out*

*for me, I might as well go for third time lucky – Canada,
America and on to New Zealand.*

* * *

Kitty rose early on Monday morning and penned a note
similar to the one she'd left at Chapin's, with the addition
of their new address.

She marked the envelope for Mr Samuel Gray, c/o Mr
Billy Botcher, and at 157 Filbert Street she pushed the letter
through the letterbox. She was home well before midday
to prepare lunch for Pa. She told herself she wasn't telling
him a lie, she was just keeping him in the dark. It was a
very slim moral distinction, but one she could live with.
She wanted Sam Gray in her life and she had to let him
know she was still thinking of him.

CHAPTER FORTY

Sam's first day at Muller's didn't begin as he'd expected. He was handed a broom by the factory foreman with instructions to help sweep the finishing room. A disgusting smell of fat assaulted his nostrils. It was dirty work. The floor was of rough boards, and something appeared to have been spilt on it. The substance had landed in the cracks between the boards and hardened.

'Is that wax?' Sam asked.

'No,' said the foreman. 'Grease got into one of the dye-pans overnight by mistake and was spat out onto the floor. Four dozen hats were spoiled. Herr Muller's gone home for his hot chocolate and biscuits in a bad mood. It's all hands on deck to get it cleaned up before he returns.'

Sam felt he was undergoing a baptism of fire. He got hold of the broom and got to work alongside several other men similarly tasked. After half an hour, most of the mess had been cleaned up and deposited into a metal waste-barrel. In the end, they'd had to use sharp serrated knives to scrape up some of the hardened grease. Sam looked up and saw Mr Bradden beckoning him from the mezzanine floor.

In the office, as well as the manager's desk there were three other tables, two of which were now occupied. The men looked up with interest when Sam entered. He was introduced to his fellow workers and directed to the vacant table. Six neat piles of paper were ready for him.

'These invoices need entering in date order in the ledger,' Mr Bradden told him. 'Just follow what's already under the column headings.'

Sam picked up the first bundle of papers and, flicking through, he saw quickly they were all out of date order, so he corrected that. Then he took the top one from the pile and, dipping his pen, made the first entry, carefully copying the system laid out in the ledger.

Name: Emmanuel Brothers, 192 Lexington Ave., New York City. N.Y.
Item: 8 dozen ladies' hats being 4 dozen felt, 2 dozen beaver, 2 dozen moleskin. 10 dozen men's caps being 6 dozen otter, 4 dozen beaver.

Amount owing: $264

Cash on delivery via our New York agent:
R. E. Fitzgerald, 743, Lafayette, New York City. N.Y.

Sam saw quickly that Herr Muller was running a thriving business and wondered what he was like. People spoke about him in hushed tones, although it was too soon for Sam to know whether that was out of respect or fear.

After fifteen minutes, the foreman came across from his desk and peered over his shoulder. 'Seems like you know what you're doing.'

For the rest of the day Sam continued making entries in the ledger. Mr Bradden made it clear all conversation must relate to work topics, which exempted him from chatting with his colleagues at the other desks. After his arrival, they didn't show much interest in him, which suited Sam. There was a short break for what Mr Bradden called breakfast, but Sam would have called dinner, during which he went for a walk and bought a hot pie. Although the work was repetitive, he found a welcome security in his new position. He didn't have to think, he could be Sam Gray again, and he could keep himself to himself. Despite the factory odours, the job promised much to recommend itself while he settled into city life and found his feet.

The next morning, Herr Muller called into the office. His clothing was that of a successful businessman who could afford an expert tailor. As might be expected, his silk hat was top of the range at Muller's Fine Felt Hat Emporium. As his dress was impeccable, so were his side-whiskers which Sam thought must be expertly seen to at least twice a week, if not more often.

Herr Muller spoke authoritatively with a strong German accent. 'The felt hats come yet from Boston?'

Mr Bradden scanned his desk. 'There's a shipment delivery note. I've just seen it.'

Herr Muller tapped his silver-topped cane on the floor and looked round the room, noticing Sam.

'You are the new one?'

'Aye, sir, Sam Gray.' Sam proffered a smile that was not returned.

'Today old hats come from Boston. We cover them in silk and make new ones. Clever?'

'Aye, sir, clever.' Sam had thought the hats were all new and probably the folk buying them thought so too. Aye, it was very clever.

'Big profits good for you. No profits, no job for you. Understand?'

Sam nodded.

Mr Bradden, having found the shipment note, waved it in the air. 'What Herr Muller is saying is, if you work hard, we'll make a profit and your job will be secure.'

Herr Muller nodded, took the delivery note, and disappeared. Sam wasn't sure what to make of him as a man, but as a businessman he was impressive.

Sam took a different route home when work had finished for the day, and he came across two entertainment halls he hadn't seen before. He was getting used to the box-office staff shaking their heads when he enquired about Kitty, but he was determined to keep knocking on doors and asking.

* * *

Kitty had even higher hopes Sam would be at the cathedral the following Sunday. He must surely have received her second note. So when he wasn't there, in her disappointment she began to think about calling in person at 157 Filbert Street. Even if Sam had commitments that kept him away, she was certain he would want to see her as much as she wanted to see him. She was busy setting up her dressmaking business, working all hours. Perhaps he was working hard too. But lately she'd been worrying he might have had an accident or been robbed or worse. A stranger in the city had to be far more vulnerable to its evils than a native San Franciscan.

After dreaming vividly of Sam wandering round the city calling out for her, Kitty awoke on the Tuesday with one single thought spinning round her head. *Today I will knock on Billy Botcher's door.* Her pa need never know, so she wouldn't be telling a lie.

Kitty primed herself to finish early that afternoon to call at Filbert Street, but as fate would have it, a well-to-do lady, Mrs Clancy, called for an alteration. On answering the doorbell, thinking it a postal delivery or something similarly mundane, Kitty found herself face to face with the one customer who loved to chat. Mrs Clancy was a pleasant enough lady and far too lucrative a customer to brush off.

'I know it's a little late in the day, Miss Muldoon, but it's my husband's birthday and this is his favourite dress of mine.'

As Kitty helped with some awkward buttons and laces, Mrs Clancy chattered away.

'I've lost so much weight, of which I'm very pleased, of course, but you will see that the sides are all swishy.' She did a quick twirl and Kitty had to agree. What should have been a figure-hugging gown was hanging loosely.

'It looks a bit drab, doesn't it?' Mrs Clancy said.

'Drab' was absolutely the correct word, but Kitty knew better than to describe a client so to their face, whatever the circumstance.

'I can see it is a little loose, but I can fix that for you.'

Kitty wanted to say, 'Hurry up, let me have the dress and then I can get on with it.' It seemed Mrs Clancy had all the time in the world. She glanced at the clock. Half past four. It would be half past five at the earliest before she could get away, and she had to be back by half past six to prepare supper. She allowed herself a silent sigh whilst maintaining a smiling face.

Just as she thought she'd finished, Mrs Clancy began fiddling in her large handbag.

'There's just one other little thing,' she said, producing a gentleman's embroidered waistcoat. 'The buckle on the tie-back has fallen off. I looked for it everywhere. Do you have one and if so, can you sew it on?'

Kitty did have one. She held her hand out for the waistcoat, glanced at the clock, and with an impatient heart realised she would have to rethink her plans. With clients until well after midday, it would be tomorrow early afternoon before she could walk up to Filbert Street.

Mrs Clancy was despatched, blissfully unaware of how she had upset Kitty's plans. Kitty began tidying the workroom. Frustrated and tired, she mouthed a prayer under her breath, half in jest and half in truth.

'Dear Lord, send me saloon gals every time. They're direct, know what they want and are easy to please. Thank you, amen.'

* * *

It was raining as it can only rain in San Francisco when Kitty woke the next morning. Frank joined her at the breakfast table and, seeing the rain splashing against the windows, remarked, 'Didn't you say you were going out this afternoon?'

'Yes, but I'm hoping rain at seven, fine by eleven.'

Frank smiled. 'I haven't heard that expression in a long while. Going far?'

'Up by Union Street. I'm following up an enquiry.' It was true, Union Street ran parallel to Filbert Street, except she was the one making the enquiry.

'Even if it's cleared, you'd best take an umbrella with you.' Frank poured himself a second cup of coffee then picked up the paper.

By midday the rain had cleared, although the sky remained dull and a thick grey fog was swirling in from the Bay. As soon as she was free, Kitty put on her coat and sturdy bonnet and ventured out. When she arrived at the house in Filbert Street, she could see straightaway, by a light in one of the upstairs rooms, that someone was at home. She was unexpectedly nervous. She'd gone over various potential scenarios in her mind, including what if Sam himself opened the door? This would be by far the best outcome.

The brass knocker had been recently polished, making Kitty think there must be a maid, or at the very least a lady of the house. She rapped on it twice, and with her heart in her mouth, waited for someone to answer. There were slow footsteps and a rattly cough, followed by the jingle of keys. It seemed an age before the door opened.

An elderly gentleman, wearing a velvet smoking hat with a short silk tassel and matching jacket, looked down at her.

'Yes?'

'I'm looking for Billy Botcher.'

The man frowned and put his hand to his ear. 'What?'

Kitty repeated her words, slightly louder and at a slower pace.

'That's what I thought you said.'

Kitty's heart went down to her feet. 'Oh,' was all she could think of to say.

The man scratched his head. 'Someone else thinks he lives here, but he don't.'

'Who is that?' asked Kitty, thinking the gentleman must mean Sam, come to track Billy down.

'I don't know. A few weeks back, maybe a bit longer, this came.' He turned to his left, where Kitty could see her note lying on a metal tray. He held it up for her to examine. 'Are you all right? You look a bit queer.'

'No, it's nothing. It's just that *I* wrote that letter.' Kitty was having a hard time getting her thoughts in order. This was one scenario she hadn't prepared for – that her letter would be sitting unopened on a metal tray in what was obviously the wrong house. She was sure Sam had said 157 Filbert Street.

'Do you know Billy Botcher?' she asked.

The gentleman shook his head. He handed her the letter. 'Well, if you wrote it, I guess it's yours. I kept it just in case someone came knocking for it and I'm glad now that I did.'

As she made her way home, Kitty's emotions were all over the place. She hadn't put her worst imaginings to bed, but at least she could allow herself the relief of thinking Sam hadn't rejected her. He had no idea she was looking for him.

CHAPTER FORTY-ONE

That same day, late afternoon at Muller's, Mr Bradden asked all three clerks to draw up a newspaper advertisement for the company. Sam set his mind to it. Anything was better than copying invoices into the sales ledger.

He thought for a few minutes then came up with:

'IN NEED OF A HAT?

The latest styles for AUTUMN or WINTER at MULLER'S FINE FELT HAT EMPORIUM on Chatham Street.

Light on your pocket and light on your head.'

Mr Bradden gathered up the three clerks' suggestions. 'I'll pass these on to Herr Muller. He'll look through them and decide if he likes one.'

When Mr Bradden told Sam the next morning that Herr Muller wanted to speak with him.. He and Mr Bradden entered what the workers referred to with awe as the 'inner sanctum' – a wood-panelled office that smelt of cigars and polished wood. In the middle of the room was a boldly carved mahogany desk that must have needed several men to put in place. Behind this, Herr Muller was sitting straight-backed, his chin slightly raised.

Mr Bradden reminded Herr Muller that this was, 'Sam Gray, our new clerk,' then stepped to one side. Herr Muller was clutching a piece of paper.

'What is this?' he asked, waving the paper at Sam as if swatting a fly.

Sam leaned. It looked like the advertisement he'd written.

'This is your writing?' asked Herr Muller.

Sam could tell by the man's manner he wasn't about to congratulate him for his efforts, but what was it that was so obviously causing annoyance?

'Aye, I wrote that. Is something wrong?'

Herr Muller ignored the question, or else didn't understand it.

'What is this "light"?' He jabbed the paper with a well-manicured finger.

Sam still had no idea what was being talked about and he looked to Mr Bradden for help.

'I think Herr Muller is upset by your use of the word "light".'

Herr Muller nodded and leaned back, which had the effect of pushing out his chest. He was looking expectantly at Sam, with an expression of annoyance.

'It's a jest,' explained Sam.

'A jest? It's what you call funny?' Now Herr Muller was looking annoyed *and* confused.

'Well, it's difficult to explain, but no one wants a hat that's heavy on their head and no one wants to pay a heavy price. So, it means easy-to-wear hats at low, affordable prices.'

'Poor quality and cheap. That's what I read,' said Herr Muller.

'No,' said Sam in horror. 'Not at all. Mr Bradden, can you help me here, please? The last thing I want to do is insult the company.'

They're going to fire me, he thought. *Just because the boss doesn't understand the play on words.*

Mr Bradden was beginning to explain to a dubious-looking Herr Muller, when a younger man entered. This had to be Herr Muller's son, since they were as alike in looks as father and offspring could be.

'Mr Muller,' Mr Bradden said. 'This is our new clerk, Sam Gray. You may be able to help us.' To Sam he said, 'He's Mr Muller Junior to you.'

'Call me Mr Hans,' the young man said. 'And how can I help?'

Herr Muller, seemingly pleased to see his son, spoke a few sentences in German, after which Mr Hans took the paper. To Sam's relief, he began laughing.

'You wrote this, Sam Gray?'

'Aye, sir, but it was never my intention to imply your hats are flimsy and cheap.'

'I think it's very clever.' He addressed his father in German again and then said, 'You must forgive my father. He is very sensitive to our reputation. He has built it up over the years and he knows it could be shattered overnight.'

'I have taken no offence,' said Sam.

Mr Hans gave the paper to Mr Bradden. 'I think we should use this. It's humorous and to the point and no hat should be so heavy that the wearer is continually aware of it.'

'As you say, sir. I will make the arrangements.'

Sam was back sitting at his desk, pondering his conversation with Herr Muller, when he heard a low rumble. The sound grew quickly in intensity until it was as deafening as if a carriage and horses were being driven through the room at full gallop. The building began shaking, no one spoke, and water in glasses on a tray set down on a table near Sam began to slosh back and forth. Pens and pencils jumped up and down on desks. Everyone started up, seeking shelter, when, just as quickly as it had started, the sound stopped.

Mr Bradden picked up his pencils from the floor. 'That was some quake, lads,' he said. 'And a bigger than normal one too.'

CHAPTER FORTY-TWO

After all movement had ceased, and when everything seemed back to normal, the staff set about with brooms, sweeping up glass shards that had fallen from the mezzanine windows onto the workroom floor. The quake had unnerved Sam badly. He'd experienced slight tremors on Vancouver Island and had felt slightly stronger ones since being in San Francisco – occasionally several times a day – but nothing like the noise and shaking he'd just experienced. It wasn't just the quake itself, but the looks on people's faces. These were seasoned San Franciscans and it had been a shock to see them visibly anxious. What he found most strange was the aftermath. It was almost as if the quake hadn't happened. There were a few comments, such as 'That was a good one' or 'We haven't had one like that for a while,' but within minutes the room and the people's faces had reverted to exactly how they'd been before the rumbling began.

He trod gingerly along the wooden boards to the stairs,

stopping halfway down to survey the damage. It seemed the mezzanine window frames had twisted as a result of being shaken apart at the corners. The glass panes had loosened and crashed to the floor.

Half an hour later Mr Bradden appeared and greeted the three clerks.

'That quake is causing me no manner of problems. Loss of production, glass everywhere. Herr Muller isn't going to like it if it's not sorted by the time he returns.' He sat down with an irritated 'humph' and began opening ledgers, glancing inside, tutting, then closing them with a loud bang.

Herr Muller could hardly blame Mr Bradden for an act of God, Sam thought. Also, to his eye, the frames had needed seeing to some time ago. It seemed to him a case of lack of maintenance, although pointing that out would not be well received. He'd noticed several areas in the workshop where, if he'd been in charge, he'd have made money-saving repairs and added a lick or two of paint. He suspected Herr Muller would regard such preventative measures as an unnecessary expense and would consider it cheaper to wait until restorative work became unavoidable.

They'd been working for half an hour, to the background noises of the sweeping up and the tinkling of glass as it hit the sides of the metal waste-barrel, when a young lad they called Runner, who delivered messages and collected goods and parcels, came in.

Mr Bradden looked up from his paperwork. 'How did you get on?'

Runner spoke quickly. 'The glazier says he can let us have glass panes and glazing bars, but he's no one can come fit them until a week tomorrow.'

Mr Bradden scowled. 'That's far too long to wait.'

'"Run off his feet" was the words he used.'

Mr Bradden tapped his teeth with his thumbnail and examined the twisted window frames.

Sam followed his gaze. 'If you can get the glass I can do it for you,' he said.

Mr Bradden stared at him as if seeing him in a new light. 'You?'

Sam laughed. 'I've not always been a clerk. In Colville we had to finish off some of the workers' homes as soon as we arrived – carpentry, roofing, drains. We all pulled together, so everyone learned some basic building skills. Then we had general maintenance to see to. For a while I worked in the coal mine, where we were always being called on to fix things. I'm good with my hands. I always have been.'

Mr Bradden looked astonished, but most definitely respectful. 'Well, what do you think? *Can* you fix it?'

Sam got up from behind his desk for a closer look. 'If you're not going to replace the wood – which I assume you're not going to, or you'd have done so before now – I can straighten them up, drop in the glass and fix it with glazing bars. I'll need to take measurements for the glazier.'

Mr Bradden looked dubious. 'What about tools?'

'The company's got a toolbox, haven't it?'

Runner spoke up. 'There's one in that tall cupboard next to the boiler. You've got the key.'

Mr Bradden opened a desk drawer and, after rummaging around, he took out a long thin key with a large label saying 'Boiler Cupboard', which he handed to Sam.

To Runner, he said, 'Take Mr Gray down and show him.'

At the back of the factory, a room had been tacked on to the main building to house the boiler. When the toolbox cupboard was unlocked, Sam was surprised to see that not only was there a wooden crate of assorted hammers, chisels and other metal implements, but stacked on a small shelf above the toolbox were glass jars holding nails of varying widths and lengths, along with several tins. He opened some of the tins to find nuts and bolts mixed in with metal odds and ends. A wooden rule with a hole in one end for a string loop had been strung up onto a nail on the inside of the cupboard door.

'I have everything I need,' he said to Runner. 'This is a surprise.' He unhooked the rule and, with Runner at his heels, returned to the clerks' office.

'I can do it,' he told Mr Bradden. 'The tools are in excellent condition. Whoever stored them put them away well-greased.'

Mr Bradden looked relieved. 'When the factory opened, we had a man who saw to all the maintenance. Those are his tools.'

'He left?'

'No, he went fishing and slipped off the wharf a year back, and that was that. He'd no family so no one came to collect his tools.'

'He wasn't replaced?'

'No. Herr Muller doesn't think we need anyone, except when the boiler goes wrong. Then we get a specialist in.'

That explained why all the jobs Sam thought needed doing hadn't been seen to. Minor repairs mostly, but ones that, if left unattended, would become major.

'If you're sure you can fix it to a professional standard, you'd better get measuring,' Mr Bradden said.

On his way home, as he weaved his way amongst the crowds, Sam, always on the lookout for Kitty, wondered if the Muldoons were all right after the quake. If he'd known where they were he'd have rushed round to offer his services, but that wasn't possible. His worries intensified when he saw several buildings showing signs of recent quake damage. Nothing disastrous, but enough to cost people good money.

* * *

The next morning, Sam was tapping in the last holding pin with his hammer when he heard Mr Hans's voice.

'You up the ladder. Aren't you the advertisement clerk?'

Sam turned his head. 'Aye, sir.'

'Then what are you doing up there?'

Sam thought it obvious, but knew better than to say so. 'I'm fixing the window and putting in new glass after the quake damage.'

'What I meant was why are *you* doing it? Why isn't the glazier seeing to it?'

'He could deliver the materials, but not send anyone until Friday, so I offered to fix it.'

'Well, this is a surprise. You can mend windows as well as write advertisements. What else can you do?'

Sam laughed and, thinking it a joke, didn't reply.

'I mean it,' said Mr Hans. 'Come down and tell me what other hidden talents you have.'

'I can do most things connected with household maintenance.' He explained, as he had done to Mr Bradden, about the settlers having to turn their hands to a variety of things.

Sensing Mr Hans was genuinely interested, Sam felt confident enough to add, 'There are lots of things that need doing here. The front door is warped and sticks; there are areas that need re-plastering.' He pointed to a workbench. 'That just needs a minor adjustment and it will stop shaking, and then the hats will stay on it without falling off every time someone passes by.'

'We've a boiler that sometimes breaks down. Can you see to that?'

'Given charge of a boiler in good working condition I'm confident I can keep it that way.'

'You would only take responsibility for it if it was declared in good working order?'

'I think anyone in my position would say the same. I worked in the coal mines in Vancouver Island and we always kept our machinery well-greased and looked after it. Boilers are like people, they need cherishing. We never allowed any machinery to get overheated. That's often where the problem lies – lack of maintenance and overheating.'

'This is most interesting,' said Mr Hans. 'My father

and I have differing ideas over how to run the workshop. I agree with you that maintenance is the key. Perhaps the quake yesterday has done us all a good favour. Opened our eyes, so to speak. Tell me, which would you prefer to see to each day – the invoices and bookwork or the maintenance of the workshop?'

Sam was taken aback. 'I've always been happiest working with my hands. Does that answer your question?'

Mr Hans nodded. 'Before I speak with my father, if we offered you a position as factory maintenance foreman, would you take it?'

'As well as my clerking duties?'

Mr Hans gave what could only be described as a guffaw. 'No, indeed not. Clerks are easy to engage, but a good maintenance man is hard to find. We would employ you for full-time maintenance. If there is not enough work here, we can supplement with work at our own homes.'

'I would be employed as the maintenance manager?'

Mr Hans guffawed again and slapped his thigh. 'I know what you're doing. You're angling for a rise.'

'Have I been successful?' Sam knew he was being cheeky, but if he could keep the conversation light, it might be to his advantage.

'We'll see what my father has to say. He's away for a few days so we'll have to wait until his return to announce this officially. You're right, there is a lot needs seeing to. I've been saying so for some time. I will tell my father you can save us money in the long run.'

'That won't be a lie. I most certainly can, but you will have to have the boiler serviced.'

That evening, his spirits lifted at the thought of the maintenance manager position, Sam took a long walk, taking in parts of the city and searching out barbershops he hadn't been in before.

When he stopped for a beer, an idea came to his mind.

CHAPTER FORTY-THREE

When Sam arrived at Chapin's, he was surprised to find the young man who'd interviewed him had been replaced by a middle-aged gentleman.

'I was here almost a month ago,' Sam told him, 'and Chapin's found me accommodation and gave me employment suggestions.'

'Are you still looking for employment?'

'No. I'm working at Muller's Fine Felt Hat Emporium. It's going well and I've been offered a managerial position.'

The man raised his eyebrows. 'That all sounds just fine. How can I help you today? Need fresh accommodation?'

'I'm wondering if someone has tried to get in touch with me recently. Perhaps left a letter or note?'

'I've a whole drawer full of notes. What's your name?'

'Samuel Gray.'

The man shook his head. 'I don't remember that name. Besides we don't pass on information from our books.'

'Well, is there any way you can check within company rules?'

'Well, I've a drawer full of notes and messages from people wanting to hook up.'

Sam tried another tack. 'Has anyone come in recently asking for a position making sewing alterations?'

The man opened his mouth to speak then, suddenly looking thoughtful, he closed it.

'It would have been a pretty girl called Kitty Muldoon,' Sam went on. 'I think she might have been looking for me.'

'There was someone said they were a seamstress. Newly arrived. I just can't remember if she left a note or not.'

'Can you look in your drawer? Please?'

The man bent down and there was the sound of a drawer being opened and then a sigh. 'They get muddled up, so it might not be on the top of the pile.'

'I can see you're busy. Perhaps *I* can take a look?'

The man pulled the drawer right out and handed it over. 'No reading other people's notes.'

Sam took a seat and began rummaging through the many messages and letters. He couldn't help reading some of them because they were only folded, and most were depressing – girls looking for lost loves, men seeking runaway wives, children seeking fathers. He was determined to check every single note, even if it took him all day. However, he didn't have to search that long, because after ten minutes he came across an envelope addressed to himself.

'I've found one for me,' he called out.

He felt dizzy in an excited way. *She's looking for me.* After reading the contents, he was jubilant.

He handed back the drawer. 'Thank you. I've found exactly what I've been waiting for.'

'You're welcome,' said the man.

Sam was in such good spirits, he didn't want to spoil the moment by falling out, but he had to ask. 'Since Chapin's found my accommodation, why didn't you forward the note to me at the hostel?'

The man had the decency to look embarrassed. 'You've got to understand, we regard those notes as being for folk who don't want to be found. You're the first person I've ever had come looking. We put the notes in the bottom drawer and every now and then we clear it out and it starts again.'

Had he not been in such a joyous mood, Sam would have taken the man to task, but his top priority was to get a bath, have his hair cut and take his best shirt to the Chinese laundry. He made to leave and had reached the top of the stairs when he turned back and to the man's surprise, he handed him a dollar and said, 'Maybe this will encourage you to follow up some of those notes in future.' He was well gratified by the look of complete surprise on the man's face.

* * *

The congregation was halfway through the first hymn when Kitty caught sight of Sam sitting across the aisle to her left. He was wearing the shirt she'd made for him and was looking unusually neat and tidy. He'd recently had his hair cut. Their eyes met and locked. Kitty felt herself short of breath. She wanted to wave, to make a physical sign that she'd seen him, but she knew he'd seen her by the happiness in his eyes. He lifted his chin slightly and grinned.

Kitty had a thousand things she wanted to ask. He must have got the note from Chapin's, after all. Was he well? Where was he living? Was he in employment? She'd promised her father they would not speak. Would he send her a note? She kicked herself for not having prepared one herself, but in her heart she'd decided he would not to be there again. How happy she was now she'd been so wrong!

The service went on forever, or so it seemed. At the end, during the organ voluntary as the priest and his entourage walked down the aisle, she looked across at Sam again. He had disappeared. She felt a sense of panic, but she just knew he wouldn't go without coming close to her.

As she came out into the street she saw him standing across the road, but she had to wait for several carriages to pass before she could cross over to him. She wanted him to embrace her, but he put a finger over his lips indicating she was not to speak.

He handed her an envelope. 'I don't want you to break your vow to your father. Our relationship must be based on honesty. All you need to know is in this letter. I've missed you.' And then he was gone.

Kitty stumbled into the nearest coffee shop and, savouring a moment she'd dreamt about, made herself wait until her coffee had arrived.

Dearest Kitty,
I received your note only yesterday when I called at Chapin's and made enquiries. I am staying at the Christian

Hostel and working at Muller's Fine Felt Hat Emporium as a clerk. The best news is that I have been offered a maintenance managerial position. It is quite a story how I got the position and I look forward to telling you all about it. I hope this will go some way to proving to your father that I am a conscientious worker with prospects.

Regarding the matter of a sense of purpose, I have two goals. One is to be able to set up my own household repair-and-building business using the contacts I will be making at Muller's, and the second, and most important goal, is to have you by my side in the years to come.

I will be here next Sunday. The days until then will seem endless.

Yours affectionately,
Sam.

Kitty wanted to skip all the way home like a ten-year-old, so happy was she in her heart. Sam had been so pleased to see her, even more than pleased, and he looked well. It was the first time she'd seen him out of his digger's uniform and he'd looked so handsome. How was she going to get through the evening and breakfast with her father without telling him she and Sam had found each other?

If Frank noticed Kitty was distracted during supper, he didn't mention it. He'd had a busy day in the barbershop and pulled several teeth, and was content to enjoy a quiet evening reading the newspaper. Kitty excused herself, saying she needed an early night.

When she was ready for bed, she knelt and prayed.

Dear Lord, thank you for this day and for the food we eat. Thank you also for enabling me to find Sam again, and please look down on us with love and kindness. Amen.

CHAPTER FORTY-FOUR

Kitty was nervous; it was the anniversary of Ma's death, with all the potential of becoming a strident day. She wished she'd someone to talk to. They had acquaintances in the city, but she didn't have any real friends and no family. Making friends in the city was hard. People were just passing through, or else stayed a year or two and moved on. Those intending to be permanent residents were busy establishing themselves. She too was building up her business, keeping ladies like Mrs Clancy appropriately clad.

When Pa appeared for breakfast in his Sunday best, Kitty's heart sank. She'd kept the day clear of fittings so she could shadow him, but he was accomplished at giving her the slip.

'I think we should visit Ma today, don't you?' she said.

Frank nodded. 'We'll go this morning, and then I have business to attend to.'

'I thought we could take a ride on one of the pleasure boats in the Bay. It's not often we spend time together.'

Frank looked out of the window at the building opposite, where lamps were being lit as the occupants began their day.

'It'll be chilly on the boats today. I'll think about it.'

'We can wrap up warm and it will be a nice way of remembering Ma. She'd be happy knowing we spent her anniversary day together doing something like that.'

'Hmm. We'll see.'

Kitty knew full well that 'we'll see' meant 'no'. She'd have to think of some other way to keep Pa by her side after they'd visited Ma's grave.

✤ ✤ ✤

Kitty thought every cemetery bleak, and her opinion hadn't changed. With the heavy rain the previous day, her ma's headstone was streaked with dirt. Frank watched as Kitty pulled out the handkerchief she always kept tucked up her sleeve and, with a few strokes, cleaned the memorial stone. It wasn't perfect, but definitely easier to read.

Frank put his arm around her. 'You're a grand lass to me, Kitty. I don't know what I'd do without you.'

'Nor me without you,' said Kitty, leaning in towards him.

They recited the Lord's Prayer aloud, as they did every time they visited, and then arranged some flowers on the grave. Frank gave a brief speech about what had happened since he'd last visited, finishing with, 'Our Kitty is such a joy.'

They were about to leave when Kitty heard a rumble. The ground began to shake beneath her feet.

'Quake, Pa,' she said, taking hold of her father's hand. The rumbling and shaking lasted no longer than ten or twelve seconds, but it frightened her and she held Frank's hand tightly until the sound receded and the ground grew still. To add to her unease, they were alone in the graveyard, with only the dead for company. Kitty had been taught that when the last trump sounded, all the tombs would open, and the dead would rise up. It was not a comforting thought at that moment, considering where they were, and a shiver ran down her spine.

It was silly, but she felt the quake was a sign from Ma that there was unfinished business at the graveside, and they were to stay until it was resolved. Kitty knew instinctively what her ma was willing her to do: she was to speak with her father about Sam. If she didn't say they'd found each other, the path ahead would be strewn with lies, and such subterfuge was not in her nature.

An oft-quoted saying of her mother's came to mind: 'Every decision I've made with my head I've regretted, and every decision I've made with my heart has taken me down the correct path.'

Remembering these words, and trusting her heart, Kitty said, 'Pa. I've been trying to find Sam Gray, because I love him.'

A short silence followed her declaration, during which time Kitty thought she'd made a mistake and that her father was going to explode, but he didn't.

He looked at her with what she read as resignation in his eyes. 'If, and only if, he's making something of his new life and isn't jobless and aimless, I will meet with him. I am prepared to give him another chance for the sake of your happiness.'

Kitty explained how they had seen each other at the cathedral, but not spoken, that Sam had passed her a note telling her about his managerial position and that he was staying at the Christian hostel. Frank looked interested when she mentioned the managerial position.

'It seems he is trying to win me over. You may invite him to afternoon tea next Sunday if you wish.'

If she wished? Kitty was ecstatic. *Everything can be mended, I'm sure of it now.* She would send a note to the hostel that very evening.

With that they walked away from the grave hand in hand. When they reached the cemetery gates, to Kitty's surprise, Frank said, 'Perhaps we should go on that boat ride after all. I'm all dressed up and nowhere to go.'

Sam was preparing to leave Muller's, as it was his half day, when he was called in to the 'inner sanctum' to see Mr Hans who was sitting in his father's chair, behind his desk. *Herr Muller Senior must have returned*, thought Sam.

'Please take a seat,' said Mr Hans. He picked up a pen and began fiddling with it, which Sam took as not a good omen.

'I have spoken with my father about the position of maintenance manager and, while he thinks the idea has potential, he is not prepared to offer it at the moment.' He paused, before adding, 'I'm very sorry. I expect you're disappointed, as am I.'

Sam's heart sank with a much greater sense of disappointment than he thought possible. It hadn't occurred to him Herr Muller Senior would not see the financial advantages he could bring the company.

'I see,' was all he could find to say.

'I should have checked with my father first,' Mr Hans went on. 'But the idea, to me, seemed such a sound one.'

'I agree, and it would save the company, at the very least, the inconvenience of things breaking down or falling apart during quakes.'

'You are right. I will continue to suggest such a position in the hope of changing his mind.'

That's that then. Sam got up to leave. Even though Mr Hans had made it clear at the time that the offer required Herr Muller's approval, it seemed so unfair to have had his hopes raised, only for the offer to be withdrawn.

'I really do think you should have the boiler serviced, if nothing else,' he said.

'I will see it is done. Thank you. And again, I'm sorry. I feel this personally.'

Despite the huge disappointment, Sam didn't hold any grudge towards Hans. He was young, like himself, and had been caught up in the moment, while Herr Muller was old and set in his ways. Sam only regretted allowing himself the luxury of thinking too far into the future. He'd imagined a maintenance job at Muller's would quickly lead to him meeting useful suppliers and making contacts which would stand him in good stead for setting up his own business. Frank would be impressed with his being a manager and he would be able to ask Kitty to marry him.

Those dreams now lay in tatters and, despite Hans Muller saying he would continue fighting Sam's corner, he had little hope things would change.

At the hostel, Kitty's invitation was waiting for him. He read the contents and grimaced. *The final nail in my coffin. Frank will be expecting to entertain a maintenance manager, but he'll be getting a lowly clerk.* He swore under his breath. It was going to be a difficult afternoon tea.

Sam was surprised at how nervous he felt as he waited on the Muldoons' doorstep, but so much depended on the afternoon going well.

Kitty answered the door and peered at him. 'You look a bit pale. Are you all right?'

'It's been a cold walk. There's a breeze coming in off the Bay and it's got right into my bones.'

She took his hands in hers and rubbed them vigorously. 'We'll soon warm you up. We've a cosy welcome for you. Pa lit the fire just before dinner and it's well bedded in.'

Sam wondered whether he should tell her there and then that the job offer had been revoked, but decided it was better he tell her and Frank at the same time. It was hardly his fault, but he knew it wasn't going to bode well for Frank's opinion of him.

Kitty led the way upstairs. When Frank didn't rise from his chair by the fire, Sam knew he was still on probation.

There was some general chit-chat about the weather and the traffic on Market Street while Kitty saw to the tea. Then, when they were settled, Frank said, 'Kitty tells me you're working at Muller's as their maintenance manager.'

Sam winced inside. 'That's not quite right now. I was offered it and accepted, but I'm sorry to say that's no longer correct.'

Frank's face fell and he leaned forward in his chair. 'Would you like to explain yourself?'

Sam glanced at Kitty, who looked taken by surprise. 'The position was offered to me by Mr Hans Muller while his father, Herr Muller Senior, was away. On his return on Friday, I was told Herr Muller had not agreed.'

'Someone else has been offered the job?' asked Kitty, looking from Sam to her father.

'No. Herr Muller doesn't want a maintenance manager. Thinks they don't need one.' Sam went on to say how short-sighted he thought it, and how it was only storing up trouble down the road. While he talked, Frank listened in silence, neither nodding nor shaking his head. Sam could see he was annoyed.

'You're still working at Muller's, though, aren't you?' asked Kitty.

'Aye, I am.'

'Maybe Herr Muller will change his mind?'

'Mr Hans said he would try and persuade him to do so.'

Frank grunted. 'Don't pin your hopes on that,' he said, in a growly voice. 'Sounds to me as if young Mr Muller stepped out of his station. It's clear the old man is in charge. I take it we can assume that you have been telling the truth about the offer?'

Kitty gasped, and Sam's jaw dropped. 'Why would I lie about something so important?'

'I can think of a good reason.' Frank looked across at Kitty. 'My daughter.'

'I've told the truth, but I see you still have a poor opinion of me.'

'These are the thoughts of a caring, loving father. You will surely allow me such? After all, your trustworthiness has been suspect before.'

Sam stood up. 'I suggest, sir, you make an appointment to see Mr Hans Muller and he will confirm everything I have said.'

'Pa,' said Kitty, 'Give Sam a second chance. Please.'

Frank sighed. 'You wanted to make something of yourself in San Francisco, young man, and so far your efforts are somewhat lacking.'

'Pa, no, it's not Sam's fault the job was withdrawn.'

Ignoring Kitty's plea, Frank went on, 'If you are the man my daughter seems to think you are, then you must prove it to me.'

Feeling any further conversation would be strained and awkward, Sam took his leave. Kitty, pale and shaking, saw him out.

'I'm so sorry. I don't know what got into him. I think he may be working up to one of his strident days. You'll keep going to Mass, won't you? So I can see you until we work things out?'

Sam nodded. He was angry at Frank's unjust treatment, but he didn't want to upset Kitty further. He bent and gave her a kiss on the cheek. 'I'll do my best.'

'I know you're trying. The city can be a hard place.'

'Thank you for your vote of confidence.'

CHAPTER FORTY-FIVE

Two difficult weeks passed slowly for Sam, broken only by snatched sightings and brief conversations with Kitty at the cathedral. On Monday December 6th he arrived at work to be called in to see Herr Muller.

'There is a problem,' said Herr Muller.

'There is?'

'The boiler-room roof is leaking.' He looked expectantly at Sam. 'You can fix it?'

Sam took a deep breath. 'Herr Muller, I am a clerk. I don't do roof repairs.'

Herr Muller frowned. 'You are an employee. You work for me.'

'Indeed, I do, but as a clerk.'

'You fixed the windows? Put the glass in?'

Sam nodded. 'I did that because I wanted to help in an emergency, but I'm not employed to do maintenance.' He wasn't going to be taken advantage of.

Herr Muller made a loud grunting sound. 'I say again, you are the employee, you do as I say.'

Sam had a vision of his money sitting in the bank, money he'd sweated for and earned by true graft. He didn't have to stay. He could support himself and there would be other jobs eventually. 'And I say again to you Herr Muller, I am employed here as a clerk.'

Herr Muller's mouth dropped open and he rattled off a long sentence in German which Sam didn't understand, but thought it probably contained oaths. 'You speak to me like this knowing I am your boss man?'

'Herr Muller, I am either a clerk or the maintenance manager. I do not do both.'

Herr Muller stood up and pointed to the door. 'You are fired,' he said, pronouncing the word as 'fire-red'. 'Take your things and go.'

Back in the clerks' office, Sam took his coat and hat from their peg. The two clerks stopped what they were doing and began looking from him to their supervisor.

'Where are you going?' asked Mr Bradden in a curious, rather than reprimanding voice.

'I'm collecting my belongings. I've been fire-red.'

Mr Bradden's jaw dropped. 'He's let you go?'

'Aye. He wanted me to mend the boiler-house roof. I told him I'm employed as a clerk, not a maintenance man.'

Mr Bradden raised both hands up to the sky in an exasperated gesture. 'I find someone who is good at their job and they are fired. Can't you wait until Mr Hans arrives? I'm sure he can smooth this over.'

'Herr Muller has fired me. I have never asked a great deal of my employers, but I do ask for respect.'

'Please allow me to speak with Mr Hans.'

'You're welcome to discuss the matter with him, but I don't see much point.'

'Mr Hans and Herr Muller do not always see eye to eye, that's a truth, but if you require a reference, I'm sure Mr Hans will give you one.'

'Thank you, I appreciate that, but I'd like my wages. Can you arrange this for me?'

'Of course, but you understand I have to check with Herr Muller first, although I see no problem.'

Sam thanked Mr Bradden, said he would call back in a day or two for the money owed him, and, putting on his coat, he turned and bade adieu to his fellow workers, who both said they were sorry to see him go.

* * *

If anyone had asked Sam at breakfast the next day which route he'd taken, in the two hours he'd walked from Muller's to reach the hostel, he couldn't have told them. He had set off to walk and his body had automatically swerved to avoid colliding with people. He had crossed roads with no conscious thought of checking the traffic, yet he must have done, for he returned to the hostel unscathed. His mind had been focused only upon his conversation with Herr Muller, and he went over and over it.

To an outsider he must seem hot-headed, impulsive and foolish, but it really had been the last straw. To refuse him the job, then expect him to undertake the duties anyway. And one maintenance job would have opened the door for more, making it never-ending. No, he'd made the right decision. To have buckled down would have been weak and he would have looked back and hated himself for agreeing to be put upon.

Sleep cleared his mind sufficiently for him to be able to carry out the important task he had set himself for the day – to see Kitty and tell her what had happened.

He waited until ten o'clock. Kitty answered the door. She was startled to see him.

'You're in luck. Pa's gone to make a house call on an elderly lady with bad toothache. I'm afraid he's still frosty towards you, but he knows I've seen you at the cathedral. I'll make us a coffee. I'm just seeing to some mending.'

It pained Sam's heart to find her so welcoming and full of good spirits, knowing he was about to deliver devastating news likely to force them apart.

Kitty tidied up some papers. 'I'll move these and you can sit in Pa's chair. You'll have to give it up, of course, if he comes back.' She was looking at him with such bright eyes he had to look away. She didn't seem to notice his discomfort and began chatting about one of her clients.

Sam lifted a hand to interrupt her. 'I need to speak with you.'

'Well, you're here and I'm listening. You look very serious. Has someone died?' She laughed, but when he didn't take up her laughter her face fell. 'What is it?'

Sam wanted to linger and savour the moment when all was well, but the time had come. He must tell her what had happened, no matter how much he didn't want to.

'Yesterday I was forced to resign from Muller's. It was a question of principle.' He didn't tell her he was fired, because in his mind he wasn't. He'd been forced to resign for peace of mind and self-respect.

Kitty stared at him, her eyes wide, as if disbelieving the words she was hearing. 'I don't understand. Why would you do that?'

He gave a short account of what had happened, ending with, 'I expect this changes everything between us. Your father won't take well to this news.'

Kitty bit her thumbnail. 'No, he won't. This is all too, too awful.'

'But you wouldn't want to marry a weak person who won't stand up for what he believes is right for himself or his family. Would you? Perhaps you can put this point to your father.'

'I know you're not weak and I admire your stand, but Pa won't see it that way.'

She began to cry and Sam took her in his arms. She sobbed against him for a few minutes then drew away.

'You... You must go. You can't be here when Pa returns. I have to tell him and you mustn't be here when I do.' She cast a glance at their mantel-clock. 'You must leave, right now.' She picked up his coat and hat and thrust them at him. 'I'll do what I can, but he's going to be angry.'

Outside in the street, hurrying away so he wouldn't encounter Frank on his way home, Sam was despondent. If Frank forbade any further contact between him and Kitty, he had a lot of thinking to do about what to do next.

CHAPTER FORTY-SIX

Sam slept badly and woke with tired, dry eyes, wondering how he was going to fill his day. He should prepare himself for some sort of confrontation with Frank. Although a face-to-face meeting was more daunting than the receipt of a written communication, he would at least be able to put his case. He was making his way back from a bland breakfast when the hostel superintendent approached him at the bottom of the main stairwell.

'Mr Gray, there's a gentleman to see you. A Mr Muldoon. He's waiting in my office.'

Sam thanked him and, with a sudden sinking feeling in his stomach, made his way to the wood-panelled room near the hostel entrance. It was the only room in the building with any claim to grandeur.

Frank was standing facing the door, with his back to the superintendent's desk. He was still wearing his hat and holding his black leather gloves in his right hand. He began speaking the moment Sam entered the room.

'Before we begin, there is no use in your trying to defend yourself. With all your fine talk about being a maintenance manager and having a purpose in life, I see now you have duped us both. You are nothing but a drifter and a wastrel. For all your supposed goodness and ability you have been unable to keep even a position as lowly as a clerk.'

'But I am a good and honest work –'

Frank scowled. 'Allow me to finish. You have duped us and others and I have no doubt you will pass through the rest of your life in a similar fashion.'

'As I say, I am a good worker and an honest one and –'

'It is pointless speaking. My ears are closed to your entreaties.'

'I have strong Christian principles –'

'Enough.' A whip-like sound ran round the room as Frank slapped his hand with his gloves. 'You will make no attempt to contact my daughter again or to attend our premises. Neither will you approach her in a public place such as St Mary's Cathedral. I thank the Lord you have finally been unequivocally unmasked as a wastrel in time for me to protect her. Good day, sir.'

Every one of Frank's verbal slurs found its mark, and because they were so unjust, their pain was greater than had his remarks been true. Sam comforted himself a little with the thought that a lesser man would have hurled insults back at Frank regarding his strident days and their effect on Kitty, but he was glad – if not, in fact, proud of himself – that he had not stooped to such a low level.

❈ ❈ ❈

Five days passed and Sam, rarely rising from a deep pit of despair following his confrontation with Frank, was only able to manage a half-hearted attitude towards finding new employment. He thought a lot about his future and decided to seek out Billy.

As usual, Billy was busy with the warehouse.

'I just need half an hour,' Sam said. 'Can you find that for me?'

'If you give me fifteen minutes to see these casks stored. I've to collect funds from the auctioneers. We can walk there together.'

It was more like half an hour before Billy was free and they set off to walk south towards Market Street.

'What can I do for you?' asked Billy. 'You've something on your mind. What is it?'

'Not to mince words, I want to come with you when you leave for New Zealand.'

Billy stopped and turned to look at him. 'I wasn't expecting that. What's brought this on? It's a bit sudden, isn't it?'

Sam related how he'd lost his job and the consequential events.

'Arguing with the boss usually ends in a firing, so you can't be surprised at that. And Muldoon is protecting his daughter.'

'I'm not surprised at either of their responses. My plan for here, or you could call it my dream, was to set myself up in my own business. Instead, I've been beholden to an employer who doesn't respect me, my savings are not being put to good use, the father of the girl I'd hoped to marry has banished me from their presence, and if truth be told, San Francisco is nothing like I thought it would be. In fact, at no other time have I felt so miserable, with no prospect of happiness.'

'I can understand how you feel, but I can't help feeling you haven't given yourself, or the city, a chance. I really mean that. You've only been here, what? Two and a half months at most?'

Sam nodded and they began walking again, dodging their way between workers and ladies with furled umbrellas.

Halting at a junction, waiting for a gap in the traffic, Billy said, 'There's no guarantee you'll fit in in New Zealand any better than you fit in here, you know.'

'Third time lucky. Canada, America and then New Zealand.'

'I don't reckon there's much truth in that "best of three" saying. You're restless and disappointed. It'll pass. Trust me.'

Sam stepped to one side to avoid a boy pushing a wide barrow. 'You moved *your* family from England to here, then on to Auckland. Surely you can understand better than most why I'm asking if I can come with you? From what I've heard, New Zealand is pretty much like where I come from, and I'm prepared to take the risk of settling in. Can't be worse than here.'

Billy took his cap off and scratched his head. 'Well, if that's the case, and you're absolutely certain, my friend, you are more than welcome to sail with me. I can put a word in for you with the ship's captain and sound him out. I've other business to see him about. We leave January 12th. A new year, a new start. Can you get your things in order in that time?'

Sam gave a hollow laugh. 'That's easy. I've not set down any roots, so there's nothing to dig up. I've only myself to please,' he said ruefully.

'It's a month before we leave and you've no job. What will you do? Use your savings?'

'I want to pick up casual work. Do you know anyone who's hiring?'

Billy shook his head. 'Not off hand, but I can ask around. If something comes up, I'll send word to the hostel.'

Sam spent the rest of the day thinking of the past and mulling over whether things might have been different if he'd had Kitty to show him around, or Frank to support him. He was now exactly where he'd begun that first day – walking the streets, his nose wrinkling from the city odours, looking for 'Help Wanted' notices. No use going to Chapin's this time. They didn't do short-term employment.

CHAPTER FORTY-SEVEN

After another fruitless morning looking for casual work, Sam decided he should write to the few people that might want to hear from him. He hadn't written to his family in Cumberland since he was in Colville in May, and the only letter he'd written in Harrison was to Stag, via Tug.

After three attempts writing to his folks, Sam leaned back in his chair and put his pen down. There was no way round the fact he'd broken his contract with the Hudson's Bay Company and deserted for the goldfields, and he knew his family wouldn't understand why. He screwed up the paper, put it to one side and picked up a fresh sheet.

December 14th San Francisco

Dear Stag,

I write to let you know I am now in San Francisco. My time in the goldfields was worthwhile and I have no regrets on that score. I have enough put by to begin a household repair business.

San Francisco is not proving to be what I expected. I have been here two months and not settled. I think city life is not for me. I have met up with Billy Botcher and decided to go on to New Zealand, where I think I will feel more at home. His family are there and we leave early January.

I will always appreciate your support leaving Victoria. I could not have managed without you.

My best wishes to the family and for your business,

Sam

Later that evening a note came from Billy.

I may have work for you. Call tomorrow by eight.

Whatever the work was, Sam was keen to take it. The wage would be welcome and, more importantly, it would keep him busy.

❄ ❄ ❄

Billy was overseeing some orders and instructing his staff when Sam arrived at ten minutes to eight.

Billy beckoned Sam over. 'Good, you got my message.' He pointed to a cart laden with boxes. 'While I was with the auctioneer yesterday, I put in a bid for some excess stock from the Eastern States.'

'Excess stock?'

'Merchants importing stock with no immediate buyer have three options: transport it to another city, store it or auction it on the wharf.'

'I'm guessing storage is expensive.'

'There's a shortage of lumber and that's led to a shortage of suitable places to store. Anyways, I saw this cutlery going cheap. I've a pitch in a warehouse courtyard I sometimes rent. Do you want a go?'

'Like a market trader?' Sam rubbed his thumb along his forehead. 'I'll give it a try.'

'You'll soon learn how to sweet-talk buyers. I'm in debt for twenty-four dollars for the dozen boxes. I'll provide the stock and you can keep twenty percent on sales. I'll lend you one of my lads for half an hour to help you get set up, then you're on your own.' He pulled a note from his pocket and handed it to Sam. 'I've priced up for you, but I leave it to you to negotiate. Get what you can.'

'When do you want me to start?'

'You can roll your sleeves up right now if you've a mind to.'

Sam didn't hesitate. Within half an hour he was walking behind Billy's lad, who was pushing the cart, on their way to set up. While the lad unloaded the boxes, Sam paid the pitch rental. He gave the lad a dime and he vanished promptly, leaving the cart.

The top layer of each box consisted of two fancy boxes of top-quality cutlery, grand enough to be labelled 'canteens'. With his stall set up, Sam needed to get rid of the cheap sets; they were taking up too much room for little profit. Better to have the good and medium quality well displayed. He piled three cheap sets in one corner and wrote out a notice in big block capitals.

THE WHOLE LOT FOR $4

A gentleman passing by offered him three dollars.

'Three dollars fifty,' said Sam.

The man frowned and picked up a spoon to examine it more closely. 'It's only worth three twenty-five.'

Since he'd only just set up his pitch, Sam repeated his earlier price, and the man took them.

Sam sold two more cheap sets in job lots. As the morning progressed, he realised quality and cheap were the sellers. At midday he reduced the price of the medium sets to one dollar seventy-five.

CHAPTER FORTY-EIGHT

While Sam was writing out labels reducing the price of the medium-quality canteens, Kitty was on her way home after delivering some lace petticoats for Mrs Clancy's daughters. Pa had said she could approach the Adelphi Theatre costume department, as it was a 'respectable establishment' of entertainment. Kitty had struck lucky there the previous week, having knocked on the stage door with some samples and been given three orders.

As she walked up Kearny Street, thinking about the dancing gals in Harrison and how cheerful they'd always been, Kitty gave a start. A commercial cart was unloading outside a household store. It was just like all the hundreds of other horse-driven carts clogging up the city's streets, but painted on the side was 'Billy Botcher, Purveyor of General Goods'. Kitty caught her breath. An idea came into her head, but she'd have to move quickly.

The delivery man moved to the rear of the cart and

lifted and secured the tailgate. It was clear he was about to leave. Kitty came to her senses and by the time the driver had got into his seat and picked up the reins, she'd run forward and placed a hand on the horse's bridle.

'Watch out, miss, he's lively,' the driver called out.

Having gained his attention, Kitty let go of the bridle. 'Can you tell me where Billy Botcher's store is?'

'It's a warehouse. We don't sell direct to the public.'

'You misunderstand me. It's Billy I want to meet.'

The delivery man raised his eyebrows. 'The boss? He's at Commercial Street.'

'Are you going there now?'

The driver nodded. He'd a kindly face and he was looking at Kitty with interest.

'Can I come with you?' she asked.

He hesitated and looked at the seat beside him, which was covered with dusty jute-sacking and bits of twine.

'I don't mind sitting on the sacking, and I won't be any trouble.'

'It's not far so I guess it's all right.' He picked up the sacking and threw it over his shoulder into the empty cart. 'You'd better hop up.'

*** * * ***

Kitty understood why she'd never noticed Billy's warehouse before – it was well off the beaten track. Three men were outside working. They looked at her with interest and one doffed his cap.

The delivery man shouted out, 'This lady's looking for the boss.'

'He's in his office,' said one of the men. He stepped forward and held out a hand to help Kitty get down. 'Who shall I say is here to see him?'

'Miss Muldoon. He's not expecting me.'

Kitty's legs began to tremble. So much depended on whether Sam had talked to Billy as a friend and, even more so, on what he had said. Her thoughts were broken by the sound of a man's voice. She turned to see a welcoming grin on the face of the man walking towards her.

'Miss Muldoon, delighted to meet you.' Billy gave a little bow.

'I'm a friend of Sam Gray's. I think you know him.'

'I know who you are. Please, come out of the cold.'

Kitty felt a warm glow inside. *He knows of me, which must mean Sam's spoken about me.*

Billy's office was a glassed-in area in the corner of what Kitty could see was a well-stocked warehouse. He picked up some papers that were strewn across a hoop-backed chair and bade her sit, while he took his place behind a distressed-oak desk piled high with what looked like invoices.

'Let me begin, Miss Muldoon, by saying any friend of Sam's is a friend of mine.'

'Thank you, Mr Botcher.'

'Call me Billy, please, everyone does.'

'I will if you'll call me Kitty?'

Billy pushed some of the invoices to one side. It was a businesslike gesture, indicating to Kitty the social niceties of their meeting were at an end. 'What can I do for you?'

'I saw your cart and…I just want to know if Sam is all

right. There was a dreadful argument and my father has forbidden me ever to see him.'

Her eyes filled with tears and she fumbled for her handkerchief. Billy waited until she'd composed herself.

'I have to tell you things are at a very low ebb for him right now,' he said. 'So low, he's booked and paid for a passage for New Zealand, to leave the first week in January.'

'New Zealand?' Kitty felt her mind and body go into shock. 'Why would he do that?'

'I can only say he has no job, no wish to stay in a city which hasn't welcomed him and – if you will allow me to say this – he's given up hope of settling down with you after your da gave him that good talking-to.'

Kitty felt the colour drain from her face. 'I thought he'd love the city, but as soon as we docked, everything went wrong.'

Billy shrugged. 'Not everyone likes it here. My own family are in New Zealand. I'm assuming it's your pa who's against Sam, and not you?'

'My feelings for Sam are as strong as ever. Unlike Pa, I have faith in him still. He worked so hard in the goldfields and I know if…' She corrected herself. '*When* he finds the right position, he'll make a success of his life.'

'I've set him up with a temporary stall selling goods. When he brings the takings this evening I'd like to tell him you'll be waiting for him in Portsmouth Square next Sunday afternoon, so you can sort your lives out. This New Zealand idea is not in keeping with the Sam I've known since four years back. He's running away from temporary pain and he needs to be made to see that. I know he'll stay for *you* if you ask him. At the moment he feels everything is hopeless. Only you can give him the hope he needs to do the right thing and stay.'

'Do you think he's too hurt to want to stay?'

'You can at least suggest he postpone for a few months. See how things work out. Will you try? I'm asking for the two of you.'

'Please tell him I'll be there at half past two.'

* * *

The winter daylight was beginning to fade and Sam was packing up. He had a small sense of satisfaction, having sold well over half the contents of the boxes, including several of the quality canteens. In his own eyes he'd done a reasonable job for a complete beginner. He'd learned a thing or two by striking up a camaraderie with the man on the next-door table, and they'd covered each other's unavoidable breaks. He'd listened to his neighbour and picked up some of his sales patter, noting that a liberal use of 'you're welcome' seemed to be obligatory. He expected Billy would be satisfied with his efforts.

But what Billy had to say took all thought of his takings from Sam's mind. His friend ignored the box of cash on his desk and opened with the astonishing news that Kitty had turned up at his warehouse to see him. Sam barely knew how to answer as he heard him out. 'You'll be at Portsmouth Square, won't you?' Billy said, handing him his commission for the day. 'You have to talk to her and explain why you're going to New Zealand. You owe her that.'

Sam hardly dared allow himself to hope. 'I'll be there.'

CHAPTER FORTY-NINE

Sam arrived early at Portsmouth Square, which was busy with folk wrapped up against the damp, greeting each other and stopping to pass the time of day. A flag waved erratically in the wind on a central flagpole, and to the east, looking out towards the wharves, the ships' masts fought for space.

When he saw Kitty walking towards him with a welcoming smile, Sam's heart leapt. She was wearing a pretty bonnet trimmed with rabbit fur which he thought had probably, at some time, passed through Muller's Emporium.

Sam took her hand in his. They were both wearing gloves, but he could feel her fingers moving within them and, he thought, she would be able to feel his.

They found a bench sheltered from the breeze drifting in off the Bay and sat for a short while in silence, holding hands. It was enough they were together.

Kitty was first to speak, voicing the subject that was

top of both their thoughts. 'Are you really going to New Zealand?'

'I've made arrangements to leave next month.'

'Arrangements that can be changed?'

'Why would I want to stay here when I can't have you by my side? It'll be agony knowing you're breathing the same air yet out of reach. What about Frank? I may have retained *your* heart but Frank has given up on me forever.'

'Don't hold his protective fatherly views against him. He just wants the best for me.'

'I understand, I really do. You're his only child and all he's got, and he wants to know there's someone to look after you when he's gone. Someone dependable. Someone with prospects.'

'When we were in Harrison, we talked one day of living in a place you loved without the one you loved. Do you remember?'

Sam remembered the conversation clearly. 'And we talked about living in a place you don't love with someone you do love.'

Kitty nodded. 'Can you do that?'

'You're talking about me staying here.' Sam paused and looked out across the square before answering. Then, not wanting to let the moment pass for him to lay his cards on the table, and speaking gently, he said, 'I think what you're really asking me is do I love you enough to stay and make this our home?'

Kitty blushed and fiddled with her gloves. 'Well, do you?'

'Of course I do, but –'

'But? But what?' Kitty made a sharp turn to look directly into his eyes.

'I've to prove I am what I say I am – honest and hard-working. And not just for Frank's benefit, but for my own self-respect.'

Kitty looked down at her gloves. 'You don't need to prove yourself to me. I'll accept the restless, jobless Englishman with no prospects who is sitting here beside me, and whom I've fallen hopelessly in love with.'

'You will?' Sam lifted her hand, removed her glove, and kissed her fingers, for a moment unable to speak. It seemed the future he'd thought he'd lost forever was tantalisingly close, after all – to have a strong partner in life who loved him, and whose love he reciprocated fully.

'I see three tasks before me,' he said, holding both her hands in his.

'Three?'

'To find gainful employment and to win over your pa, and at the same time to learn to see the city through your eyes.'

'No one can say you don't have a sense of purpose now, and I can help with finding the real San Francisco. Tomorrow you can go to Chapin's and find a job with prospects.'

Kitty was making it all sound so easy. Of the three obstacles – finding permanent employment, settling in to the city and gaining Frank's respect – Sam knew which was the biggest.

✻ ✻ ✻

The next morning Sam was at Chapin's as soon as they opened. It was the same young lad he'd seen on his first day.

'I'm sorry, Mr Gray, but there's not much happening now until after Christmas.'

'There must be some businesses hiring?'

'Some retailers are taking on extra staff, but you say you want something permanent and, with you having left Muller's under what seems to have been a bit of a cloud, it won't be easy to find you a position.'

'I have a reference.'

'Sometimes people write glowing references to get rid of folk.'

'That's not the case with me, I can assure you.'

The clerk took a pencil from behind his ear and made some notes. 'If you leave things with me, I'll make some enquiries.'

Sam stood up to go. 'When shall I call again?'

Without looking up, the clerk said, 'I'll contact you at the hostel if something turns up.'

Sam took that as a dismissal and made his way downstairs.

Despite his disappointment, out in the street he took a moment to look at his surroundings with a more open mind than previously. Ignoring the people, the smells, and the sounds of the passing traffic, he took in the fine buildings with fresh eyes. There was a dignity and strength about them, a solidity that indicated the city had put down strong roots in the soil upon which it stood. Perhaps he had been too hasty to overlook such grandeur. He set forth for Botcher's Stores.

✳ ✳ ✳

Billy, all ears about Sam's meeting with Kitty the previous day, offered Sam another day's work for Friday.

'I'm sorry I can't offer you more, but things are a bit slow now until the New Year, and I'm winding down a few operations to make the business simpler to run while I'm away. I guess you're rethinking leaving now your love life's picked up?'

'My life is in a state of flux right now on all fronts.'

'Flux or not, San Francisco, from where I'm sitting, looks a better bet for you than it did last week. You can always come to New Zealand later if it don't work out for you and Kitty. But if you're not planning on coming with me next month, you'd best withdraw now or you'll lose your deposit.'

'I'll do that.'

'How are you getting on at that hostel?'

'It's a place to lay my head.'

'I'm thinking when I leave next month, Rosie'll have a spare room while I'm gone. I can ask her if you can have it at a fair rent. Might be a bit more than the hostel, but it'll be a lot homelier. You'll have a room to yourself with a warm bed, company of all ages and home-cooked grub, and I'll know Rosie's got a trustworthy man looking out for her while I'm away.'

'I'll leap at it if you think she'll be all right with that.'

'I can but ask. She'll appreciate the rent, that's for sure.'

The thought that Rosie might welcome him as a paying guest gladdened Sam's heart. He left to cancel his New Zealand passage. How different his life seemed now to the dark days when he'd thought of leaving forever.

* * *

Kitty was busy adding festive à la mode touches to old ball gowns and making new Christmas ones for show gals. Pa had relented over 'respectable establishments', but still wouldn't entertain any of these clients at the barbershop.

In the meantime, Sam was finding it hard to remain positive about his employment prospects. As he walked the streets alone, looking for work, sometimes he chastised himself for having been too quick to leave Muller's. He yearned for Kitty's company; he thrived on her optimism that there must be opportunities for him in the city, if only he could find them or they find him.

CHAPTER FIFTY

On Thursday December 23nd everything changed. A letter for Sam from Hans Muller arrived at the hostel, dated the previous day.

Dear Mr Gray,

My Compliments of the Christmas Season to you and I trust this letter finds you in good health.

I appreciate your feelings towards Muller & Company may well be tinged with some umbrage and deservedly so. However, I am writing to offer you the full-time position of maintenance manager for the company workshop. Since you were so hastily dismissed, there have been several occasions when your services would have been much appreciated. As a result, my father has realised he made a grave error of judgement and he is prepared to apologise for this. If you are not already suitably and gainfully employed, perhaps you will consider this offer to return to us at a salary commensurate with the skills you possess - a rise of ten percent on your previous wage.

I shall be at the offices tomorrow (the 23rd) and the next day, when I will be happy to receive you without the necessity of you making an appointment.

Yours, in truth and trust,
Hans Muller.

Sam read the letter twice, then, being alone, read it aloud, just to make sure he'd interpreted it correctly. Addressing himself, he said, 'To think Muller's are now coming to *me* cap in hand. This is a turnaround.'

Judging by the tone of the letter Hans Muller was on his side. He imagined the loud exchanges in German that must have occurred on those 'several occasions' when their premises needed maintenance. He checked his watch. Eleven o'clock. There was time to call on Hans Muller before he left for his dinner.

As Sam strode out, he formulated a plan. He didn't want Hans Muller to think he was desperate for the job, even though he was.

On his arrival at the emporium he was ushered straight into the 'inner sanctum'.

Mr Hans stood up, walked round to the front of his father's desk, and shook Sam's hand. 'Have you considered our offer, Mr Gray?'

The respectful use of 'Mr' did not go unnoticed by Sam.

'Aye. It has come as a surprise. Since I left I've made alternative arrangements to leave the city.'

Hans Muller frowned. 'Ah, you're moving further along the coast? Perhaps where they're building?'

Sam shook his head. 'No, further afield than that. To New Zealand. Auckland.'

'New Zealand?' Mr Hans looked startled, before quickly recovering himself. 'Then you will not be accepting the position of maintenance manager here?'

Sam was pleased to see Herr Muller looking disappointed. 'Had you asked me a week ago, that would have been my answer.'

'Things are different this week? Have you been offered employment?'

Sam nodded. There was no need to say it was their maintenance manager job he'd been offered.

'Ah,' said Hans, looking thoughtful. 'So now your prospects are better you may be persuaded to stay?'

'Aye.'

'We are perhaps then talking about salary?'

Sam felt his mouth go dry. He wondered if he was overplaying his hand. He knew Hans Muller wanted him, but there were other men who would leap at the salary. 'I haven't yet accepted the position offered to me so terms remain negotiable.'

'I'm assuming the position is more than we have offered. As we feel you are well suited to Muller's I can raise the salary by five percent a week.'

'What are my prospects?'

Hans raised his eyebrows. 'This is a reputable company.

Your position will be secure for years to come and…but you don't need me to tell you that. You are familiar with our accounts. Will you accept the position?'

Sam made a show of thinking the offer over, then said, 'Aye. When shall I start?'

'A week today?'

He shook Mr Hans' proffered hand. 'And you'll have the boiler serviced?'

Hans nodded. 'Yes, we'll have the boiler serviced. We'll expect you to use your judgement for what is required immediately. Would you like to inspect the premises now? Then you can report back on any tools or supplies you need. You will be reporting to me, not to Father.'

On the way to inspect the boiler-house tool cupboard, they brushed shoulders with Herr Muller in the workshop.

'Mr Gray has accepted the position of maintenance manager, Father,' said Mr Hans.

Herr Muller gave a curt nod. 'I look forward to you joining our firm. Again.' Then he carried on his way.

Sam took that as the promised apology.

After inspecting the tools and discussing the jobs that needed seeing to immediately, Sam, feeling very pleased with himself, walked to the nearest bar and bought himself a beer to celebrate. He couldn't wait to see Kitty's face when he told her he was no longer the restless, jobless Englishman who had fallen in love with her, but a young man with good prospects. Then he had a better idea.

CHAPTER FIFTY-ONE

It was three o'clock on Christmas Eve when Sam opened the door to Muldoon's barbershop. A familiar jangling bell announced his arrival. With his eyes shut, he could have imagined himself back in Harrison.

A voice came from behind a half-open door. 'Take a seat. I'll be with you in a minute.' It was Frank and, as Sam had hoped, there was no sign of Kitty. He pulled down the corners of his waistcoat and cleared his throat.

When Frank appeared, his eyes widened when he saw it was Sam. He closed the barbershop door. 'What is it you want?'

Sam drew in a deep breath. This wasn't going how he'd planned it at all. He hadn't anticipated feeling so nervous. The conversation was too important to make a mess of, but he was too far forward to stage a retreat under Frank's cool stare.

'I've come to lay my credentials at your door.'

'You'd better come into the parlour, then.' Frank turned

and led the way. With the door into the hallway closed, he placed himself, legs astride, in front of the fireplace, with his back to the heat. Sam didn't feel he could sit without being invited, so he remained standing. He was about to speak when Frank said, 'What is this talk of credentials?'

'In the past you've had reason to regard me as dishonest. Feckless, even.'

'If I recall correctly, I said to Kathryn you needed to find a purpose in your life, and suitable employment. Then you gave a trumped-up version of your employment prospects and, a little later, it turned out you had no employment at all.'

'The facts, while not being trumped up, are more or less correct. I would add that my sense of principle was the reason I lost my position at Muller's. I was not afraid to take a stand against something I thought wrong. I'm here today to provide you with proof of sound employment and purpose.' He took out Mr Hans's letter. 'I now have a permanent position, which was offered to me based on my reliable work record for this company.'

While Frank was reading the letter, Sam added, 'And I was able to negotiate an increase upon the offered wage.'

Frank handed the letter back. 'You appear to have met the employment credentials. What about your purpose in life?'

Sam straightened his back. 'My purpose, sir, is to marry your daughter. With your blessing.'

Frank's bearing did not change, but he sucked in his cheeks. 'She has agreed to this?'

Sam thought he saw a slight softening in Frank's features,

but he couldn't be sure. 'I haven't proposed officially to her yet and I will not do so without your permission, for without it I know she will not accept me. But I am confident she will accept if a proposal is supported by yourself.'

Frank moved away from the fire. 'It may surprise you, but I have been expecting this. Over the last two months or so there has been a sadness in Kathryn's mood and a noticeable loss of spirit. For a while I saw her demeanour lifted when things were well with you. Recently she has withered before my eyes.'

'That tells us both something, sir.'

'Now here you are in our home, asking for her hand, suddenly respectable. I accept that despite your dishonesty you did us a good turn in Harrison by rescuing me from Bulley. I regret I have never referred to it and I thank you for it now. You also sought me out when I was going to miss the ferry. Over the last weeks, I've realised I am to no small degree indebted to you financially.'

Sam began to protest, but Frank raised a hand to pause him. 'As well as my revised thoughts, there is the subject of love – that state of mind when hearts are fragile, emotions take charge and decisions are oft-times made in haste. I am guilty of the latter. My father's love for my daughter made me seek to protect her from what I saw as fraudulence. I have no doubt my daughter loves you, and you have always appeared to care for her. You may not think it now, but in my opinion the forced separation I insisted upon has proved this love for you both.'

Sam had mixed feelings about Frank's assessment of the value of their separation, but he made no comment, not wishing to rock the boat. 'I may ask her for her hand?'

'With one proviso that I cannot insist upon, but which I hope you will respect.'

Sam had a feeling he knew what was coming.

'I ask you to put your roots down here and, if you are blessed with children, to raise them here. This city is going to be great in future years. I sense you can't feel that now, but you will, and Kitty shares my vision.'

At the door, as Sam went to leave, Frank put his hand on his arm. 'You have arrangements for tomorrow's Christmas celebrations?'

'I've been invited to Rosie's – that is, Billy Botcher's sister. You've heard us speak of them both. I'm to rent Billy's room when he leaves for New Zealand. So I'll have a sound base to work from.'

'That sounds a good arrangement. You may wish to know Kitty and I shall be beginning the day together with early Mass at the cathedral.'

It was only as Sam was walking back to the hostel that the suggestion within Frank's words became clear.

✽ ✽ ✽

Sam arrived at the cathedral in plenty of time and stood in the shadows slightly to one side, near the font. The sweet aroma of incense hung heavy in the air. All the candles in the four elaborate brass candelabra above the nave had been lit to celebrate the birth of Christ. An usher approached him and offered to guide him to a seat.

'I'm waiting for someone, thank you,' said Sam, his eyes remaining fixed on the entrance doors. He watched the congregation arriving, greeting each other, embracing friends and relatives, and choosing their places. All were in their fanciest clothes, as was Sam himself.

Ten minutes before the service was scheduled to begin, Sam saw Kitty arrive on Frank's arm. He waited until they had finished kneeling in prayer and were seated, then squeezed past several people to take his place beside them. Kitty, eyes wide with surprise, looked first to her father, who smiled and leaned forward to kiss her forehead, and then back to Sam. With a wicked grin on his face, Sam silently handed Kitty his hymn book, then placed a small be-ribboned parcel beside her on the pew.

The hymn book fell open in Kitty's hands at a place where a marker was protruding, to reveal a note written on expensive writing paper. It was dated December 25th 1858, and the handwriting was Sam's.

Kitty looked at Sam and, receiving a small nod of encouragement, her eyes returned to the note.

Your father and I have made our peace. Please accept this small Christmas gift as a token of my love. I also offer you my heart.

She blinked away what Sam interpreted as happy tears.

'Marry me,' he said, in a voice louder than he'd intended. Several folk nearby turned to look at them.

Kitty giggled nervously. 'What did you say?'

'I asked you to marry me,' he said, again a little louder than he'd intended.

'Yes, of course,' replied Kitty, all smiles, whereupon Sam leaned forward and kissed her on the cheek.

A soft ripple of amused laughter passed through the few people around them.

'Open the parcel,' Sam whispered.

Kitty undid the ribbon and removed the wrapping paper with great care. By the time the contents were revealed, the priest and his entourage, the gold and silver threads in their vestments sparkling, had processed halfway up the nave.

Kitty was holding a triangular packet of Halahan's cough candy in her hand. Her shoulders began to go up and down and it was only with a great effort that she managed to contain her laughter.

'You're right,' whispered Sam. 'It really is delicious.'

EPILOGUE

After working at Muller's for six years and forging valuable connections within the building trade, Sam set up his own home-maintenance business, Samuel Gray & Company. By dint of excellent workmanship and service, and through valuable introductions from Mr Hans to the owners of some of the grander houses, Sam built up a sound business. Kitty gave up her dressmaking alterations to raise their children. Their two daughters were musically gifted, playing in orchestras and ensemble groups from an early age, before turning their talents to teaching. Two of their sons, like Sam, were good with their hands, and in later years the nameplate outside the company offices was taken down and repainted as 'Samuel Gray & Sons'. Their third son entered the legal profession and graduated as a lawyer, working in one of the tall red-brick buildings Sam had noticed his first day in the city. The building was completely destroyed in the 1906 great earthquake which, fortunately for his son, struck at 5.12 am, when he was safely asleep at home.

Sam being Rosie's lodger, she and Frank were introduced and, with his strident days becoming few and far between, they established a strong relationship, leading to a joyful marriage. Frank enjoyed great happiness sharing his grandchildren's company. He died peacefully one Sunday afternoon, while taking a nap after lunch. His great-granddaughter singing nursery rhymes in the next room were the last sounds he heard.

Tug Tait retired when he was seventy and lived into his eighties, telling all who would listen that he put his longevity down to 'a life on the river'. Over the years he received several letters from Sam, and after he'd read them, he always had a smile on his face. In his final days he was cared for by his sister in New Westminster and died peacefully in his sleep.

Billy's wanderlust for ocean-going tall-ship adventuring gradually faded as he grew older, but he never lost his eye for a good deal. After selling off his San Franciscan interests, he settled full time in Auckland, buying up property. As his investments bore fruit, he donated both land and dollars to charitable causes. He continued carving wooden animals in his spare time, and Rosie eventually received the Noah's Ark he'd promised her and her children years before. Her grandchildren loved it and played with it endlessly. Billy died a rich and happy man.

The Frenchman, Pierre, went looking for Sam Jenkins in San Francisco in 1862, but could find no trace of him. It was as if he'd never existed – as indeed he never really had.

SELECTED BIBLIOGRAPHY

Adams, John, *Old Square Toes and His Lady*, Canada: Touchwood Editions, 2011.

Akrigg, G.P.V. and Akrigg, Helen, B, *British Columbia 1847–1971: Gold and Colonists*, Vancouver: Discovery Press, 1977.

Bowen, Lynne, *Boss Whistle: The Coal Miners of Vancouver Island Remember*, Lantzville: Oolichan Books, 1982.

Bown, Stephen R., *The Company: The Rise and Fall of The Hudson's Bay Empire*, Canada: Doubleday, 2020.

Cornwallis, Kinahan, *The New El Dorado; or, British Columbia*. Reprint of the 1858 edition, Charleston, SC: BiblioBazaar Reproduction Series.

Decker, P. R., *Fortunes, and Failures: White-Collar Mobility in Nineteenth Century Sam Francisco, Harvard University Press*, 1978.

Erdnase, S.W., *The Expert at the Card Table: Artifice, Ruse and Subterfuge*, Hey Presto Publishing, 2023.

Evanosky, D., and Kos, E.J., *Lost San Francisco*, Harper Collins, Dublin, 2011.

Fardon, G.R., *San Francisco in the 1850s*, Dover Publications,New York, 1977.

Fisher, Robin, *Contact & Conflict: Indian–European Relations in British Columbia, 1774–1890*, Vancouver: University of British Columbia, 1986.

Hagelund, W. A., *The Dowager Queen: The Hudson's Bay Company SS Beaver,* Surrey, BC: Hancock House Publishers, 2003.

Hayes, Derek, *British Columbia – A New Historical Atlas,* Douglas and McIntyre, 2013.

Howay, F. W., *The Early History of the Fraser River Mines,* Legislative Assembly – Archives of British Columbia, 1926.

Hutchings, *The Miner's Own Book: California Mining,* Hutchinson & Rosenfield, San Francisco, 1858.

Lillard, Charles, *Seven Shillings a Year: The History of Vancouver Island,* Ganges: Horsdal & Schubart, 1986.

Lower, J. Arthur, *Western Canada: An Outline History,* Vancouver: Douglas & McIntyre, 1983.

Norcross, E. Blanche, (ed.,) *Nanaimo Retrospective: The First Century,* Nanaimo: Nanaimo Historical Society, 1979.

Norcross, E. Blanche, (ed.,) *The Company on the Coast,* Nanaimo: Nanaimo Historical Society, 1983.

Peterson, Jan, *Black Diamond City Nanaimo: The Victorian Era,* Surrey: Heritage House Publishing Company, 2002.

Pethick, Derek, *Victoria, The Fort,* Vancouver: Mitchell Press, 1968

Thomas, R. S., *Blacklegs, Card Sharps, and Confidence Men,* LSU Press, 2010.

Waite, D. E., *British Columbia and Yukon Gold Hunters,* Heritage House Publishing, 2015.

ACKNOWLEDGEMENTS

My intention was to write two books about colliers emigrating from England to Vancouver Island, but this was not to be. There is truth in the saying 'My characters speak to me' because after I had finished *Called to Vancouver Island*, I could hear Sam asking 'What about me?' Over time he became more and more insistent until, after two years, I just had to sit down and write his story.

As with my other novels I have received much help and encouragement from my beta readers – Mike Bird who prompted me to make more of my epilogue to good effect, Susan Elston who read the opening chapters (and the rest) and encouraged me to continue, Pat Langridge who always helps me with the Irish side of things and the historian and lawyer Dr Christopher Roberts who reads with a critical, extremely helpful eye.

I thank Matthew Davies for taking time out from his busy schedule as a film production designer to create the map.

Writing can be a lonely occupation and my buddies in the Leicester RNA Belmont Belles & Beaux Chapter and in the Retford Authors' Group are a huge source of support and information both face to face and online.

My loyal production team consisting of my editor Helena Fairfax, my proofreader Julia Gibbs and my publisher Sarah Houldcroft of Goldcrest Books, have smoothed out the plot slip-ups, and the textual errors and I thank them.

Thanks too to my children – Kathryn, Thomas and Hannah who are always interested in how things are progressing. Jim, my husband with whom I share my #authorslife, is happy to discuss the plot anywhere, anytime. We don't always agree on the way forward, but he makes me think more deeply about my characters and their lives while being happy to accept that I have the final say.

ABOUT THE AUTHOR

Lorna was born and brought up in Lincolnshire. Her Canadian mother would often talk about growing up on Vancouver Island in the 1930s, and the family's early history there. This sparked an interest for Lorna that continues to this day. After raising a family Lorna studied and taught history at the School of Oriental and African Studies in London. She now lives in Stamford in a very old house with stone walls and lots of beams.

Contact Lorna:

www.lornahunting.com

X: @lornahunting

Facebook: @huntinglorna

Instagram: lornahunting

ALSO BY LORNA HUNTING

New Beginnings on Vancouver Island

The year is 1854 and Stag Liddell, a young collier from Whitehaven, signs up to work in Vancouver Island's new coal mines. Whilst waiting for his ship to Canada, he meets ambitious school teacher Kate McAvoy who is also making the trip.

As the ship nears its destination, Stag and Kate's relationship begins to blossom, but damning information comes to light and a pact made years before comes into play.

Will their budding romance survive these devastating revelations? And will they both achieve their dreams in this new land?

Called to Vancouver Island

Grace Williams, a young English missionary, arrives in Colville, Vancouver, in 1857 to find the community neither wants nor seems to need her. When her superior, Reverend Palmer, disappears into the snowy woods, on a foolhardy mission to seek converts amongst the Salish First Nations people, Grace is left behind to oversee their mission. There are no half-measures in this place where they do things differently, and she is forced to find self-confidence and rise to the challenge.

Grace is grateful to Sam Gray, a widower, and Long Ben Sloane, the sawmill manager, who befriend and aid her in her mission to improve people's lives and find acceptance. In this wild outpost, the two men become an invaluable support, but only one will win her heart…

Will book-loving Fergus Shackleton find success in business and love despite his overbearing father, Hector?

By forging his own path is Fergus going to turn into his father, the very person he is trying to escape?

Is chasing success going to change Fergus so much that his girlfriend, Becky, is forced to doubt their future together?

Will the price of success be a broken heart?

5* Review for *The Shackletons of Whitehaven*

'The characters were relatable, the setting vivid, and the plot highly engaging. The book is beautifully written and as I was drawn into the story I found I couldn't put it down. I highly recommend this book and can't wait to read more by this author! Five stars!

The Shackletons of Coates Lane

It's 1861 in Whitehaven, and Fergus Shackleton is about to marry his sweetheart, Becky. With a new house to maintain, and a wife and ward to look after, money has never been so important, but Fergus's shipping line is rapidly losing business to the railways. The days of sail are numbered. For the sake of his family, Fergus is forced to risk everything on one throw of the dice.

Helping her ma behind the bar of the family pub is no longer suitable for the young wife of a Shackleton, and Becky soon finds herself with time on her hands. That is, until a stranger arrives who could change everything for their beloved ward.

In an era of rapid change, there is much at stake for the newlyweds – and no guarantee they won't lose everything...

The Shackletons of Chapel St

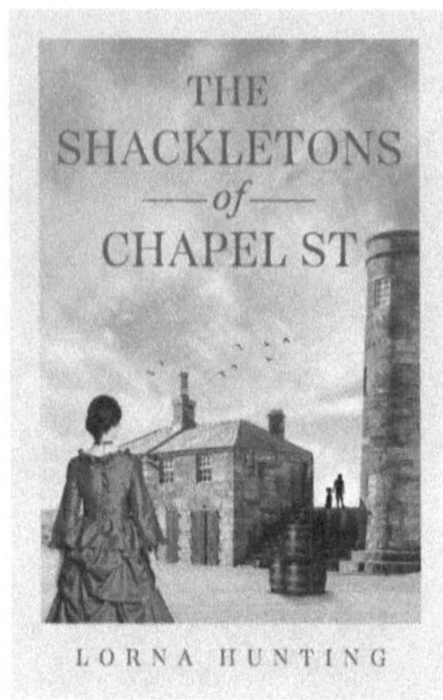

Whitehaven is thronged with out-of-work weavers and their families. The American Civil War means no cotton is reaching the country. For Fergus and Becky Shackleton, the war threatens to have a devastating effect on their lives, and they stand to lose the home they've worked for as newlyweds.

Fergus has staked everything on the exotic goods imported by his ship, the SS Ketton – but it seems his venture may fail. When Becky sees an opportunity to help Fergus's business prosper, and at the same time to support the weavers she's grown to respect, she seizes it with both hands. But will the Shackleton family allow a woman to set her hand to business? And will her efforts be enough to save them losing their home?

A turbulent era in nineteenth-century maritime history forms the backdrop to Book Three in the brilliantly researched Shackleton Saga.

If you've read and enjoyed this book, please leave a review on Amazon or Goodreads.

www.ingramcontent.com/pod-product-compliance
Lightning Source LLC
Chambersburg PA
CBHW050615170726
48283CB00001B/257